PRAISE FOR THE AMISH COZIES
OF AMANDA FLOWER

"As it turns out, Amanda Flower may have just written the first Amish rom-com."
—*USA Today*

"Flower has hit it out of the ballpark . . . and continues to amaze with her knowledge of the Amish way of life."
—*RT Book Reviews*

"At turns playful and engaging as the well-intentioned Englisher strives to rescue her Ohioan Amish friends from a bad fate . . . a satisfyingly complex cozy. Alan is a pseudonym for librarian-author Amanda Flower."
—*Library Journal*

"Reading the book is a visit to a town that feels like home."
—*Kings River Life*

ASSAULTED CARAMEL

Amanda Flower

KENSINGTON PUBLISHING CORP.
http://www.kensingtonbooks.com

KENSINGTON BOOKS are published by

Kensington Publishing Corp.
119 West 40th Street
New York, NY 10018

Copyright © 2017 by Amanda Flower

All Kensington Titles, Imprints, and Distributed Lines are available at special quantity discounts for bulk purchases for sales promotions, premiums, fund-raising, and educational or institutional use. Special book excerpts or customized printings can also be created to fit specific needs. For details, write or phone the office of the Kensington special sales manager: Kensington Publishing Corp., 119 West 40th Street, New York, NY 10018, attn: Special Sales Department, Phone: 1-800-221-2647.

Kensington and the K logo Reg. U.S. Pat & TM Off.

ISBN-13: 978-1-4967-0639-3
ISBN-10: 1-4967-0639-0
First Kensington Mass Market Edition: September 2017

eISBN-13: 978-1-4967-0640-9
eISBN-10: 1-4967-0640-4
First Kensington Electronic Edition: September 2017

10 9 8 7 6 5 4 3 2 1

Printed in the United States of America

For the staff at the
Hudson Library & Historical Society

Acknowledgments

Writing is solitary craft, but it takes a team of dedicated dreamers to publish a novel. I'm lucky to have one of the best in the business.

Special thanks, as always, to my super agent, Nicole Resciniti. She is more than an agent. She is my friend, dream maker, and spirit guide in writing and in life. Thank you is never enough. Special thanks, too, to AJ Trauth. I never would have written this series if not for his persistence and enthusiasm for the story.

Thanks to the wonderful team at Kensington Books, starting with Peter Senftleben, who acquired my Amish Candy Shop Series when it was a mere idea, and Alicia Condon, who steered it in the right direction with her thoughtful comments and encouragement.

Thanks, too, to my wonderful assistant, Molly Carroll, who read the novel when it was raw and unwieldy, and to my dear friend Suzy Schroeder for her advice on recipes and all things candy making.

To my dearest friend, Mariellyn Grace, love and thanks for listening to hours and hours of plot twists and turns during the drafting of this book. And love to my family—Andy, Nicole, Isabella, and Andrew—for their unwavering support.

Finally, to my Heavenly Father. The path you put me on is truly amazing, and I am grateful for every story I'm given the opportunity to tell.

Chapter 1

"I still can't believe you left!" Cassandra Calbera shouted into my ear. "They're making the announcement Monday. You have to be here!"

I held the phone away from my face and imagined my best friend standing in the middle of Jean Pierre's test kitchen in the back of JP Chocolates in Midtown, New York. She'd be in her chef whites and have her short, purple and black hair pinned behind her ears to keep it out of her eyes. I prayed that she was alone, considering the direction of our conversation. The fewer people who knew I'd left the city, the better.

While Cass continued to tell me all the reasons why I should immediately return to New York, I parked in the first spot I could find on Apple Street, which ran perpendicular to Main Street. Apple trees lined either side of the narrow lane. In the spring, they looked like flowering white torches marching up the road, forming a beautiful canopy. When I was a little girl, I had asked my grandfather why the apple trees never had any apples. He replied that the English residents of the village didn't like the apples because they made a mess on the street and sidewalk, so the Englishers made the trees sterile. At the age of five, I had no idea what sterile meant, but it sounded bad. *"It is the* Englisch *way,"* he had said. *"To change what Gott created into something more convenient."*

This late in September, the tree's leaves had turned yellow-gold, and a few fell to the sidewalk in the breeze that rolled over the green hills surrounding the village.

"Bai, are you listening to me?" Cass demanded.

I took a deep breath. "I explained to Jean Pierre before I left. This is a family emergency. My grandfather is sick. Jean Pierre understood. Besides, it's only Thursday. I'll be home in time for the announcement on Monday morning."

"Jean Pierre might understand, but the selection committee will not. They're looking for any excuse to give that skunk Caden the head chocolatier job. Just because he's French, and they think it goes better with the brand of Jean Pierre's empire. Do you think I should run the mob just because I'm Italian?"

"You probably wouldn't be bad at it."

"First of all, that comment is both flattering and insulting. Second, you are completely missing my point."

"What would that be?" I asked, rubbing my forehead and staring out the windshield of the rental car I had picked up at the tiny Akron-Canton Airport. There hadn't been much selection, and the inside of the car smelled faintly of stale cigarettes. The smell was giving me a headache. As I stared out the window, an Amish buggy clopped down the cross street. Inside, an Amish man with a long dark beard chatted with the Amish boy in the passenger seat. The boy was laughing. I couldn't be farther from Midtown if I tried.

"Are you listening to me?" Cass asked.

I blinked. I hadn't realized she was still talking. As much as I loved my best friend, she had a tendency to ramble when she was really passionate about a subject. "I'm listening," I lied.

"You not being here the week before their final decision as to who will be Jean Pierre's replacement only makes it easier for them to give it to that jerk. Is that what you want?"

"Jean Pierre won't let them do that." I had been Jean Pierre's first chocolatier and protégé for so long, that everyone, even me, assumed that I would be appointed as head chocolatier at JP Chocolates when Jean Pierre retired.

"It's not Jean Pierre's decision," she argued. "When the chocolate company went public, all the power went to the board of directors, which is the selection committee. Sure, they may listen to Jean Pierre's suggestions, but they can do whatever they want."

She wasn't telling me anything I didn't already know. I rubbed my temples. I had to get out of the car. "Cass, I'm not going over this again with you. My grandfather is ill. He's more important than some job."

"It's not just some job, Bailey. You've been working for this for six years. *Six years*. Do you want to throw away all the thousands of hours you spent on perfecting your craft?"

I drummed my fingers on the steering wheel. "Of course not."

"Then, come back—"

"Oh, Cass, can you hear me? You're breaking up," I said. "I'm way out in the country now . . ."

"Bailey? Bailey, can you hear me? Bai?"

I hung up the phone. As a native New Yorker, Cass

questioned cell phone reception anywhere west of Manhattan.

I scrolled through my text messages for a response from Eric Sharp. Nothing. The last text messages had been from me to him, telling him I was heading to Ohio to visit my ailing grandfather, telling him I was at the airport, and telling him I had landed in Akron. No response to any of them. I reminded myself that between his two pastry shops, television show, and thousands of other obligations, Eric didn't have time to text his girlfriend, especially since he and I were the only ones who knew we were dating. I threw the phone into my purse. Despite Eric's impossible schedule, a short "thinking of you" text would have lifted my spirits considerably, because I was pretty certain Cass was right. My rash decision to drop everything and fly to Ohio *did* put my promotion to head chocolatier at JP Chocolates at risk. I shook my head. I'd had no other choice. When my grandmother had called to tell me my grandfather was ill, I had to go. My grandmother only called if it was an emergency. The Amish didn't use the telephone for chitchat.

Through the windshield of my rental car, I watched as a second horse-and-buggy rolled by. I had told Cass that I was in the country; I hadn't told her I was in Amish Country. The village of Harvest in Holmes County, Ohio to be specific. I wasn't sure what my fashionable coworker would have said if she knew I had Amish relatives. She'd probably wonder if I had a bonnet hidden somewhere in my apartment.

My grandparents might be Amish, but I wasn't. Neither were my parents. My father had grown up Amish and then left his district to marry my mother. Right now, Mom and Dad were having the very un-Amish adventure of traveling through Europe to celebrate their thirtieth wedding anniversary. Judging by the number of vacation photos in my email inbox, I could safely say that Mom and Dad had mastered the selfie and were on a personal mission to snap a photo of themselves with every major landmark in Europe. The last one I had received included the Leaning Tower of Pisa.

I took a deep breath and stepped out of the car. I would have to buy an air freshener if I was going to spend any significant amount of time in the rental car, or risk asphyxiation. As I walked to the corner of Apple and Main Street, I hoped that *Daadi* and *Maami* would be happy to see me. My grandparents didn't know I was in town. My grandmother had called to tell me *Daadi* was ill, but she'd asked me not come. She said *Daadi* would not wish me to leave my work on his account.

I turned the corner onto Main Street, passing an Amish woman pushing a double stroller. Two plainly dressed toddlers sat in the stroller, kicking each other with their small feet. The mother said something to them in Pennsylvania Dutch. The children giggled, and I felt myself relax. I had made the right decision. The selection committee members wouldn't change their minds about choosing me as the head chocolatier just because I took a couple of vacation days that were owed me. I hadn't taken a single day off from work since last year, when Jean Pierre had announced his planned retirement.

Main Street was the primary shopping district in the tiny village of Harvest, Ohio. Gas-powered lamps marched down the street, alternating with more apple trees, and store fronts advertised Amish-made products—everything from quilts to baskets to pretzels and brooms.

Returning here felt like stepping back in time. Not into a former century, as many people misperceived the Amish culture, but into a bustling community of shops and merchants, where clothes and home goods and foods were locally harvested and handmade. Cass would be horrified—there wasn't a Starbucks or a department store in sight. Me, I rather liked the simplicity and authenticity. I specialized in chocolates, so it made me smile to think that people specialized in furniture and cheeses and even blank-faced Amish dolls.

My grandparents' store—Swissmen Sweets—was in the most coveted spot on the street. It was right across from the town square, where the village held the Apple Blossom Festival in the spring, community picnics in the summer, farmers' markets in the autumn, and ice-skating in the winter. Everyone in town wanted *Daadi's* location, but he had owned it for well over fifty years, and he was way too smart to sell.

I was about a block from Swissmen Sweets when I spotted my grandfather leaning on a walker in front of his candy shop. His snow-white Amish beard hung to his chest, and his black felt hat sat primly on the top of his head. He spoke to a non-Amish man wearing a business suit that could have been sold in any number of the New York department stores Cass loved to frequent.

I took a deep breath, happy to see *Daadi* was no longer in the hospital as he had been when my grandmother called, but the walker frightened me. *Daadi* was a proud man, and he must hate having to rely on the contraption to keep him from toppling over.

I started to wave to attract my grandfather's attention,

but stopped myself when I was close enough to overhear their conversation.

Daadi gripped the sides of his walker until his knuckles turned white. "I have told you before, we're not interested."

The man in the suit appeared to be in his late forties. He wore his brown hair combed back in a wave and his tan had the slightest hint of orange. "You're a fool. No one is going to make you a better offer than I am."

"That is *gut*," *Daadi* said. "Because I do not want any more offers. I'm happy with what I have. More importantly, *Gott* is happy with it. Now, if I cannot interest you in any fudge, I must ask you to leave."

The man pointed at my grandfather. "You're just prolonging the inevitable. When you're gone, this property will belong to me. There'll be no one to stand in my way. You don't have any family to take it over."

My chest constricted. *Daadi* did have family. He had *Maami,* and he had me. I clenched my teeth and started walking toward the pair at a fast clip.

The man spun around and headed directly for me. Not watching where he was going, he ran smack into my shoulder. "Hey!" I shouted at him, so loudly I wouldn't have been surprised if they heard me back in New York.

He blinked at me. In Harvest, pedestrians didn't yell at each other like they did in the city. I could use this to my advantage. "Watch where you're going."

He straightened his jacket. "Get out of my way."

I was going to say something else, but then I saw *Daadi* over the man's shoulder. *Daadi* was bent over his walker. He held his chest and crumpled to the sidewalk.

I ran to him. "*Daadi!*" I held him in my arms and looked back up the sidewalk. The man glanced at me, shock registering on his face, before he turned the corner onto a side street and disappeared.

"Bailey." *Daadi* touched my cheek. "What are you doing here?"

Before I could answer, he lost consciousness.

Chapter 2

My grandparents' family doctor was an English man in his late fifties with a wide, kind face that immediately put me at ease. He put his blood pressure cuff in his medical bag and adjusted his wire-rimmed glasses on the long bridge of his nose. "Jebidiah, I do think you should go to the hospital for some additional tests."

Daadi shifted his position on the nest of pillows my grandmother had made for him on their bed in the small apartment above the fudge shop. "*Nee*, I have been to the hospital too many times. They always tell me the same. My heart is weak. I don't have much more time. I do not need to hear this again. When *Gott* calls me home, I will be ready. Going to the hospital won't change that."

It felt like someone reached into my chest and squeezed my own heart in a vise when my grandfather stated this so matter-of-factly. I agreed with the doctor. *Daadi* should go to the hospital. After he had collapsed on the sidewalk, I started to call 911 when my grandmother asked me to stop. She said *Daadi* didn't want the ambulance called. Instead, she called their family doctor,

Dr. Brown, who had an office on the other side of the square and was there in a matter a minutes. During that time, *Daadi* had come to, and Dr. Brown and I half led, half carried *Daadi* up the stairs to his room.

The doctor sighed. "I expected you to say that." He glanced at my grandmother, who stood on the opposite side of the bed, holding *Daadi*'s hand. "Clara, please call me day or night if you need me. I'll be here as quick as I can."

My tiny grandmother nodded. "*Danki*, Dr. Brown." The white prayer cap on her head blended in with her soft, silver hair. Her hair had once been brunette like mine, but it had been silver for as long as I had known her.

The doctor nodded and headed for the door.

Before he reached the bottom of the back stairs, I rushed out of the room. "Doctor, what's wrong with my grandfather?"

Dr. Brown looked up at me from the middle of the narrow staircase. The gas-lit wall sconce illuminated his broad face. There was a sadness in his eyes that I hadn't noticed when he had been in the bedroom with my grandparents. "Congenital heart disease."

My chest tightened as if an unseen hand had cranked the vise just a little more tightly, and even though I didn't want to, I asked, "The prognosis?"

He only shook his head. Then he turned and descended the stairs to the shop's main floor.

I stood there, staring down the narrow stairwell with a hand covering my heart. I didn't know if I was covering it in protection or prayer. I glanced over my shoulder at the doorway that led to my grandparents' bedroom. Maybe now was a good time to start praying, assuming I still knew how to do it. I dropped my hand and headed back to the bedroom.

"No, Clara," *Daadi* said. "I am not going back to the hospital. They have told us before there is nothing more to be done. Let it be. I would rather spend what little time I have left on this earth with you, here in our home."

Tears gathered in my grandmother's blue eyes, the same color as my own. "*Ya*, you are right, Jebidiah."

He gave her a weak smile. "I will savor that, because it is a rare thing, indeed, for you to tell me I am right."

She frowned. "Do not joke at such a time."

"Jokes are always welcome. Even the *gut* Lord laughs." He noticed me standing in the doorway. "There's my girl. Come closer and tell me why you are here."

I sat on the edge of his bed, careful not to disturb him. "I came to see you. I heard you were unwell."

Weakly, he shook his finger at *Maami* and me. "I think the two of you have been up to something."

Maami lifted her chin. "I called Bailey when you were in the hospital. She is your granddaughter and has a right to know."

"I agree. Bailey has a right to know," *Daadi* said, and then turned his head on the pillow toward me. "But you should not have come. Don't you have the chocolate man vote this week?"

I smiled, touched that my grandfather would remember the pending head chocolatier announcement at such a time. "I've never heard it called that before, but yes, the selection committee is voting on who will be the next head chocolatier at JP Chocolates. The announcement will be made Monday morning."

Daadi tried to sit up, but *Maami* and I both pushed him back onto the pillows. "Then why are you here?" he asked. "You should be in New York, making chocolate castles to wow the committee. Don't give them any reason to consider another chocolatier."

My hand remained on his shoulder. "It's not as important as being here with you."

"Hogwash," *Daadi* snapped, some of the fire back in his eyes. "It's all you have written to us about for the last five years. You can't fool me into thinking it is no longer important to you, now that I am under the weather."

"You're more than under the weather, *Daadi*." I held his cold, wrinkled hand in mine. "And you're more important than a silly job."

He grunted, but his face broke into a smile. I found myself smiling too.

Maami stood up and smoothed a wrinkle out of her plain lavender dress. "I'll let the two of you argue about this and make some tea. I'll put double sugar in yours, Bailey." She winked at me. "Don't think I forgot your sweet tooth."

I smiled my thanks.

Maami closed the door after her. When I heard her footsteps fade, I asked, "*Daadi*, before you fell, you were talking to a man. Who was that?"

Daadi opened his eyes and stared at me like he was looking through me. It was almost as if he was searching his mind for the memory. That frightened me, because the incident in front of Swissmen Sweets had been less than three hours ago. He smiled. "Oh, *ya*, that was Tyson Colton. He's a developer in the county. He wants to buy the candy shop. He's already bought the two shops on either side of me."

There was a cheese shop on the right of Swissmen Sweets and a tiny pretzel shop on the left.

"What? Why?" I wondered if I should be questioning him about this Tyson Colton character at this time.

My grandfather focused on me. "Because he wants to make money. What other reason do *Englischers* need to take away Amish property? He knows that I have the best location in the village, and since it is the best, he wants it."

"How much is he offering?" I held my grandfather's hand a little more tightly.

"More money than I would ever have a use for, or want. I told him he could double his amount, and I still wouldn't sell."

I knew he wouldn't like to hear what I had to say next, but I had to share it. "If he is offering you a significant amount of money, then you could retire and take it easy. You could take better care of your health. You work too hard."

My grandfather frowned. "*Gott* made us to work for His Kingdom. I will rest when I pass on."

I bit the inside of my lip. I didn't like the sound of that. My grandfather's mind was made up, and arguing the point with him would only upset him more, which wouldn't be good for his failing heart.

He covered my hand with his. "Do not worry, my girl. All will work out as it should. *Gott* has had this moment planned from the beginning."

What moment did he mean? The offer from Tyson? Or *Daadi's* failing health? All will work out as it should? To quote my grandfather, *hogwash*! If the doctor's frown had been any indication, that was not to be.

"Do you want me to email Mom and Dad?" I asked. "They're somewhere in Italy right now, but they would want to know you are ill."

He struggled to sit up some more. "*Nee*. Don't bother

them. They have waited for their trip for a very long time. Your *maami* should not have bothered you either. I will be fine. You go back and make those fancy chocolates. It's your dream. I'm not going to get in the way of what you've worked so hard for. I like to think it's a little bit of me that makes you so *gut* with chocolate."

"It's more than a little bit," I whispered.

"Then go back and get that head chocolate person job for me, if you can't do it for yourself."

Tears sprang to my eyes. "If your strength is up, I'll leave the day after tomorrow, but I'll be back just as soon as I can after the head chocolatier is announced."

He smiled. "All right then, if returning will make you feel better, you have my blessing."

Maami pushed opened the bedroom door and came in with a tea tray. "I brought you some hot broth too, Jebidiah."

My grandfather grimaced.

Maami squinted her blue eyes at him. "Don't you make that face at me, Jebidiah King! You will drink this broth. Nothing warms you all the way through like hot chicken broth."

Grandfather winked at me. "She is always telling me what to do."

Maami set the tray on a side table and cupped the bowl of broth in her hands.

I reached for it. "Let me."

She smiled and gave me the bowl. I dipped the spoon into the hot broth and held it up. "Here, *Daadi*."

He smiled. "Clara, did you see how beautiful our Bailey has become?"

"I did," my grandmother said.

I felt myself blush, and I fed my grandfather the broth.

Chapter 3

A little while later, after *Daadi* had drunk enough broth to satisfy my grandmother, he dozed off.

I picked up the tea tray and crept down the stairs. The stairs from the living quarters ended in a short hallway that opened directly into the candy shop. I stood there for a moment, admiring the room in which I had fallen in love with chocolate as a little girl. Along the walls, maple shelves held glass jars filled with every kind of candy you could imagine, from mints to licorice to caramels.

However, the pride of the shop was my grandfather's signature fudge, and it was displayed front and center in a ten-foot-long glass case that doubled as the sales counter. Inside the display case there were dozens of trays of fudge: milk chocolate, rocky road, Neapolitan, maple, pumpkin, blueberry, peanut butter, and so many more. Even though I worked with chocolate every day, my mouth still watered when I saw all those trays of fudge, and the memories of my grandfather sneaking me pieces of fudge on summer evenings before dinner when *Maami* wasn't looking brought a smile to my face.

As many times as I tried to duplicate my grandfather's fudge in New York, it didn't taste quite the same as that made by his own hand. I bit the inside of my lip. How much longer would he be able to make it?

Maami smiled at me over the glass counter. "Want a piece?"

I nodded. If anything, eating the fudge would give me something else to do other than worry over my grandfather's health.

She laughed and lifted the plank of wood at the end of the counter that divided the work area from the public. "Then come on back and pick your own. Being a chocolatier, I suppose you know how to cut chocolate."

"I sure hope so, or JP Chocolates will be in big trouble." I stepped around the counter, slid the glass door back on the display case, and removed a tray of fudge. I set the tray on the counter behind me and picked up the chocolate knife from the white cutting block. It had a long, curved eight-inch blade with a sharp hook on the end, which pointed back toward the handle. It was perfect for cutting huge blocks of chocolate. I had found it in a specialty cooking shop in New York. It had cost me a small fortune.

"*Daadi* uses the knife I gave him?" I asked, feeling pleased. Finding Christmas and birthday gifts for my grandparents was always a challenge. The Amish only wanted practical things, and their estimation of what was practical was far different from any English person's I knew.

She smiled. "He refuses to use any other knife. If it is dirty, he waits for me to wash it before he will cut anything."

I grinned and set the knife on the cutting board next to the piece of fudge. "I'm glad."

Maami hugged me. "And I'm glad you're here. You being here, even for a little while, lifts Jebediah's spirits so."

I hugged her back. "*Danki.*"

She laughed when I used the Pennsylvania Dutch word for thank you.

I cut a generous piece of salted caramel fudge—my favorite of *Daadi's* recipes—and was taking a huge bite when a man in a sheriff's department uniform stepped into the shop.

He was followed by an older, bald officer who hung back by the front door. The men wore identical khaki uniforms, but the man by the door had a golden eagle pin on the breast pocket. I noticed it because it caught the sunlight streaming in through the candy shop's front window when the older man turned away and walked back out the door.

My heart skipped a beat when the first officer smiled at me. He had dark brown hair and eyes, and he was tall, really tall. In his case, what they say about a man looking good in uniform was spot on.

"Hello there," he said.

I tried to swallow and nearly choked on the piece of fudge.

Maami smiled at the tall man. "Aiden, are you here to pick up your mother's order?"

His face broke into a wide smile. "That's right, Mrs. King."

I coughed and spurted.

My grandmother cocked her head. "Bailey, are you all right?"

I nodded and covered my mouth. I shoved the piece of fudge into my cheek, so I resembled a greedy chipmunk, which is always the look a girl wants to shoot for in front of an attractive man.

My grandmother smiled at Aiden. "I have your mother's order right here." She spun around and picked up a large brown shopping bag. "Have you met my granddaughter, Bailey?"

He arched his eyebrows at my blue jeans and sweater. "Your granddaughter?"

I nodded. My mouth was still full. My cheeks burned as the image of a foraging chipmunk returned to my mind.

He smiled. "It's nice to meet you." Reaching over the counter, he accepted the bag from my grandmother.

I nodded again. I couldn't stop myself. It was like I was a marionette on strings.

"Tell your mother I threw in a couple of extra blocks of maple fudge," *Maami* said. "I know the ladies in her quilting circle love their sweets."

"You bet they do," the deputy said. "And Mom is going to need it. She plans to keep the quilting circle at the church tomorrow for however long it takes to finish Mira's quilt. There's not much time left before the wedding."

"Two days isn't much time at all."

I wanted to ask who Mira was and whose wedding they were talking about, but since my mouth was still stuffed with fudge, it was next to impossible. I turned away from them and forced down what was left of the fudge.

The radio on the deputy's duty belt crackled.

He smiled. "I'd better run. Thanks for the extra treats, Mrs. King. You're always so good to me." He tipped his sheriff's department ball cap at me, nodding at the chocolate knife in my hand. "You be careful with that."

As soon as he left, I ran into the kitchen and poured a glass of water to wash down the piece of fudge caught in my throat. My throat felt raw from swallowing the fudge so quickly.

As I sipped on my water, my thoughts immediately went to Eric. I wondered where he was, and if he'd noticed that I had left the city. There was a fifty-fifty chance he'd never read any of the texts I'd sent him. A warm blush crept up the back of my neck over the embarrassing incident with the sheriff's deputy. How could I even look at another man when I had a boyfriend, even if he was a secret one? I chalked the reaction up to stress over the head chocolatier announcement and my grandfather's poor health.

I continued to sip my water in an attempt to regain whatever dignity I had left, and I surveyed the kitchen. The floor was plain white, vinyl tile. The walls were white, and the one window in the back of the room next to the metal door that led to the alley behind Swissmen Sweets, was adorned with a navy blue, cotton curtain.

There were no electrical outlets in my grandparent's apartment. In their Amish district, like most, electricity wasn't allowed in the home. However, they were allowed to use electricity for their business. There were a number of outlets around the room, with two industrial mixers and three ovens plugged into them. There weren't any of the fancy molding machines I had back in New York. My grandparents made their candies with the barest essentials. I wondered what they would make of my chocolatier test kitchen back in New York with every modern gadget one could imagine.

At the moment, the room was spotless, and all of the appliances were off. I knew that my grandparents did most of their candy making in the early morning before the shop opened at nine. And by early morning, I mean from four in the morning right up until opening time. The fact that my grandparents were early risers was another way in which we differed.

"Bailey?" *Maami* poked her head into the kitchen. "Are you all right, my girl?"

"I'm fine, *Maami*." With my head high, I walked back through the kitchen door.

She studied me.

"What?" I asked as I started to pack up the piece of fudge I had cut.

"You seemed to be a bit flustered when Aiden was here." She made no attempt to hide her smile.

I picked up *Daadi's* knife again. "You seem to know him well."

She smiled. "I do."

Before I could ask her how, she said, "You might want to cut a smaller piece next time. You never know who might drop by."

I felt my cheeks grow hot again as I bent over the fudge.

Chapter 4

A little before one in the morning that night, I woke and reached for my cell phone on the nightstand. It wasn't there. Then I remembered I wasn't in my apartment in New York, but in the spare room of my grandparents' home above their candy shop in Harvest, Ohio. My phone sat in the kitchen below, plugged into the wall. The night before, my grandmother had unplugged one of the mixers before we went to bed, so I could charge my phone.

I lay there, debating whether to walk down to the kitchen to check my messages. Part of me was afraid to, because if there wasn't a message from Eric, I would be crushed. That evening before going to bed, I had stepped outside and tried to call him. There had been no answer. The excuses I had made for him the day before had run out when I still hadn't heard from him before falling asleep. I told myself he was busy, and maybe he wasn't somewhere he could text privately. Our relationship was a secret, so we had to be extra careful, and I reminded myself that it was a secret at my request. Eric was on JP Chocolates' board of directors and, because of that, was a member of the head chocolatier selection committee. If it was discovered that I was dating one of the committee members and I landed the job, someone would claim that I had gotten the head chocolatier position out of favoritism. Nothing could be further from the truth. Eric didn't cut me any breaks when it came to my desserts. In fact, he was my greatest critic. If anything, he was harder on me than anyone else.

I rolled over and punched the pillow, but I couldn't fall back to sleep. The situation with Eric bothered me, but not as much as my grandfather's failing health. What would become of Swissmen Sweets if the worst happened, and he died? I couldn't imagine *Maami* running the shop alone. Maybe she could have ten or fifteen years ago, but she was seventy herself.

I punched the pillow again with a little more force this time. After giving the innocent pillow a thorough pounding, I gave up, threw back my grandmother's quilt, and sat up. I yelped when my bare feet touched the ice-cold floor.

I grabbed my tennis shoes, slipped them on, and wrapped a lap blanket over my shoulders before tiptoeing to the bedroom door. It creaked as I opened it, and I winced. I didn't want to wake my grandparents.

Finally, I opened the door wide enough to slip through. I tiptoed down the hallway past my grandparents' bedroom. Every step I took made the floorboards squeak. I paused at the top of the narrow stairs, and when I didn't hear anything, I went down.

In the front room of the shop, ambient light from the gas-lit lampposts outside shone through the large front window and reflected off the refrigerated fudge case. The many flavors of fudge stood in perfectly straight lines on the glass shelves. My grandmother had straightened each tray before she went upstairs for the night. The kitchen and the sales counter were always spotless when she left them for the night. Nothing was put off for the next day in my grandparents' shop.

I lifted the board that separated the main room from the work area and stepped behind the counter. I pushed the swinging kitchen door in, but something stopped it. Frowning, I pushed harder, and again it wouldn't budge. Frustrated, I hip checked the door, and the something on the other side gave. I stumbled through and had to grab the edge of the door to stay upright. The floor was sticky with some kind of liquid. Perhaps a jar had fallen off one of the white shelves lining the wall and shattered.

I hit the light switch, half-expecting to find an over-turned crate of jam or chocolate syrup at my feet. Instead, I saw Tyson Colton lying in the middle of the floor, still wearing the suit I had seen him in when I arrived in the village. I didn't pay much attention to his suit though, because my eyes were zeroed onto my grandfather's chocolate knife sticking out of his chest.

I screamed.

So much for not waking up my grandparents.

Chapter 5

When I finally stopped screaming—which seemed a long time but was probably only seconds—I heard a commotion above me. My grandparents were awake. I wouldn't be surprised if half the neighborhood had been frightened out of their beds by my screech.

I pushed back against the door, planning to run up the stairs to tell them what I'd discovered. A sickening sticky sound stopped me. I stood in blood, Tyson Colton's blood. I couldn't move without tracking it all over the store.

I covered my mouth with my hand, physically holding back a second scream. I spotted my cell phone sitting on a milk stool next to an electrical outlet, just as I had left it only a few hours ago. Its green notification light blinked at me, telling me I had a new message.

I closed my eyes. "White chocolate, milk chocolate, dark chocolate, sweet chocolate, semi-sweet chocolate, bittersweet chocolate, cocoa, couverture, vermicelli." When Jean Pierre had chosen me as his first chocolatier, he made me memorize the different types of chocolate and recite them back to him every day for an entire year. He said the first order of business of being a chocolatier was knowing chocolate and all it was capable of, and before I could discover that, I needed to know the chocolates.

Of course, I knew all the types of chocolate from visiting my grandparents' candy shop and from my years in culinary school, but Jean Pierre had made me list the chocolates so many times, it was a mantra I fell back on whenever I was stressed. And nothing was more stressful than finding a dead body in my grandparents' kitchen.

"Bailey?" my grandmother called from behind me.

I opened my eyes and pivoted in place. A second later, my grandmother stood behind me in her plain blue nightgown and bare feet. Her usually bound hair fell all the way down her back in a silver wave. "Bailey, are you hurt? We heard such a terrible scream. It scared us so."

Fear gripped me, and for a moment, I forgot Tyson lying at my feet. "How is *Daadi*? Did my screaming startle him and hurt his heart?"

"*Nee,* do not worry about that. I'm worried about—" She gasped. "What has happened?"

My grandmother gaped at my feet, which brought me right back to the reality of my situation.

I began to shake. "I came down to check my phone for messages, and I found him like this."

"What is he doing here?" *Maami* sounded like she was talking to herself, so I didn't bother to answer. "And why are you still standing there next to him?" She directed this question at me.

I grimaced. "I don't want to track blood all over."

My grandmother straightened her back. "Then give me your arm, and I will help you step out of your shoes."

I did as my grandmother instructed and was freed. My white tennis shoes remained in the kitchen. Their laces fell onto the floor near Colton's head. They were as much a goner as Tyson himself.

I stumbled into the relative safety of the main shop and away from the kitchen. Since I was no longer holding it open with my body, the kitchen door closed after me, sparing us the view of the gruesome scene.

"*Ya*," my grandmother said into the telephone at the counter. "Come as quick as you can."

Daadi hobbled into the shop holding onto the wall. I ran over to him. "*Daadi*, you shouldn't be out of bed."

He scoffed. "I cannot stay in bed when it sounds like the two people I love most on this earth are in trouble. What has happened?"

I shared a look with *Maami*. There was no point in hiding it from him. He would learn when the police arrived. "I found Tyson Colton in the kitchen."

Daadi's face flashed red. "What is that scoundrel doing in my shop? I knew he wanted this place, but I never thought he would stoop so low as to break in. Where is he? I want to tell him what I think."

The muffled sound of approaching sirens filled the air.

I put my arm through my grandfather's to support him. "*Daadi*, you can't tell him anything. He's dead."

My grandfather, in his simple pajamas, blinked at me. "What? How is that possible?"

I took one of the wooden chairs, which was turned upside down on a round table, and set it on the floor. "Please sit down, *Daadi*." I helped him into the chair.

Maami wrung her hands. "What are we to do? Should we call the bishop?"

Daadi held onto the end of his long beard as if it was some sort of lifeline and he needed it to steady himself. "*Nee.* Let's not involve the bishop just yet." He released his beard. "The deacon will learn about it soon enough. It's best first to talk to the police."

As if on cue, banging shook the store's front door. *Maami* moved to open the door. Two uniformed sheriff's deputies marched inside. One was the bald, middle-aged man with ruddy features who had briefly stepped into the candy shop the afternoon before while Aiden collected the treats for his mother's knitting circle. The other was Aiden himself.

"We got a call that you've discovered a body in the building," Aiden said, directing his comment to my grandfather.

I stepped forward. "Yes, I found him." I pointed to the swinging door on the other side of the counter. "He's in there with my shoes."

The deputy gave me a strange look. "You talk."

Terrific. He had thought I was a mute.

I bit the inside of my cheek. I pointed at the door again. "There is a dead man in there."

"Right," he said, all business now.

Maami touched her hair and whispered something in Pennsylvania Dutch, as if she'd just realized her hair was down, and she didn't have her prayer cap on. She spun around and headed for the stairs that led up to the apartment.

"Where are you going?" the middle-aged deputy asked. "No one leaves the scene until we say so."

My grandmother froze in the doorway leading to the back stairs.

Aiden bumped the other man in the upper arm with his fist. "Relax, Carpenter. Mrs. King is only going to get dressed. Go ahead, Mrs. King."

My grandmother nodded and disappeared into the short hallway that led to the stairs.

I dropped my grandfather's arm and glared at Deputy Carpenter. "You should be more respectful of the Amish who live in your county."

The older deputy glowered back at me. "A man is dead. He's the one who deserves respect."

"I know that," I said. "And I'm sorry for Mr. Colton."

"Mr. Colton?" Aiden asked. "Tyson Colton?" His eyes darted to the closed kitchen door. "In there?"

I nodded.

The two deputies shared a look, and I got a feeling that this case had just become a whole lot more complicated.

Aiden cleared his throat. "Miss King, I think we got off on the wrong foot. I'm Deputy Aiden Brody, and this is Deputy Gordon Carpenter."

I didn't say anything in response. "Nice to meet you" didn't seem appropriate under the circumstances.

After a beat, Aiden added, "Miss King, why don't you take your grandfather upstairs? We can talk to him and your grandmother there. There is no reason for them to be uncomfortable down here while we investigate the scene. However, since you found the body, I would like you to come back down once they're settled, if you don't mind."

Daadi braced his hand against the wall. "Now, this is my business, Aiden. You know that as well as anyone. I should stay down here with Bailey. I have a right to know what has happened."

I took my grandfather's arm again. "Don't worry,

Daadi. I'll tell you everything just as soon as I can." I led him to the doorway at the base of the stairs.

"Don't be long, Miss King. We have many questions to ask you." This came from Deputy Carpenter.

I felt my grandfather bristle at the sound of the man's voice, but he made no more attempts to argue with me about going back upstairs. He was wobbly on his feet without his walker, and surely he would have fallen over if I hadn't been there to support his arm. It seemed that he had expended all his energy to come down the stairs to make sure *Maami* and I were all right. I refused to let myself think about what all of this upset must being doing to his already failing heart. Even in the dim light, I could see that there was a gray cast to his lined face. "*Daadi*, should we call your doctor?"

He grunted. "My doctor? Why?"

I helped him up another step. "You have had a shock. Your heart."

He shook his head. "Just don't let them misplace that knife you got me. I love it so."

I winced. There wasn't much chance of the police losing the knife since it was sticking out of Tyson's chest. I decided *Daadi* didn't need to know that particular detail.

I helped him to the second step. "How about I set you up on the sofa in your sitting room? If the deputies want to speak to you, they can do it there."

"*Ya*, that would be all right. I don't want the police speaking to me while I'm in my bed like an invalid." His arm quivered as he gripped the railing.

After I got *Daadi* settled into the tiny sitting room at the far end of their apartment, I stopped in my own room to find a new pair of shoes and throw on a hoodie over my pajamas. As I headed back down the hallway, I ran into *Maami* as she came out of her room, fully dressed with her hair up and prayer cap firmly in place.

I reached for her hand and squeezed it. "I put *Daadi* in the sitting room. The police said you could stay with him. They'll talk to you up here."

She shook her head. "*Nee,* I should go with you. You will need me."

I placed a hand on her arm. "*Maami*, let me take care of this for you. *Daadi* needs you."

Her eyes darted back in the direction of the sitting room where *Daadi* was. "I suppose that it will be all right with Aiden here," she relented.

I frowned and wondered at some of the comments that both the young deputy and my grandparents had made. They seemed to know each other better than a county deputy and an elderly Amish couple normally would.

Maami squeezed my hand even more tightly. "But you will come and fetch me if you need me, won't you?"

"I will," I promised.

I waited until she disappeared through the doorway that led into my grandfather's sitting room before I went downstairs.

In the short time that I had been upstairs, more police and several crime scene techs had arrived. The flashing lights of an ambulance reflected off the shop's front window, illuminating the glass candy jars on the wall.

I was about to enter the front room when I heard the two deputies speaking about my grandfather. I slid back into the shadow of the stairway.

"That old guy killed the richest man in the county," Deputy Carpenter said, sounding exasperated.

"Gordon, there is no way Jebidiah King had the

strength to stab anyone. You saw him. He can barely walk across the room," Aiden said.

"I'll give you that. The old man does look like he could drop dead at any second," the older deputy replied, as if he were discussing the weather.

I balled my fists at my sides and repeated the kinds of chocolates in my head again.

"But," Carpenter said. "That doesn't mean he didn't put someone else up to it. His granddaughter, for example. She looks scrappy. I bet she could have stabbed Colton if challenged."

"Why would any of the Kings want to kill him?" Aiden sounded angry now, and I liked him a little bit better for it.

"Everyone knows Colton wanted to buy this place. He's bought every other Amish business on Main Street, and Jebidiah King was the last holdout. Maybe Colton pushed the old man too far. Maybe he even threatened King's family. You know Colton would do whatever it took to get what he wanted."

"We shouldn't jump to conclusions," Aiden said.

"I'm not jumping to anything," Carpenter said mildly. "I'm only pointing out the obvious."

"Let's see where the evidence leads," Aiden replied. "The evidence is what's going to solve this case. Not wild speculation. If Bailey King killed Tyson Colton, the evidence will show that."

My former approval for the deputy dissolved in an instant.

I tiptoed halfway back up the stairs and called over my shoulder as if my grandmother could hear me, "Don't worry, *Maami*. I'll take care of everything." Then, I walked the rest of the way down the steps and into the front room of the shop like I had just come down the stairs.

The two deputies stood about three feet apart from each other. If I hadn't heard it with my own ears, there would have been no way for me to know that they had just been discussing the possibility that my grandfather and I were killers. I had no intention of letting them know that I was eavesdropping on them either.

I folded my arms over my chest. "My grandparents are in the sitting room upstairs. They'll wait there until you're ready to speak to them."

"Thank you, Miss King," Aiden said with a kind smile, but after overhearing his conversation with his fellow deputy, it wasn't a smile I trusted.

"I'll go consult with the crime scene boys," Deputy Carpenter said and walked around the counter into the kitchen.

Aiden gestured to one of the café tables in the front of the shop. The chairs had been flipped over onto the tabletops for the night. He removed two chairs off the top of one table. "Why don't we sit down to go over what happened?"

I slid into one of the chairs, and he took the other.

The deputy studied me with his dark brown eyes. If I were asked to identify their chocolate color, I would say milk chocolate. It was a standard in any baker's kitchen, but I preferred dark chocolate. With dark chocolate, I could better control the amount of sweetness.

"Can you tell me what happened?" he asked.

They think I did this, and Daadi put me up to it. The thought crept into my head. Even silently listing the types of chocolate didn't make it go away.

"Bailey? May I call you Bailey?"

I nodded dumbly.

Aiden leaned forward in his chair. "Are you all right?"

I wasn't all right, but I wasn't going to admit that to him. I looked into his milk chocolate eyes. "I'm fine." I sat up straighter in my seat. "Ask me whatever you like."

He nodded, all business again. "Tell me how you found Tyson Colton, from beginning to end."

I took a deep breath, and told him about waking up in the middle of the night and going downstairs for my phone in the kitchen. I ended with what I found when I got there. The image of Tyson Colton's body lying on the floor crossed my mind, but two details seemed to stand out to me the most, my grandfather's knife sticking out of his chest and my shoes in his blood. I shook the memories from my head. "I never got my phone. It's still in there."

"Depending on how close it is to the body, and if it could be related to the crime, we might have to hold onto it for at least a day or two."

"But—" I began to protest. I couldn't imagine getting through an hour without my phone, let alone a day or two.

"Brody!" Deputy Carpenter poked his head out around the side of the open swinging door.

Aiden turned to see what the other deputy wanted.

Deputy Carpenter carefully stepped through the doorway, avoiding the blood just as I had. "The tech says the murder weapon is some type of curved knife. He's never seen one like it before."

Aiden's dark gaze fell back to me. "I have."

Chapter 6

The police started to pack up just as dawn broke over the gazebo on the village square, and I was still in my pajamas. Fatigue seeped into every muscle of my body as I watched the officers and techs carry their equipment out the front door of Swissmen Sweets, but as much as I wished for it, I knew I wouldn't be able to sleep after they'd gone. One of the crime scene techs cut long strips of crime scene tape and crossed them in an X over the doorway leading into the kitchen. Tyson's body had been carted away two hours ago, shortly after the coroner arrived and did his preliminary examination.

Aiden approached me. "Here." He handed me my cell phone.

I balanced the phone in my hand. "I thought you needed to keep it for a few days."

He smiled, and a dimple I hadn't notice before appeared in his right cheek. "Do you want me to take it back?"

I closed my fingers around the phone and pressed it to my chest. "No."

"Didn't think so." The dimple flashed at me again. "Excuse the powder on there. We had to dust it for prints to make sure neither the victim nor anyone else had touched it."

"Were there any prints on it?" I asked.

"Just one set. We assume they're yours. You and your grandparents will have to come to the station to be fingerprinted for a process of elimination."

I swallowed. Fingerprinting sounded a lot more serious than just a process of elimination. "My grandparents won't want to go to the station. It would make them uncomfortable."

"I understand. As police, we're used to dealing with the Amish in the county. I can send an officer over later this morning with a portable fingerprint kit."

"Thank you." I noticed the blinking green light that indicated a new message. "Did you check my messages?"

"No. We'd have to acquire a court order to do that, and besides, we can't get beyond your passcode."

The passcode comment made me wonder if perhaps they had tried.

I frowned, hoping that there wasn't a text message from Eric on my phone after all. Not that my relationship in New York had any bearing on the tragedy unfolding in Harvest, but the fewer people who knew about Eric and me, the better.

Aiden held onto his duty belt just in front of his gun. "You won't be allowed into the kitchen until the scene is released. That will take a couple of days. My best guess is you all will be allowed back in there on Saturday."

I shoved the phone into the pocket of my hoodie. "How are my grandparents supposed to run their shop?"

"We will release the scene as soon as possible. We have no intention of harming your grandparents' business, but do remember a man died here." His voice was stern. "And when the time comes, I can recommend a company that can come in and clean the kitchen. It will need to be professionally cleaned."

I bit the inside of my lip and tried not to think of the state the kitchen must be in. "Thank you."

"I'm glad you're here to be with your grandparents through this. They need you." He paused as if debating whether or not he wanted to say what came next. "Your grandparents are good people. I know that more than anyone. I'll make sure they're treated fairly. You have my word."

My forehead wrinkled as I puzzled over what that meant.

Before I could ask him, he pulled his sheriff's department ball cap out of the back pocket of his uniform. "I'll be in touch, Bailey." He put the hat on his head and marched out the door.

Through the front window, I watched as Aiden climbed into his cruiser and drove away.

I was headed for the stairs when my cell phone rang. The readout said Baker. It was my code name for Eric. That was how deep my paranoia over anyone finding out about my romantic relationship with Eric Sharp went. Even in my own cell phone, I used a code name for him. It was in case he ever called, and someone spotted the readout before I did.

The name—Baker—was a bit of a joke too. Eric hated it. As he told me countless times, he was not a baker, he was a pastry chef, and there was a world of difference.

The phone rang again.

I put it to my ear. "Hello."

"Bailey, for the love of God, what are you doing outside of the city?" Eric yelled into my ear.

I barely heard him over the hard rock playing in the background. From the music, I knew Eric must be working in one of his pastry shops, probably the one in SoHo—it was his favorite. Eric always listened to loud music while he worked. He said it helped his muse. I suspected he played it to reinforce his "bad boy of the pastry world" image. It was the persona the media just couldn't get enough of, which was why a major network had just offered him his own reality TV show. Eric hadn't agreed to anything yet, but I knew it was only a matter of time. He loved the limelight.

"Can you turn the music down?" I asked, holding the phone away from my ear.

A second later there was silence, which came as a relief to my ringing ears.

"Where are you?" he demanded.

"I sent you a text," I said defensively. "I'm visiting my grandparents in Ohio. My grandfather is sick."

"You left during the most important moment of your life. The committee is about to name Jean Pierre's replacement, or did you forget?"

I gripped the phone. "I didn't forget, but my gran—"

"Hey!" Eric yelled. "I said brown sugar in that tart, not cane sugar. I don't share my recipes with you so that you can change them!"

I winced for the sous-chef who was about to be verbally flogged the moment our call ended. I had been on the receiving end of Eric's chef rants more times than I cared to count.

"You jump on the next plane for home," Eric said into the phone.

"But—"

There was a crash in the background.

Eric swore and ended the call without saying good-bye.

I didn't even have a chance to tell him that I'd found a dead guy in my grandparents' kitchen. Maybe I should have led with that.

"Bailey, dear, are you all right?" *Maami* asked.

I jumped and juggled my phone, catching it before it hit the floor.

"I'm sorry if I scared you," *Maami* said. She stood in the doorway leading to the stairs to the apartment. "Who were you talking to on your little phone?"

I smiled. *Maami* always called cell phones "little phones." I shook my head. "It's not important."

She straightened her apron. "It sounded important."

"It's not," I reassured her, and stuck the phone back into the pocket of my hoodie.

Maami's eyes widened as she saw the large X of crime scene tape covering the door that led into the kitchen. "Oh my."

"Deputy Brody said we can't go into the kitchen until the scene is released. He said it'll be released as soon as possible, and thinks we will have it back Saturday. It's only one day of business lost." Then I thought of how the kitchen would need a thorough cleaning. "Maybe you will be able to open on Monday."

"Aiden is a *gut* man, and I know he will do what he can." The corners of her mouth turned down. "A few days closed for us is nothing compared to what that poor man's family will suffer when they are told the news." Tears gathered in the corners of her eyes.

"Did Tyson have a family?"

"Oh, yes." She brushed the tear away from her eye. "A son. I hope that Aiden will be the one who will tell him. Aiden will deliver the news with compassion."

I frowned, momentarily distracted from wondering what the unlikable Tyson Colton's family must be like. More than once *Maami* had hinted at some kind of relationship with the brown-eyed deputy. The last comment the deputy had made to me before he left Swissmen Sweets had given me the same feeling.

I was about to ask my grandmother about it, when she clapped her hands. "I've just had an idea," *Maami* said. "There is a farmers' market in the square this afternoon. We can set up shop there to sell our candies and fudge. The fudge in the refrigerated display case should be enough for the day."

"Maybe it would be better if you and *Daadi* rested after your ordeal," I said.

"Nonsense. Sitting here and dwelling on what's happened won't change anything. Work is the best medicine for troubled thoughts. I will need your help setting up. We have a small canopy in the shed in the back alley along with a cart that we can use to move the candy across the street. We must do as much as we can without involving your grandfather. I don't want your *daadi* helping—it wouldn't be *gut* for his heart. We'll give him the job of pricing the items for sale after we have the booth set up. Considering the circumstances, I think we could price everything at a discount, but I will talk that over with Jebidiah to make the final decision."

I smiled. "I knew you would think of something to do."

She grinned back at me. "It wasn't my idea. It was a gift of the *gut* Lord. I'm certain of that, and He will help us through all of this. You will see."

I wished I had her confidence.

Chapter 7

As the farmers' market wasn't until that afternoon, *Maami* and I spent the morning packing up treats to transport across Main Street. I arranged shiny truffles in a bakery box. My grandparents sold milk chocolate and dark chocolate varieties. Back at JP Chocolates we made over fifty varieties every day, from orange cream to saffron. Saffron was out of the question for Swissmen Sweets, but I wondered if I could talk my grandfather into some other flavors when we got the kitchen back. I was creating a list of possible truffles in my head when there was a rapid tapping on the front window.

"Oh dear," *Maami* said.

I looked up from my truffles. A round woman with wire-rimmed glasses had her nose pressed up to the windowpane as she tried to peer inside.

"Oh dear," *Maami* repeated.

"Who is that?" I asked.

"Ruth Yoder, the deacon's wife." *Maami* wiped chocolate from the edge of a plate with a clean rag.

Ruth spotted us standing at the counter and waved.

"She's seen us," my grandmother said, disappointed.

"I suppose I have no choice but to let her in." She removed the gloves she wore while working with the chocolate.

My hospitable grandmother didn't want to let a member of her district into the shop? "Why don't you want to let her in?"

Maami stepped around the counter. "You will see."

A moment later, *Maami* opened the door, and the large woman flounced into the shop holding a casserole dish in her hand. She pulled up short when she saw the kitchen door with its X of crime scene tape. "Oh, Clara, I've heard about what happened, but I hoped the news was horribly exaggerated. I came as soon as I was able. As you know, the deacon is very busy, and as his wife, I have many responsibilities. He's heard about the tragedy in your shop, but I assured him I would comfort you. What a terrible, terrible thing to have happened in our district. The deacon and the other church elders are meeting now to discuss what the district response should be."

The deacon's wife lowered her voice. "How is Jebidiah doing with all of this? I hope it's not affecting his heart. Poor man. It must be just awful being told that you're about to pass on, but, it's something we all will face someday." She paused in front of me. "Who is this now? Did you hire a new girl?" She frowned. "I would have hoped that you would hire a young lady from our district. You know how important the deacon believes that to be."

I stared at her openmouthed. I don't think she had taken a single breath since entering the shop.

Maami jumped in before Ruth could say another

word. "This is my granddaughter, Bailey. She's visiting from New York."

"I see." Ruth studied me. "This must be Ben's daughter then. It was such a shame when he decided to leave the community to marry that English woman. It breaks a mother's heart when any of her children choose another path." She placed her hand over her own heart. "It would break mine, but as you know, Clara, none of my six children have left. They're married and settled in our district with children of their own. It must be extra difficult for you, since Ben was your only child." She nodded at me. "I'm Ruth Yoder, the deacon's wife."

"It's nice to meet you," I forced myself to say out of politeness. As for it actually being nice to meet her, I wasn't so sure. And my grandmother was right; I did see why *Maami* had been reluctant to let her into the shop.

"This is sure to affect your business, Clara. You wouldn't want anyone coming into your store with that," she said as she pointed at the crime scene tape, "on your door. Present company excluded, as you know I'm only here to lend my support out of duty and friendship."

I mentally snorted. If this was what the deacon's wife considered friendly support, I didn't want to know how she treated people she didn't like.

"We will be selling our fudge and candies at the farmers' market later today," *Maami* said as she walked back around the counter and resumed packing fudge into disposable plastic containers.

Ruth pulled out a chair from one of the café tables and sat. "I'll be here to support you."

My eyes widened as I made eye contact with *Maami*. Was this woman serious? She was going to camp out in the shop while we prepared for the farmers' market?

There was another knock at the door.

"I'll get it, *Maami*," I said, and squeezed her arm as I passed her on my way to the front door.

Through the glass door, I saw Deputy Aiden Brody standing on the sidewalk with another man in uniform. The second man was much younger than Deputy Carpenter, and I was relieved the surly deputy was absent. I opened the door.

"Hello, Bailey," Aiden said. "This is Matt Larkin." He nodded at the other man. "He's here to take the fingerprints."

I inwardly groaned. I had only known Ruth Yoder for fifteen minutes, and I knew my grandmother would not want her around while the police fingerprinted us.

Matt held up a black case that was the size of a toaster. "I have everything I need right here."

I opened the door wider and let the two men inside.

Ruth jumped out of her seat. "What is going on? Are you here to arrest someone?"

"No, ma'am." Matt stumbled back. "We're just here to collect fingerprints from the King family."

If a forceful Amish woman like Ruth barked questions at me like that, I might have taken a couple of steps back too.

"Fingerprints?" Ruth yelped. She glanced at *Maami* and me with suspicion.

Aiden stepped around the fingerprint tech. "It's only to eliminate their fingerprints from our evidence."

Ruth smoothed her apron over her skirt. "I had better be off. The deacon would not like it if I were here at the same time as the police." She turned to my grandmother. "Don't you worry, Clara, I will make sure everyone in the district knows about your predicament."

She marched out of the shop, taking the casserole she'd brought with her.

"I'm sure you will," *Maami* muttered under her breath. I stifled a chuckle.

Matt placed his case on one of the café tables and unzipped the top. "I'm sorry to have scared off your guest."

"It's quite all right," *Maami* said. "It might keep her away for a little while at least. Let me find my husband while you are setting up your contraption. He's upstairs resting." *Maami* walked to the small hallway that led to the stairs.

Matt pulled out a black box that appeared to be the weight and size of a television remote control. He caught me watching him. "It's a portable fingerprint scanner. We got it last month. It's awesome." Matt gave it a loving pat.

Aiden laughed. "Matt likes his toys."

Matt grinned. "Especially the new ones. I just need to enter some data, and we can get started."

While Matt tapped on his screen, I looked at Aiden. "Do you have any leads on what might have happened?" I asked.

He shook his head. "No, but it is still very early in the investigation."

Part of me wanted to ask him about the conversation I had overheard between him and Deputy Carpenter. The older deputy had seemed pretty certain that I'd murdered Tyson Colton. I thought better of it and instead asked, "Why was Tyson inside of my grandparents' shop?"

Aiden's eyebrows knit together, and he studied me. "That's a good question. The answer might lead to the killer. We'll find out who did this. Don't worry."

"Was there any forced entry?" I couldn't believe I hadn't thought to ask that before. How, exactly, had Tyson entered Swissmen Sweets?

He arched an eyebrow at me. "Forced entry?"

"How else could Tyson have gotten inside the kitchen other than to break in? My grandparents didn't let him in, and I sure didn't."

He nodded. "Someone broke the lock on the back door to the shop."

Even though it was what I had expected him to say, it was still shocking. "What's the status of the lock now? Is the door secure?" I asked. "Can someone get into the shop from that way?" My eyes darted in the direction of the kitchen door, still blocked with those glaring strips of yellow crime scene tape.

Aiden shook his head. "We took the lock with us for evidence and had it replaced with two deadbolts. No one is getting into the shop from that direction."

"Why didn't you tell us this before?"

"I told your grandparents when I went upstairs to interview them. I assumed that they would have told you." His voice was even.

I wondered why *Maami* hadn't thought to mention that little detail. But, no matter whether or not my grandparents had told me about the broken lock, it was very good news. "Doesn't that take my grandparents and me off the hook?"

"I'm afraid not." He removed his departmental baseball cap and tucked it into the back pocket of his uniform. "It only proves that someone broke into Swissmen Sweets through the back door. It doesn't tell us anything about what happened after he entered, or who he was with in the kitchen."

I read his thoughts in those dark eyes. *He thinks that person with Tyson in the kitchen could have been me.*

His brow knit together as he studied me. "Don't worry. I'll find out who did this."

I frowned. Aiden's telling me not to worry only made me worry more. I still didn't quite understand Aiden's history with my grandparents, but no one was going to care about this case as much as I did. I couldn't allow my grandparents' good name to be tainted in their Amish district or in the village as a whole. Unfortunately, it seemed the deacon's nosy wife had already taken on gossiping about the murder as her personal mission.

I watched Aiden as he and Matt put their heads close together, looking at the fingerprint reader's small screen, and I came to a decision—I needed to do a little poking around on my own. My grandparents seemed to trust Aiden. I wasn't as sure about him, and I didn't trust Deputy Carpenter the least little bit. The only person I trusted to find out what had really happened to Tyson Colton was me.

"Miss?" Matt pointed to the chair. "I'm ready for your fingerprints."

I sat at the table and gave him my hand.

Chapter 8

After Aiden and Matt—still cradling his beloved fingerprinting machine—had gone, *Maami* and I finished packing up everything we would need to sell fudge and candies at the farmers' market. My grandfather, who seemed to be rejuvenated after his rest, sat at one of the café tables writing a price list by hand. His lettering was careful and precise. Penmanship like my grandfather's was a lost art in the English world of keyboards and smartphones.

Maami closed one of the plastic fudge containers with a piece of Scotch tape. "I'm going next door to ask Esther if we can borrow her cart to move all this chocolate across the street. With two carts, the job will go much more quickly."

I wiped my hands on a dish cloth. "I'll go. You stay here with *Daadi* and help him price."

Maami cocked her head. "If you don't mind. Esther owns the pretzel shop next door."

I removed my cell phone from my back pocket. "I don't mind, and besides, I should probably call Jean

Pierre and give him an update about how long I'll be gone."

Daadi looked up from his list. "You aren't going home tomorrow?"

I shook my head. "I can't with everything that's going on. You can't even enter your own kitchen."

My typically smiling grandfather frowned. "We're not going to allow what happened to Tyson to ruin your life as well. If you don't return to New York this weekend, what will happen?"

I shook my head. "I'm sure as long as I'm there by the time they make the announcement on Monday, everything will be fine," I said, even though I knew nothing of the kind.

Maami closed another fudge container. "But you may lose your chance."

I walked around the counter. "I'm staying at least until Sunday, and that's final."

Daadi chuckled, and he marked a box of taffy with a price. "She gets her stubborn streak from you, Clara."

"Jebidiah!" my grandmother exclaimed.

I kissed *Daadi* on his wrinkled cheek before I went out the front door. "I think both of you have enough stubbornness to go around."

They were still gently bickering over who was more stubborn when I went out the front door of the candy shop.

Instead of going straight to the pretzel shop, or even making the call to Jean Pierre I'd said I would, I walked behind Swissmen Sweets. I wanted to look at the back door where Tyson had broken in. I came around the side of the building, but before I could make it all the way, I was stopped by a small orange cat, who couldn't have been more than a year or two old. "Well, hello there."

The small cat meowed and rolled back and forth on the ground, exposing his white belly to me. I squatted next to him and held out my hand. He sniffed it, and then pressed his orange striped cheek into my hand.

"You're a friendly little guy, aren't you? Where's your owner?"

As if on cue, a young Amish girl came running up the alley. "There you are! I've been looking for you everywhere." The girl was in her late teens or early twenties, tall, and slim. Her hair was honey blond, and her features were small and delicate, as if they had been painted on her face with a light hand. Even her plain, navy dress and black apron couldn't hide how beautiful she was.

"Is that your cat?" I asked.

She scooped up the cat. "*Ya.*" She scratched the cat under the chin, and he began to purr. "I mean no . . . he's not . . . not really."

I raised my eyebrows.

"He showed up in my family's barn this week. I think someone just dropped him along the road, and he wandered onto our property. It happens more often than you would think. My *bruder* said that we couldn't keep him, because the other barn cats didn't seem to take a liking to him. Barn cats can be very territorial. The other cats howled the entire night he was in the barn. They kept us all up. My *bruder* said the new cat had to go, but I just couldn't part with him. My sister said that I could keep him at the pretzel shop until I found a home for him. It's only temporary," she added regretfully.

"Does he have a name?" I asked.

Her face broke into a wide smile, making her even more endearing. "Esther said that I shouldn't name him, but I've been calling him Nutmeg."

I smiled. "I think Nutmeg is a perfect name."

She scratched the cat behind the ear. "I think so too, but I can't keep him." She said this more to herself than to me, as if she were trying to prepare herself for the pending separation from Nutmeg.

"Esther is your sister?"

"*Ya*, Esther Esh is my sister." She said this as if Esther's was a name I should have recognized.

"I'm Bailey," I said. "I'm Jebidiah and Clara King's granddaughter."

"I'm Emily." She studied me curiously over the cat's head. "Esther said that the Kings had an *Englisch* grand-daughter, who never comes to visit."

I flinched when she said that. "I'm here now."

"That is *gut*." She nodded.

"I'm supposed to ask your sister if I can borrow her cart. My grandparents are going to sell their fudge and candy in the farmers' market this afternoon, and it would be a great help to have the cart to move every-thing across the street."

Her eyes flitted onto a spot somewhere behind me. "I heard about the *Englischer* who died in Clara's kitchen. How terrible for your grandparents that it had to happen there."

I couldn't help but note that she didn't mention she felt sorry that Tyson was dead. She was only sorry that it had happened in my grandparents' kitchen.

"I'm sure my sister will let you borrow the cart. The Kings have always been *gut* neighbors to us." She turned away from the sidewalk and toward the street that faced the village square. "I can introduce you to her."

Checking on Swissmen Sweets' backdoor would have to wait. I followed Emily back to the front of the building. Across Main Street, dozens of Amish farmers had set up white tents and canopies to protect their produce and homemade jams and jellies from the afternoon sun. There was a late September bite in the air, but the sun was still strong. I stood there for a moment watching them work. Young Amish men handed down crates of vegetables from buggies and horse drawn wagons. Amish women neatly arranged their goods on wooden folding tables decorated with dark plain cloths or nothing at all.

Emily turned. "Are you coming?" She still held Nutmeg in her arms, and the ginger-colored cat appeared perfectly content in her embrace.

"Right."

ESH FAMILY PRETZELS was stenciled on the window of the shop's front door. Emily opened the door to the pretzel shop; there was a petite woman behind the counter with the same coloring as Emily. I knew at once it must be Esther. While the honey-blond hair on Emily made her beautiful, the honey-blond hair on this woman—who I guessed was close to my own age of twenty-seven—was almost too close to the color of her complexion, and it washed her out.

"I see you found him," Esther said as we walked into the shop. "If that cat keeps running away, we'll have to take him to a shelter. I can't have a cat running loose in the shop."

"He won't run away anymore," Emily said, holding the cat a little more tightly. "I promise."

Her sister shook her head as she spun a long piece of dough into a pretzel with such ease, I knew that she must have done it a thousand, if not a million, times before. "It doesn't do any good for you to promise. It's up to the cat to behave." Esther raised her eyebrows at me. "What would you like, Miss? Can I make you a fresh pretzel?"

The granite counter in front of Esther was covered with a layer of white flour.

In a display case to the left of the counter there were dozens of soft pretzels of varying sizes and flavors waiting to be sold. My stomach rumbled as I stared at the display case, and a cinnamon-sugar pretzel caught my eye. Earlier that morning, my grandmother had attempted to feed me breakfast, but I had been too upset by Tyson's death to eat. I was surprised how quickly my appetite had returned. Had I already gotten used to the idea that a man had been murdered in my grandparents' candy shop?

"Esther," Emily said. "This is Bailey King, Jebidiah and Clara's granddaughter."

Esther's brows rose, and she studied me with renewed interest. "You're the *Englisch* granddaughter from New York they speak so highly of. You're some kind of chef."

"A chocolatier, actually," I said.

"What's that?" Emily asked as she set the cat on the floor.

Nutmeg walked across the room and curled up on a pillow under the front window. It wasn't hard to guess which of the two Esh sisters had placed the pillow there for the cat.

"It's just a fancy name for someone who makes things out of chocolate." I smiled at the girl.

"So you are a candy maker like your grandfather," she said.

That wasn't exactly true, but I nodded anyway. "Basically."

Esther twirled another pretzel into shape. "I'm sure that your chocolate is much more expensive than what your grandfather sells in his shop."

I shrugged. "It's a different place," I said, thinking it

was a different planet. "Actually, I'm here because my grandmother sent me. We would like to borrow your cart. Swissmen Sweets is closed today. I'm sure you know why." When she didn't say anything, I went on. "So we're going to sell what chocolates and candies we can at the farmers' market across the street."

"I'm happy to lend my little cart if it will help." She dusted flour from her hands. "Emily, go fetch the cart for Bailey, will you?"

The girl disappeared through a door into a backroom.

While Emily was gone, Esther walked over to the display case and plucked out the largest cinnamon-sugar pretzel. She wrapped it in a piece of thin wax paper and held it out to me. "Here. I saw you eyeing it while we were talking."

I took the pretzel from her hand, and my mouth was already watering. "How much is it?"

She shook her head. "Your grandparents have been *gut* neighbors to us. It is a gift."

"Thank you." I took a bite of the pretzel and closed my eyes. "This is the best pretzel I've ever tasted. You would stomp all the bakeries in New York with this." I wiped cinnamon and sugar from my mouth.

She laughed and held out a napkin to me. "It is *gut* to hear that that the Amish can do something better than the *Englisch*."

"You certainly make pretzels better. How long have you been in business?" I asked.

She beamed. "*Danki*. The pretzel shop was started by my grandfather and has been passed down through the family to my siblings and me. My *bruder* would much rather farm than work in the shop, so he gave it to me to manage, day to day."

I remembered coming into this very shop during the

summers I spent with my grandparents when I was a child, and there had always been an elderly Amish man behind the counter, whom my grandfather would chat with while I took an inordinate amount of time deciding which of the pretzels I wanted. I realized now that he must have been Emily and Esther's grandfather.

"Is your farm far from here?"

She shook her head. "It's on Barrington Road, just two or three miles from here."

I remembered my grandparents had been friends with an elderly couple who lived on that road. We had visited them often. They had since passed away, but I knew the road well. There wasn't much else out there except for the farm.

"How long have been minding the shop?" I asked.

"Since I was sixteen," she said proudly.

"I'm impressed." I wiped more sugar from my face. I was starting to believe that it was a futile act, and that I would need to wash my face when I got back to Swissmen Sweets. "I can't imagine running a business when I was sixteen. I could barely make it to class on time."

She smiled. "It's not very Amish to say, but I am proud of it."

I saw my opportunity. "If you are so proud of the shop, why would you sell the building to Tyson Colton?"

She stepped back and her eyes narrowed. In an instant, all the goodwill I had won by complimenting her pretzels was lost. "Pardon me?"

I wrapped what was left of my delicious pretzel, which admittedly wasn't much, in the piece of wax paper. "My grandfather told me that the merchants on either side of him had sold their buildings to Tyson, and that was why Tyson wanted to buy Swissmen Sweets."

"The building isn't sold yet," she corrected me. "Not officially. We had just begun the process."

This was interesting. I tried to keep my face neutral. "Will you find another buyer now?"

Esther glared at me.

The cowbell hanging from the front entrance's doorknob rang behind me. I glanced over my shoulder and a large Amish man entered the shop.

Nutmeg jumped off of his pillow as if someone had stepped on his tail and dashed into the back room. The fur on his back stood on end.

The man was clean shaven, his head uncovered, and he had red hair. By his lack of beard, I knew he wasn't married. He ignored me and spoke to Esther in Pennsylvania Dutch. I couldn't understand his words, but it was clear that he was upset.

Esther replied in kind and then caught me staring at them. "Abel, we will talk about this later. Emily is in the back."

He fisted his large hands at his sides.

"We have a guest," Esther said through clenched teeth. "Bailey, this is my *bruder*, Abel. Bailey is Jebidiah and Clara's granddaughter."

Abel looked me up and down with obvious interest. "We have met."

I blinked at him. "No, I don't think we have." I had been in Harvest for less than twenty-four hours. I would remember if I had run into a red-headed, burly, Amish man.

"When we were children." He watched me.

The memory came back in a rush. Heat flushed my cheeks as I remembered an encounter with a young red-headed boy behind the village gazebo. The pretzel maker's grandson had taken a liking to me when I was ten, but I'd wanted nothing to do with him. He was older than I was, Amish, scrawny, and I was in love with a boy in my class back in Connecticut. One summer day, he'd tried to steal a kiss me from me behind the gazebo, and I'd run away. That was the last time I had seen him until today. Abel wasn't scrawny anymore.

He scowled as if he didn't enjoy the memory either.

At that moment, Emily returned, pushing a small silver cart. "I'm sorry that took so long," the young Amish girl said breathlessly. "There were a bunch of bakery supplies piled on top of it, and I had to find a place to put them." Emily looked from one of us to the other. "Is everything all right?"

Esther broke eye contact with me. "Everything is fine, Emily." She turned back to me. "Please tell Clara she can have the cart for as long as she needs it."

I stepped back at the abrupt change in her demeanor. "I'm sorry if I upset you."

"Like I said, she can keep it as long as she needs," Esther said, still with her body turned away from me.

"Thank you for the pretzel, and thank you for the cart." I grabbed the handles of the cart and rolled it to the door. "It was nice to meet you both."

"Bye." Emily gave me a little wave, and her older sister went back to twirling dough into pretzels. This time she used a little more force than she had before.

Abel leaned on the counter and folded his arms, watching me all the while.

Before I left the pretzel shop, I wondered where Nutmeg had gone when he'd fled. I hoped for Emily's sake that he hadn't run far.

Chapter 9

Before entering my grandparents' shop, I needed to call Jean Pierre. It wasn't a conversation I looked forward to, and I still wanted to look at Swissmen Sweets' back door. I left the cart at the corner of my grandfather's building, and walked between the candy shop and Esther's pretzel shop to the alley behind my grandparents' store.

I walked up the three short steps to the back door and peered at the lock. There did seem to be tool marks around the door's handle, but not knowing what condition the handle was in before Tyson died, it was difficult to determine what was new and what had been there previously. I was happy to see two new deadbolts installed in the door, so I reassured myself that at least what Aiden had said about the new locks was true.

I tried the doorknob, and it was locked. I stared at the tool marks a little harder, but nothing came to me. I didn't know what I had expected to learn by staring at the lock, and I had put off my call to Jean Pierre long enough. It was time to get it over with. I felt the same way I did when I was asked to supply a chocolate

fountain at a wedding or anniversary party for one of
Jean Pierre's wealthy clients. I hated chocolate foun-
tains, but I always did it first during set up, because the
sooner I started it, the sooner it would be over.

There wasn't anywhere to sit other than on the steps
themselves, so I perched on the back stoop and removed
my cell phone from my pocket. I looked at my text messages for the first time. I had at least a dozen from Cass
demanding to know when I would be returning to New
York, but none from Eric. I supposed he thought his
abrupt phone call early that morning was sufficient. I
didn't need a therapist to tell me that our relationship
was doomed. Perhaps I had even known it when I'd first
accepted Eric's invitation to go out. I wasn't any better
than the countless girls who had fallen under the spell
of a famous man's attention, but my trip to Ohio was a
hard slap to the face, waking me up to the truth. I would
worry about Eric when I returned to New York. I had
enough problems to cope with in Ohio.

I scrolled to Jean Pierre's cell phone number in my
favorites. The phone rang and rang. It wouldn't be too
long before the call clicked over to voicemail. I didn't
know if that was better or worse. It would certainly be
easier to leave Jean Pierre a message, but there was
always a chance he would never hear it. As he had told
me many times during my tenure as his first chocolatier,
*"A famous chocolatier does not have time to check his
messages."*

I was about to give up and call back later, when he
picked up. "Hello?" he asked in a heavy French accent.

"Hi, Jean Pierre," I said.

"Bon sang, I need you at the shop. Caden is not your
worthy replacement." He added some French curses to

the end of that statement. I knew French profanity well from working with the famous chocolatier for so long.

A small part of me was happy Jean Pierre was dissatisfied with Caden's work. That meant that Cass had to be wrong about the selection committee giving the head chocolatier job to Caden. They would never choose anyone without Jean Pierre's support. You did not make a world famous chocolatier—one who could carve a block of chocolate into a replica of Michelangelo's David with one knife—angry, if you knew what was good for you. If what Jean Pierre said next was any indication, apparently this was a lesson I still needed to learn.

"When are you coming home?"

Home. I wished that it was possible to go home. Even if I was willing to leave my grandparents at a time like this, I didn't know if the police would let me go.

"You have left at an uncomfortable time," he complained. "I need you here. Are you back in the city?" He blew out a frustrated breath.

"No. I'm still in Ohio with my grandparents," I said.

A creative string of French swearing assaulted my ear.

When he finally wound down, I interjected, "I can explain. Just give me five minutes to speak, and then you can yell at me again."

"All right, *ma chérie*, but when you finish speaking, I will resume my shouting." He was matter-of-fact.

A smiled curved my lips. "Deal." I took a deep breath and told him everything that had happened since I had arrived in Ohio, except I left out any reference to Eric Sharp, because, of course, Jean Pierre didn't, and couldn't, know about my relationship with the pastry chef.

Jean Pierre swore as I finished my tale.

Silence hung between us until I couldn't take it anymore. "That's all you are going to say? You aren't going to rant and rave?"

"*Ma chérie,* I would not yell at you at a time like this. Do you think I am some kind of *animale*? You have been through a terrible shock. I will not make it worse."

To my surprise, the fact that Jean Pierre wasn't yelling at me about abandoning him was even more disturbing than his curse-laden rant would have been. Tears stung my eyes. For all his rants and complaints, he really did care about me.

"And you must stay there and take care of your grandparents. They need you now." He gave a long-suffering sigh. "Even more than I do."

I hesitated. "What about the selection committee?"

He called the selection committee a particularly terrible name, which made me feel better. "Let me take care of them. They can postpone their decision a few days, until you are able to return."

"Thank you, Jean Pierre." I brushed a tear from my cheek.

"Ah, do not thank me now," he said. "Thank me later, when you assume my role in my great *chocolat* empire."

I laughed. "Okay. I'll thank you then."

I ended the call and shoved the phone back into my pocket. My hand fell to my side on the cement stoop.

"Ow!" I yanked my hand back as a sharp pain coursed through my index finger. There was a tiny piece of glass, a sliver really, stuck in my finger. I pulled it out, and blood gathered on my fingertip.

I jumped to my feet and stared at the stoop. The sunlight glittered on other minuscule shards of glass on the edge of the stoop. I moved around the landing and found several larger pieces in a small patch of grass. The glass was very thin. I squatted in front of the pieces. I didn't dare touch them. I glanced up at the back door.

"What are you doing?" someone demanded.

I screamed and rolled onto my back like an overturned turtle. Aiden stared down at me. He offered me a hand, but I ignored it and scrambled to my feet. "Don't you know better than to sneak up on a person like that?"

He held his hands up in mock surrender. He held a plastic sack of apples in one hand. "Sorry. I didn't mean to scare you." He showed just a hint of the dimple with that remark.

"You didn't scare me," I lied.

His face morphed from amusement to concern. "You're bleeding."

I looked down at my hand and saw blood trickling down my index finger to my palm and wrist. "It's nothing." I moved my hand above my heart to slow the bleeding.

"You might need stitches."

I shook my head. "No. I have had far worse cuts, which didn't require stitches."

He blinked at me.

"I'm a chocolatier," I explained. "Anyone who works in a professional kitchen has cut him or herself once or twice."

He rested the hand not holding the sack of apples on his duty belt. "I still think you should have it looked at."

"I'll bandage it up when I go back inside." I held my wrist with my left hand. "What are you doing back here?"

He scanned the alley. "I thought I would take another look around."

"That's what I was thinking too," I said. "And look what I found. Broken glass. There's some on the stoop, but there are some larger pieces in the grass. Though even the larger pieces are small. None are much bigger than a matchbook. I think whoever broke this glass cleaned it up in a hurry, and didn't care that they missed part of it." I paused. "Or they didn't have time to care."

Aiden stood next to me. "The glass is very thin." He nodded to my hand. "Is that what cut you?"

I nodded.

"You're lucky it didn't do more damage. Glass that thin could have really hurt you." He held the piece of glass under his nose and sniffed. "Just what I thought."

"What?" I asked.

"Kerosene. This glass came from a kerosene lamp."

"So someone Amish brought a kerosene lamp here," I said.

"Why do you say they're Amish?" he asked.

I sidestepped away from him. He was too close. I cleared my throat. "Who else would carry a kerosene lamp?"

He stepped back from the stoop too. "Good point."

"You didn't know about this glass before?" I asked.

Aiden shook his head.

"Didn't you search the back alley for more signs of a break-in?" My tone was accusatory.

He frowned. "Deputy Carpenter searched the alleyway early this morning."

"But he didn't find this," I said.

He shook his head. "He may have missed it."

"Or he didn't want to see it," I muttered, remembering Deputy Carpenter's accusations against my grandfather.

Aiden's gaze snapped in my direction. "Deputy Carpenter is a good cop. He would have reported something like this if he'd noticed it."

I didn't bother to argue with him. "Doesn't this prove

that whoever broke into the shop with Tyson was Amish? Maybe Tyson and the killer even entered together."

"No, this proves nothing," the deputy said simply. "We don't know how long that glass has been there."

I took a deep breath and recited the types of chocolate in my head. "I know it looks bad for my grandfather, but I'm telling you he didn't do this. He's sick. He even passed out yesterday. His family doctor had to make a house call to check on him. He's in no condition to kill anyone, let alone have the strength to stab a grown man. That takes a lot of force, which my grandfather doesn't have, and he didn't ask me to do it either, if that's the other theory you have going."

"Miss King," he began.

"I thought you were calling me Bailey," I said. "Every time you say Miss King, I feel like you're about to administer a chocolate sculpting test. My instructors in culinary school always called me Miss King."

The lines around his mouth softened into a smile. "Bailey, first take a breath."

I glared at him.

"Go ahead." He smiled encouragingly. "I'll wait."

I scowled, but finally, I relented and allowed myself to breathe.

The deputy removed an evidence bag and a set of tweezers from the breast pocket of his uniform. He set the bag of apples on the step as he collected the pieces of glass from the ground. "Did that help?"

"Nope." I folded my arms, taking care not to bump my finger, which was beginning to throb. But I wasn't going to let Aiden know that.

"I'll have the crime scene guys come back here to take pictures and collect whatever glass I missed. They are better equipped to pick up all the tiny pieces." He sealed the bag and put the tweezers back in his pocket. "I don't believe that your grandfather did this either, but I have to follow wherever the evidence leads. Right now, he is the best suspect we have, but you're right that his health almost immediately eliminates him. I'll talk to his doctor about his strength and his ability to stab anyone the night of the murder."

I grimaced.

"But even if your grandfather is eliminated from the list, it still leaves you and your grandmother as suspects." He picked up his bag of apples from the step.

I felt sick, because I knew he was right.

The radio crackled on his hip. "I have to go." He opened the plastic sack in his hand and removed an apple from it. He held it out to me.

I stared at it. "What's that?"

"A Honey Crisp." He grinned. "I just picked these up from the farmers' market before coming back here."

I still didn't move to touch the apple.

"Take it. They're the best apples you'll ever eat."

I accepted the apple, feeling a little bit like Snow White accepting a snack from the evil queen. This time, she might be disguised as a handsome prince instead of an old hag.

Chapter 10

I stared at the apple for a long time after Aiden left the back alley.

"Bailey!" I heard my grandmother call me from the front of the shop.

I glanced from the apple to my cut finger, which was no longer bleeding, but still throbbed. Of the two, I thought my *maami* would be more upset about the cut, and I didn't want to give her any more reason to be upset that day. Heavens knew, she'd already had enough to cause her worry that morning.

With my hand in my pocket, I came around the back of the building. My grandmother stood beside the metal cart that I had borrowed from Esther Esh and smiled at me. "When I saw Esther's cart here with you nowhere in sight, I was afraid something might have happened to you." She chuckled, but her eyes were worried. "I know that's silly."

I rushed over to her and gave her a hug, taking care to not to show her my injured finger. "That's not silly at all. I'm sorry. I was just wandering around outside the shop, thinking about all that's happened this morning."

She gave a great sigh. "There is certainly a lot to worry us."

I stepped back and shoved my hand back into my pocket before she could see my cut. My grandmother had a sharp eye, and I knew she would realize there was something wrong with my hand at just a glance.

Her brow creased. "Where did you get that apple?" she asked, proving my theory that there was little she missed.

"From the farmers' market," I said breezily.

"Oh, that's nice. I didn't know that you already went over there."

I didn't correct her.

She patted my arm. "It's at times like these that *Gott* reminds us to cast our cares on Him. I don't know why this happened. I don't know why Tyson died in our home, but I do know our Lord can use an evil act for His purpose and for *gut*."

I bit the inside of my lip to stop myself from questioning my grandmother's faith. I didn't know that I believed the same, or if I ever could. How could a man's murder—even if that man was as universally disliked as Tyson seemed to have been—be turned into anything good?

"Now," she said, her face breaking into a smile, "we should get to work loading the carts and opening our booth. Until we know how *Gott* will use what has happened, we must be faithful in the *gut* work the Lord has assigned us for the here and now."

I smiled, still uncertain over what my grandmother had said. "Let me just take this inside." I held up the apple.

Maami stared at the apple a little harder, as if she suspected that there was more to the story.

"Clara! Clara, dear!" A woman with short black curls waved a stack of papers at my grandmother from the other side of Main Street. "You will need to set up your tent quickly, if you want to open with the rest of the farmers."

Grateful for the interruption, I asked, "Who's that?"

"Margot Rawlings. She's the village chairwoman in charge of the square and all the activities that are held there. I spoke with her this morning about having a booth at the farmers' market, and she was kind enough to grant us that," she said, just barely above a whisper.

"Why are you whispering?" I asked in an equally low voice.

"Clara! Hurry up now, dear. Chop, chop." Margot tapped an imaginary watch on her wrist. "The farmers' market won't wait for you to open."

My grandmother waved to acknowledge she had heard the other woman.

Margot marched across Main Street straight toward us, crossing right in front of an Amish buggy. The driver had to pull back hard on the reins to avoid hitting her, not that she noticed.

"Clara, are you almost ready?" Margot asked, half out of breath.

"*Ya*, Margot, we are all but ready. We will be ready to open when the market begins as promised."

"Wonderful," Margot said, seemingly only slightly more relaxed at this news.

"Margot, have you met my granddaughter, Bailey?" my grandmother asked.

Margot's curls bounced on her shoulders like Shirley Temple's might have in the middle of a dance number.

"No, I haven't. It's nice to meet you, Bailey. Will you be helping your grandparents in the booth this afternoon?"

"That's the plan," I said.

"I'm glad to hear it." She turned back to my grandmother. "I was sorry to hear about what happened in your shop. What a terrible situation for you, but I can't say that I'm sorry Tyson is dead. He was a horribly greedy man. You should have heard about the plans he had for Main Street after he bought everything up. He was going to turn us into a Disney version of Amish Country. The very thought of it makes me sick to my stomach. He even had plans to tamper with the village square, *my* square. Can you imagine?"

"Margot," *Maami* said, aghast. "You should not say such things."

The English woman sniffed. "Why not, if it's the truth? You will be hard-pressed to find anyone in the village who is sorry that he's dead."

I studied Margot with renewed interest. It looked like I had a suspect. How far would Margot go to protect her control of the village square? But then I remembered the glass from the broken kerosene lamp behind the candy shop. Margot definitely wasn't Amish, and wouldn't be carrying a kerosene lamp to light her way in the dark. Then again, as Aiden had said, we didn't know how long the glass from the broken lamp had been there. Margot remained on my list.

Margot glanced over her shoulder. "Oh no, Ephraim Schmidt is setting up his honey stall in the wrong place. I told him it must be on the south end of the square." She started back across the street without saying goodbye and nearly got hit by an Amish buggy a second time.

My grandmother sniffed. "Insufferable woman."

I bit my lip to hold back a laugh.

My grandmother eyed me. "Are you laughing at your *grossmaami*, Bailey King?"

"No." I giggled. "I just have never heard you speak badly of anyone. Ever."

"You haven't met Margot. The woman would drive a saint to distraction." She frowned. "I am sorry. I shouldn't say such a thing. It's unkind."

"But is it true?" I couldn't help but ask.

She grinned. "Maybe a little, but Margot was good enough to give us an open spot in the farmers' market. I should be kinder with that in mind." She sighed. "And she's right. We do need to set up the booth."

I headed for the door. "I'll be back out in a minute."

I ran into the shop, feeling grateful for busybody Margot. At least she kept me from having to explain the apple to my grandmother. I stopped in the bathroom and cleaned my cut. In the medicine cabinet, I found an old-fashioned tin can of Band-Aids. Thankfully, the bandages didn't appear to be as old as the tin.

I tucked the apple in the crook of my arm and wrapped the bandage around my wounded finger as I made my way down the hall to the spare room, where I set the apple on the nightstand beside my bed, doubting that I would ever be able to eat it.

Chapter 11

Once the Swissmen Sweets' tent was set up at the farmers' market—with some help from my grandparents' friends who were also selling their wares on the village square that day—*Maami* and I stood back and admired our work. My grandmother smiled brightly at me, and I knew I had the same expression on my face.

Daadi was sticking the last of the price tags onto the plastic containers of fudge. When that was done, all we had to do was wait for customers to drop by the booth. I didn't doubt that the candy shop's booth would do well. Who didn't like chocolate and candy?

Maami patted my arm. "*Danki*, my girl. You were a big help to me today. I love you so."

I hugged her. "I wish I could help with all of it," I said, knowing that my grandmother would know that I also meant the murder and *Daadi's* failing health.

"I love you too," *Daadi* said, looking up from his fudge pricing.

I went over to him and kissed the top of his fluffy white head. His hair felt like cotton against my cheeks.

Unfortunately, the glow of our accomplishment was short-lived.

"Clara King!" A high-pitched voice rung out across the square. "I would like to have word with you!"

My usually pleasant grandmother muttered something under her breath in Pennsylvania Dutch. I didn't understand the words, but from her tone, I got the gist.

The thin woman who'd spoken didn't walk toward the Swissmen Sweets' booth, she glided. Her dark, bobbed hair fell to her chin and made her look striking in a 1920s sort of way. She wore a dark yellow dress with a thin black belt around her narrow waist. She looked like so many of the women who floated into JP Chocolates to order desserts for their daughters' sweet sixteen celebrations or for dinner parties, I almost forgot I was in Ohio.

"Eileen, how can I help you?" my grandmother asked in her most pleasant voice.

Eileen waved her hand as if in exasperation. As she did, a cloud of too-sweet floral perfume wafted over the booth.

I had to shove my hands into the back pockets of my jeans to keep myself from covering my nose.

"You can help me by telling me what is going on with the final tasting this afternoon for the wedding."

I glanced at my grandmother. Tasting? What was this woman talking about?

Maami's hands flew to her mouth. "Oh, Eileen, I'm so very sorry. I forgot that was today."

"How could you forget that was today when the wedding is tomorrow? We scheduled this tasting months and months ago, and you promised to make it a wonderful event for my daughter and her future husband."

Mother of the bridezilla. I recognized the signs. As Jean Pierre's assistant, I had met more than my fair share, and a wedding dessert tasting for a mother of the bride was the worst. Many times, the mother of the bride was much harder to contend with than the bride and groom.

"I can't tell you how sorry I am," my grandmother said. "But I'm surprised."

"Surprised about what?" Eileen's tone was sharp.

I peeked over my shoulder to see if my grandfather was following this conversation, but he had wandered off and was speaking in Pennsylvania Dutch to an elderly Amish man in the neighboring stall. Both men sat on lawn chairs and had their heads bent together. I wondered if my grandfather was telling him of the morning's events.

Maami lowered her voice. "Surely, you have heard by now about what happened to Tyson. I would have thought Jace would know, and he must have told you and your daughter, Mira."

In my head, the players were beginning to fall into place. Had this been the wedding that Aiden and my grandmother had been discussing yesterday afternoon? That seemed so long ago.

Eileen sniffed indignantly. "Yes, of course. Mira was Jace's first call. He insisted the wedding should go on as planned. After the farmers' market is over today, and everyone leaves, the reception tent will be put up."

"They're getting married here?" I asked, speaking for the first time.

Eileen's icy blue eyes slid in my direction. "And who are you, exactly?"

I immediately bristled and was about to fire back a response when my grandmother interjected, "Eileen, this is my granddaughter, Bailey. She's visiting from New York."

Eileen examined me from the top of my head to the bottom of my black, calf-high boots. "I had heard that you have English family, Clara."

The way she said it almost sounded like an insult, but I couldn't figure out why that would be. She was as English as I was. Perhaps everything Eileen said was meant to sound insulting. I made up my mind that I didn't like her. Anyone who yelled at my sweet grandmother was immediately filed into the dislike category of my mind.

"Eileen's daughter," my grandmother explained to me, "is getting married tomorrow evening, here on the square at sunset. It was to be the wedding of the year in the county."

"It still will be," Eileen snapped.

My grandmother looked like she wanted to argue with that, but instead, she pressed her lips together. My Amish grandparents believed that if you don't have anything nice to say, you should say nothing at all. I wasn't of the same mind.

"There's no reason to yell," I said. My voice was hard. "What exactly was it that you needed from my grandparents for the wedding?"

Eileen appraised me with renewed interest. Maybe because I talked back to her, I had earned a speck of her respect. I suspected that it wouldn't last long. "If you must know, Swissmen Sweets was to cater the dessert for the wedding. Jace, my daughter's fiancé, hates cake, so instead of cake there will be a dessert bar. It was against my wishes, of course. A wedding should have cake, but Jace wouldn't budge on this one piece of the wedding planning. My daughter," she said with a disparaging tone, "took his side in this argument. I see no reason why she would. We could have a dessert bar *and* cake. He doesn't have to eat the cake. Clara promised us a final tasting today before the wedding tomorrow evening, so you can guess why I am so upset to see that, not only is she not ready for the tasting, but Swissmen Sweets is closed."

My grandmother blinked rapidly, as if she was trying to digest everything Eileen had just said and it wasn't adding up. "I'm sorry that I forgot about the tasting. I suppose in the back of my mind, I assumed that the wedding would be postponed, so with all the disturbing events of the day, it flew clean out of my head. That is no excuse."

"That's all well and good." Eileen twisted the strap of her purse in barely contained anger. "But what are we to do about the tasting now?"

"Why would the wedding be postponed?" I asked. I knew I was missing a large piece of this conversation.

My grandmother glanced at me out of the corner of her eye. "Jace, Mira's fiancé, is Tyson Colton's son."

Chapter 12

"His what?" I asked. Maybe I had misheard her. She'd said Jace was Tyson's what?

Eileen glared at me. "He's Tyson's son. Didn't you hear her?"

I hadn't misheard her at all. I had only hoped that I'd heard wrong. "And Jace is still getting married tomorrow, the day after his father died?"

Eileen's eyes narrowed into icy slits. "We've already been over this several times. I don't know why you keep asking me the same question over and over again." She lowered her voice. "He and his father weren't close. I didn't even know if Tyson was coming to the wedding. We invited him, of course. It was the right thing to do, but I never received his RSVP, and I suppose now I never will."

My grandmother wrinkled her nose, and I felt myself recoil at the woman's callousness over the death of the man who would have been her daughter's father-in-law. At the same time, my ears perked up at this news. An estranged father and son? Jace sounded like the perfect murder suspect to me. I hoped that Aiden and the rest of the sheriff's department planned to take a good, hard look at Jace Colton.

"So." Eileen clasped her hands a little more tightly around the stiff handle of her box-shaped purse. "We would like the tasting to go on as planned, promptly at noon. As it is already after eleven, I expected you to be in your shop, already setting up for the tasting."

Maami's mouth fell open. She was clearly at a loss for words.

I stepped forward. "There's one little problem."

Eileen glowered at me. "And what could that be?"

I glanced at my grandmother, but since she seemed unable to speak, I answered the question. "Swissmen Sweets is closed."

"Closed? Why on earth would you close before the wedding?" She glared at my grandmother.

I stopped myself just in the nick of time from clapping my hands to get her attention focused back on me. "The candy shop is closed because I found Tyson Colton in the kitchen this morning."

She sputtered. "Wh-what? How can that be? Jace said that his father was found dead just this morning. He couldn't be in the candy shop's kitchen."

I shot another glance at my grandmother. "That's just it. I was the one who found his body."

She covered her mouth with her hand, and color drained from her face. "He died in the kitchen with the wedding desserts? They'll be ruined. What are we going to do? We can't have a wedding without dessert. It's too late to order a cake worthy of my only daughter's wedding. I knew this dessert bar idea was terrible from the get-go. I should have insisted that we order a cake."

I stared at her with my mouth hanging open. A man

was dead, and she was more concerned with the wedding desserts.

Eileen turned back to my grandmother. "Had you even started the dessert?"

"We had," *Maami* said regretfully. "But as you said, they are in the kitchen, and even if we were able to enter the kitchen, I wouldn't want to give them to you for the tasting. And we don't have the use of our kitchen to finish preparing the desserts for the reception tomorrow."

The farmers' market had officially opened during our conversation with Eileen, and I couldn't help but notice that a small crowd of curious shoppers had gathered around us. They stopped just short of leaning in and cupping their ears. I was certain the mention of Tyson Colton had attracted them. Murder wasn't a common occurrence in Harvest, Ohio, and everyone wanted in on the latest gossip.

"You don't have anything for the reception?" Her voice was barely below a screech.

My grandmother gestured at the table. "Maybe something here will suit you. Most of what we have available is here."

Eileen wrinkled her nose at the containers of fudge and other candies that my grandparents had for sale at the farmers' market. "This will never do. You promised me a unique menu. There is nothing unique about this!"

I balled my fists at my hips and tried to hold my temper. If I had been in New York, I might have told her off for being so rude, but I knew in Ohio, manners were different. I didn't want to do anything that might hurt my grandparents' business or embarrass them in front of the members of their district.

Eileen threw up her hands. "What are we going to do? You can't expect me to disappoint Mira and Jace, especially on today of all days, when they are reeling from such a tragedy."

I wrinkled my brow. Reeling from tragedy? Did she really mean that? Hadn't she just said that Jace hadn't been that close to his father and wanted to go on with the wedding?

"Clara," Eileen said in a harsh whisper. She leaned across the sales table so that her face was just inches from my grandmother's. "You know I have much influence in the village. If the news gets out that you failed to deliver for my daughter's wedding, you won't have another English customer come through the doors of Swissmen Sweets. You have my word on that."

Maami stiffened her spine. "Eileen," she said evenly. "A man, a child of *Gott*—likeable or not—has died in our candy shop. There's really nothing more damaging than that which you can do to us."

A solution that might solve everything came to my mind, and it might even give me the opportunity to catch a killer. Besides, I couldn't let this show on the square go on much longer. Soon, one of the Amish farmers would be selling their kettle corn and breaking out folding chairs for the growing audience.

"I—" Eileen began, but I cut her off.

"I have an idea," I said.

Both women stared at me as if I'd just said I saw a cow fly by, like in the movie *Twister*.

"I can make your dessert menu, and even have a tasting for you later this afternoon if we can bump back the tasting until three."

"You?" Eileen looked me up and down. "How are you going to create the dessert bar that my daughter and her future husband want for their wedding?"

I bit down hard on the inside of my cheek to keep myself from snapping back. If nothing else, my time in Ohio was giving me lots of practice in holding my tongue. I wasn't sure if I would be able to carry that habit back to the city with me.

"She knows more about desserts than all of us put together," my grandfather said as he shuffled through the grass back to our booth. The old man in the neighboring booth watched him make unsteady progress, but held himself back from offering *Daadi* any assistance. I did the same. I knew that it would only embarrass him in such a public setting.

"My granddaughter is a prize-winning chocolatier, and she is next in line to be the head chocolatier at JP Chocolates in New York City. Your daughter's wedding will be the envy of the county to have a sweets menu made by her gifted hands." He finally reached us, and *Maami* helped him back into his folding chair. Hers was the only help he would accept.

I felt a blush creep up from the base of my neck to the top of my head. "It's not for sure yet. It's not a done deal that I got the job," I said automatically.

Daadi waved away my clarification. "It's all but done."

Eileen studied me with renewed interest in those icy blue eyes. "JP Chocolates. I visited there once when I was in the city. Their chocolates are quite expensive and more exclusive than Godiva. I believe I had one of the saffron truffles. It was divine." She appraised me with those cold eyes again. "*You* are the next chocolatier?"

"It's not official yet."

"But you work there, and you would know how to

do a tasting of a much higher caliber than your Amish grandparents ever could."

I stopped just short of grinding my teeth. "My grandparents and their shop, Swissmen Sweets, taught me a love for chocolate long before I ever worked for Jean Pierre."

Tears welled in my grandfather's eyes. He smiled at his hands.

"I'm Jean Pierre's first chocolatier," I told Eileen. "As his first chocolatier, I can do everything Jean Pierre does. Your tasting will be no trouble. All I need is to gather my ingredients and supplies, which is why I am asking for a little more time to prepare, and I need a kitchen."

She clapped her hands together. "Splendid. Mira will be absolutely thrilled when she hears the news. She loves JP Chocolates as much as I do."

I blinked at her. All of Eileen's anger over the tasting seemed to have disappeared now that she knew who I was. I tried not to let that bother me, but it did. Eileen reminded me too much of many of the stuck-up women and men who came into JP Chocolates in New York and fell over themselves to chat with Jean Pierre, but sneered at anyone else they perceived to be of lesser importance. The way they treated not just me, but the entire staff, never sat well with me. Cass said it was my Midwestern roots. Even though my parents were from Ohio, I grew up in Connecticut, but she always seemed to glaze over that piece of my personal history. She said it was impossible for me not to assume that every new person I met would be kind and reasonable because of my Midwestern heritage. That might be true. I didn't expect it, but I hoped for it. I didn't see anything wrong with hoping for kindness in the world.

Eileen opened her purse and removed a cell phone. "How about we do this—you can use the church kitchen. All I need to do is make a quick call, and it's yours."

"What church is that?" I asked.

"That one." With a long manicured nail, she pointed to the opposite side of the large village square, toward a broad white church with a dark purple front door and an iron cross at the very top of the steeple.

It was a beautiful building nestled in between two enormous oak trees on the church's expansive lawn. As a village landmark, it was the most photographed building in the village. I wasn't the least bit surprised to learn this was Eileen's church. It was the best in the village, at least judging strictly on the outward appearance. I wouldn't doubt that Eileen had chosen it solely based on that.

"We have a meeting with the pastor at the church later this afternoon anyway. If you can set the tasting for two, that will work well."

When I had asked for three o'clock, I had cushioned my request with an extra hour. I knew I would need several hours to make all the desserts I had planned. I already had a running menu in my head. My only wish was that Cass, who was a gifted chocolatier in her own right, was there to back me up.

"Will your pastor mind if we use the church kitchen? Don't you have to ask his permission?" I inquired.

"Of course not. My family almost single-handedly keeps his offering plate full on Sundays. He more than owes me this little flavor." Some of the venom had returned to her voice. I had suspected Eileen wouldn't be able to stay as sweet as sugar for long, even if she was impressed with my chocolate credentials.

"What's the name of the church?" I asked. "Who will let me inside?"

"First Church of Harvest, but everyone just calls it First Church. I'll call and let them know that you are coming and will need the kitchen. There will be someone there to greet you." She picked an invisible speck off of the sleeve of her dress. "I should let Mira know the change of plans. We'll be there at two PM sharp. I'll expect to be wowed, as you are the first chocolatier from JP Chocolates. I have very high expectations now. I hope that you can deliver." With that, she flounced away. Only the sickly sweet scent of her floral perfume remained.

Chapter 13

"She's a charmer," I muttered after Eileen had gone. The crowd gathered around our booth had dispersed when it was clear there weren't going to be any further arguments involving Tyson Colton.

"She's a menace," *Daadi* said from his spot on the folding chair.

Maami shook her head. "Now, Jeb, you can't call people names like that no matter how unkind they might be. *Gott* teaches us to turn the other cheek."

"*Ya*, he does, but he didn't say we had to enjoy it," my grandfather replied. There was still a slight gray cast to his complexion, but I thought he looked better overall. He also had the twinkle back in his eye that he always had when he was trying to get a rise out of my grandmother. I suspected that my grandmother was as aware of the twinkle as I was, and I had a feeling that she had rather enjoyed my grandfather's teasing during the last fifty plus years of their marriage.

Daadi tried to adjust his sitting position on the chair but couldn't seem to get comfortable. I made a move to help, but he waved me away. "I'm all right. These old bones just don't settle into place as well as they once did." He shook his head, and his long white beard waved back and forth. "It was very difficult for me to sit back and listen to her insult both my wife and my grand-daughter. Had she been a man, I would have given her a piece of my mind."

I walked over to my grandfather and patted his shoulder. "You're my hero, *Daadi*, but I don't need pro-tecting. I can handle her. If I can handle Upper Eastside supermoms planning their daughters' million-dollar birthday blowouts, I can handle Eileen and her small country wedding in Harvest, Ohio."

He frowned. "A million dollars for a birthday party? Surely, that can't be right."

"Maybe I exaggerated." I paused. "A little. You would be surprised at the amount of money some parents spend on their children. I don't think it's exclusively a New York thing though."

He shook his head again, this time much more slowly, as if contemplating a mystery as deep as outer space. "It seems silly to me, but I have long given up trying to understand how the *Englisch* spend their money."

I patted his shoulder again. "That's probably a good policy. Now, I had better get to work on that tasting menu and gathering everything I might need. I assume there isn't a kitchen supply store in the county?"

Both of my grandparents stared at me.

"I'll take that as a no." I sighed.

"What are you going to do?" *Maami* clenched her hands in front of her apron. "You can't use anything from our kitchen."

I sighed again. "That is a problem, but a church kitchen should have the basics. If I was able to make a sampling in my studio apartment that impressed Jean Pierre enough to give me a job, I can make a tasting in a church kitchen that will wow Eileen and her daughter."

Maami worried her lip. She didn't seem as sure as I was. If there was something I was one hundred percent confident in, it was my skill with chocolate.

"At the very least we will be able to give you a start," my grandfather said. "We have extra sugar, salt, baking soda, and other dry ingredients stored in the closet beneath the stairs, so those will be safe to use."

"That's perfect, and I think the farmers' market will have a lot of what else I need. Can you purchase some fresh berries and jams and anything else that you can find that might be put into a dessert? I'll go collect those dry ingredients from the candy shop. Hopefully, there won't be much that I'll have to purchase from the store, which will allow me more time in the church kitchen." I pulled my cell phone out of my jacket pocket. It was already past eleven. That didn't leave me much time.

Maami nodded and the wrinkle in the middle of her brow smoothed. I think she was relieved that we had a plan to appease Eileen, and it was nice to have something pressing to focus on instead of the murder, although I did plan to take the opportunity to do a little investigating of my own.

As my grandmother went off to buy fruit and preserves from her friends, I headed across the street to the candy shop, taking my grandmother's cart with me. From my pocket, I removed the shop key my grandfather had given me, unlocked the door, and went inside.

The front room, which was usually bustling with activity in the middle of a Friday morning, was eerily quiet. As I parked the cart by the front door, I tried to avert my eyes from the kitchen door with the huge stretch of crime scene tape across it, but its bright yellow color attracted my eye much like a moth to a lamppost at night.

"Focus, Bailey, focus," I told myself, shaking off the creepy feeling that inched its way up my back. I didn't want to be frightened by my grandparents' shop. It held my best childhood memories, but now, because of Tyson's death, they were tarnished by what I'd found in the kitchen that morning. I knew I'd never be able to erase that memory completely, but the sooner we got the kitchen back, the sooner the memory would fade.

I knew exactly where the closet under the stairs was. As I child, I had hidden there on more than one occasion, usually when my parents said it was time to head back to our home in Connecticut. I never wanted to leave my grandparents back then. *Daadi* always knew where to find me, and he would climb into the cubby space with me and coax me out. I opened the door and peered inside the crawl space. It was a wonder that I had been able to fit inside there even as a child, and even more amazing that *Daadi* would go in there after me. I had to remind myself of how spry he had once been.

I squatted in front of the crawl space, and the memories of me crying inside came back to me in a rush. In my mind's eye, I could see my grandfather, his hair just beginning to turn white, crouching in the doorway like I was now. He'd smiled at me and asked what I was doing in the closet under the stairs.

In a pouty voice, I answered, "I'm hiding from Mom and Dad. I don't want to go back home. I want to stay here with you and Maami.*"*

His face broke into a smile. "It makes me very happy that you want to be with Maami *and me. We wish you all could stay in Holmes County to be near us, but this town doesn't offer the life your parents want for you."*

"It's my life," I protested. "Why can't I decide where I want to live it?"

"You can someday." He chuckled. "You only have to wait until you're grown."

"I don't like to wait." I pouted.

He laughed a little harder. "You sound just like your father at your age. He didn't want to wait either." His face clouded over for just a moment. "That was the Englisch *that was always in him. I suppose I knew then that the Amish way of life wasn't for him. There was too much he wanted to do, too much of the world he wanted to see, more than our way of life could give him." He patted my knee. "But you, I wouldn't be the least bit surprised if you ended up back in this very spot someday."*

I stared into the crawl space, lost in the memory. He had been right. I was back in this very spot. I remembered another conversation with my grandfather under the stairs.

"Other kids can talk to their grandparents on the telephone or they see their grandparents because they live nearby. I never get any of that. I never talk to you on the phone."

"We talk on the phone from time to time."

"Not very much," I said.

He nodded as he seemed to think this over. "In the Amish way, the phone is a tool for work. It is not for idle chitchat."

"You think talking with me is chitchat?" I couldn't keep the hurt out of my voice.

He laughed. "Of course not, but it is not work. As a tool, the telephone is meant for work. And we have our letters, don't we?"

I nodded.

"The letters keep us close at heart," he said.

"Letters aren't the same," I muttered, determined to stick to my argument.

He shook his head. "Letters are better. With letters you can read my words and hear my voice over and over again. It will be a reminder to you when I'm gone. Those who love Gott never die. I will be waiting for you with Him."

I had every one of my grandfather's letters stored in a shoebox under my bed in my New York apartment. He was right—reading the letters was like hearing his voice, and I would always have them. My eyes drifted back to the crime scene tape marring the kitchen door. I couldn't let anything happen to my grandparents' business. I needed to figure out who Tyson Colton was with when he entered the shop. He couldn't have stabbed himself in the chest like that, and I knew my grandparents and I were innocent. Someone else had to have been in the kitchen with him. Amish or English, I had to find that person. Maybe by learning who the other person was, I would discover who the killer was.

There was something else nagging me about Tyson's death. Why hadn't my grandparents or I heard anything while we were upstairs? It seemed there would have been a scuffle or some type of argument if Tyson was murdered while we slept in our beds. Surely if someone had been trying to kill him, he would have fought back and tried to save himself. Wouldn't he have cried out in pain when the knife entered his chest? I felt sick at the thought. Maybe he had been taken by surprise or incapacitated in some way. Tyson wasn't a small man. Who could have been strong enough to attack him and win?

I tried to think back to the crime scene—the little bit of it I'd seen other than Tyson's body on the floor. In my head, all I could see was the body and that horrible puddle of blood. I squeezed my eyes shut, just as I used to when I was a child in the middle of a spelling test, trying to remember the letters of the word I needed to spell.

My memory was too fuzzy. The only aspect of the room I remembered with one hundred percent certainty was the blood on the floor. That, and the fact that my cell phone had been plugged in across the room in an outlet reserved for one of the large mixers in the back of the kitchen. I was tempted to break through the crime scene tape for another look. The deputies hadn't mentioned any signs of struggle, but I doubted they would have told me if there had been any. At least I knew Deputy Carpenter wouldn't have. Aiden, I wasn't so sure of. He acted like he wanted to help my grandparents and me. He'd even said as much, but was it some kind of trick to earn my trust, a trust that he'd be able to use against me later?

Assuming there was no struggle, did that mean Tyson had entered the shop with his attacker, and the attacker was someone he knew? That possibility gave me even more motive to do the tasting for Tyson's estranged son and his fiancée. I needed to know if Jace Colton had been in the shop with his father. Why the two men would choose my grandparents' candy shop for their family argument was beyond me, but I would worry about that minor detail later. I couldn't rule any of the suspects out at this point.

Again, Aiden came to mind. Maybe I should tell him about the tasting and Jace. My grandparents seemed to trust him, so why shouldn't I? I immediately squashed that idea. Even if Aiden was on our side, he wouldn't want me snooping around the Colton family's affairs, and if he knew I was doing that, he might suspect me even more. I didn't want to give the police any more reasons to suspect me. If they did, they might watch me a little too closely when I needed the freedom to find the real killer.

I began to pull the large bags of sugar and flour and containers of salt and baking powder out of the storage space. *Maami* had been right—the spot was well stocked. I removed my cell phone from my pocket and shone the flashlight app into the space. In the very back, I saw a large tin of cocoa powder and a crate of evaporated milk. It was just what I needed to make the chocolate creations I knew Eileen and her daughter would love. I was almost as determined to impress the fussy woman as I had been to impress the board picking Jean Pierre's replacement. When it came to chocolate, I always wanted to be the best.

I crawled deeper into the space, lying on my stomach to slip under the shelves. I had no idea how my grandparents had been able to reach the supplies this far back into the cubby.

I grabbed the crate of evaporated milk and pulled. Half of my body was inside the closet, the other half, outside. I could only wriggle back and forth on my stomach like a worm. There was no room to move left or right.

Then, I heard what sounded like footsteps coming from the front room.

I tried to scramble back out of the tight space and managed to bang my head on the shelf just above it.

"Is someone in here?" a gruff voice yelled.

I froze, unsure what to do. If I fled, I would only draw more attention to myself. There was no way I could escape the storage closet without making noise.

The footsteps approached and stopped right at my side. Even though I couldn't see who was beside me because I was still lodged halfway inside the cubbyhole, I could feel his presence.

"Why don't you come out of there?" the man asked.

I crawled backward out of the crawl space, dragging the crate of evaporated milk with me. Worst case scenario, I could use one of the cans as a projectile to fling at my would-be attacker. I wrapped my hand around one of the potential weapons on my way out of the closet.

I wriggled backward. When I could straighten up, I turned with the can raised and came face to face with the barrel of a gun.

I have to say a can of milk is no match for a gun.

Chapter 14

I was more than a little dismayed to find Deputy Carpenter staring down at me with his gun drawn.

"What exactly are you doing inside there, Miss King? Hiding evidence of the murder?" Carpenter asked, holstering his gun.

I scrambled to my feet and went on the offensive. "What are you doing in here, deputy?"

He rubbed his bald head. "You may remember that a murder occurred here this morning. I'm investigating. It's what I do."

I brushed the dust from the closet floor off of my shirt the best I could. It was a lost cause. I would have to change before I headed to the church to prepare for the tasting. "I'm well aware of that. Are you back because you need to reexamine the crime scene? I'm sure by now that Deputy Brody has told you about the broken glass behind the candy shop. He said that it was most likely from an Amish lantern. Perhaps whoever broke into the shop's kitchen with Tyson Colton was Amish. We both know that Tyson would have no use for an old-fashioned lantern like that. It fits with the forced entry that was already in evidence, doesn't it?" I was quite proud of myself for coming to that conclusion.

That pride was short-lived as he took a step toward me. "I heard about your little discovery in the back alley. We can't know when the kerosene lamp was broken. Maybe it's completely unrelated to the murder. Maybe someone left it there to throw us off. Maybe it was even you."

I clenched my teeth. "How many times do I have to tell you that I had nothing to do with Tyson Colton's murder? Don't throw accusations at me because you're embarrassed that you missed an important clue in the homicide investigation."

"Clue?" he scoffed. "This isn't a whodunit, and you aren't Nancy Drew." He took another step toward me so there were only about eighteen inches between us. It felt like much less. "And, Miss King, I don't miss anything. I especially don't miss a hoity-toity city girl who thinks she can get away with murder in my county."

As much as I wanted to hold my ground, I couldn't stand his closeness, and I took a big step back. "I didn't kill anyone." My voice shook, and I wished that I could control it.

He seemed to relax now that it was clear I was visibly shaken by my encounter with him, and a slow smile spread across his lips. "That's yet to be determined."

While I gathered the ingredients that I would need for the tasting, Deputy Carpenter looked on. I started to pick up the case of evaporated milk from the floor. He held up his hand. "Let me get that."

I stepped back.

He picked up the crate. "I apologize if I sounded

harsh earlier, Miss King. I know that you must be worried about your grandparents."

"I am."

"And please know that I worry about them too. I'm worried for the safety of everyone in Harvest." He leaned closer to me. "There is a killer in our midst. I will find him." He paused. "Or her."

After that, Deputy Carpenter helped me load the cart in silence. When all the supplies were loaded, I said good-bye to the deputy. I felt his eyes on my back while I waited for an Amish pony cart to clomp down Main Street and then pushed my cart across the street to the Swissmen Sweets' booth at the market.

Thankfully, my grandmother's cart had rubber wheels, so I was able to push it easily over the grass.

I parked the cart in front of the Swissmen Sweets' booth and was happy to see that *Maami* had found everything that I needed from the farmers' market. There were four different preserves, strawberries, apples, dried fruits, and fresh clover honey. All made or grown by Amish hands.

"Was that Deputy Carpenter who came out of the candy shop with you?" *Maami* asked.

I nodded. "He was looking over the crime scene again. I'm sure the police will be popping in and out of the shop over the next few days." I didn't share any of the details of my less than friendly encounter with the deputy. I saw no reason to worry her any more than she already was.

"I suppose so." Her face fell, and for the first time, she looked her age.

I squeezed her hand and began loading the ingredients that she had collected from the market onto my cart. There was just enough space for every last thing.

I was happy about that. Fewer trips meant more time in the church kitchen preparing, and I needed time the most. Every second that went by meant less time for the chocolate to solidify and hold the shape necessary to impress Eileen and her daughter. Even though I had never met Mira, I knew Eileen would be the harder of the two to win over. Or so I hoped.

"I'll take this to the church and make a shopping list of what I need from there. I think I will have a better understanding of the menu I want to create once I have all the ingredients spread out on the kitchen counter." I couldn't keep the excitement from my voice. There was nothing that I liked better than a chocolatier challenge, and this might be the biggest one of my life. I not only had to make my chocolate shine, but I had to gather information on a killer. No small feat.

Daadi watched me from his lawn chair in the shade of the tent. "Are you sure you want to do this? Eileen isn't the easiest person to work with."

There was an understatement.

"I'm sure. I want to help, and if Eileen is impressed with my desserts, it will rebuild some local confidence in your business."

Maami patted my cheek. "All right, my girl, you win. We'll let you help us just this once."

I smiled. "Thank you. You won't be disappointed. After I'm done with Eileen's tasting, she will rave over Swissmen Sweets."

"I'm sure that's true," *Daadi* said from his folding chair under the tent.

I waved good-bye to my grandparents and pushed the cart toward the church. As I passed the gazebo, I could have sworn I saw the orange tail of a cat slink around the side of the structure. It appeared that Nutmeg was on the loose again. I hoped Emily would be able to track him down.

I crossed the street that separated the square's green from the churchyard. The church appeared even larger up close. The front of the building was whitewashed wooden siding, but a brick addition extended behind it. The bricks were also painted white to blend in with the rest of the church.

Leaving my cart in the churchyard, I climbed the front steps that led to the church's deep purple double doors. I was about to reach for the massive knocker on one of the two doors when both of them were flung open.

"There you are! I've been waiting to see your pretty face," a petite woman with a slight southern accent proclaimed.

Before I had the chance to speak, she went on. "You must be Bailey, Clara and Jebidiah King's grand-daughter. I have heard so much about you from your grandparents, so when Eileen said that you were coming to our church today, I was just tickled." Her cheeks flushed a pretty shade of pink. Her dark hair was just beginning to gray around her temples, and she had it pulled back from her face with a pink butterfly clip. I guessed she was in her late forties or maybe even early fifties. She beamed at me, but even her glowing smile wasn't enough to distract me from the pig standing at her side. "Do you need any help carrying things in?" she asked, as if there wasn't anything unusual about our current situation. "I'm Juliet. Did I tell you that yet? How rude of me not to introduce myself. The ladies from my quilting circle are here, and we are happy to help you in any way."

"Umm . . ." I stared at the pig. I couldn't help it. Not

only was a pig greeting me at the church door, but it was black and white polka-dotted. One of the dots made a perfect black circle around his right eye. The creature was the size of a toaster oven, and came up to the middle of the petite woman's calf. I had seen many strange things during my time in New York City, but nothing quite like this. "Umm . . ." I repeated. The pig's presence stole my words.

She laughed. "I see Jethro has you tongue-tied." She patted the top of the pig's head. "He has that effect on people."

Yes, yes, I could understand why.

"He'll be a perfect gentleman. He always is. You won't find a kinder, gentler soul than Jethro." She smiled brightly, and there was something about her smile that was vaguely familiar, even though I knew I had never met her before. I certainly had never met Jethro before. I would remember Jethro.

Before I could stop them, the words popped out of my mouth. "He has polka dots!" As soon as the words flew out of my mouth, I regretted them. I didn't want this cheerful woman to think that I was insulting Jethro the Pig.

She laughed, and her laughter sounded like the tinkling of the wind chimes hanging from my next door neighbor's balcony back in the city. "He does. I know. That's what made me fall in love with him. When I saw those polka dots, I knew I had to take him home. I love polka dots." She held out her arms. "As if you couldn't tell."

For the first time, I noticed she wore a yellow and red polka-dotted dress.

She let her arms fall to her sides. "He's a pinto."

"Like a horse?" Again, the mouth had a mind of its own.

She grinned as if I had come up with the perfect answer. "Just like a horse. Potbellied pigs like Jethro can be pinto. Not many of them have such distinctive dots. He's special that way."

The pig looked up at his mistress in adoration. If I didn't know better, I would say that he understood every word she'd said.

Juliet cocked her head at me and put her hand on her narrow hip. "I heard you were from New York City, but you act like you've never seen a pig before. Don't they have pet pigs in the city? They're great for apartments."

I stared down at Jethro and tried to imagine him living with me in my tiny apartment back in the city. "I've never had one greet me at a church door before."

She threw back her head and laughed, and again I was reminded of my neighbor's wind chimes. "I suppose not. Why don't you come inside? I'll show you where the kitchen is. I know the other ladies are eager to meet you too. We're all so fond of Jebidiah and Clara. It's an honor to meet their granddaughter."

I stepped inside the church and stood in the dim entryway for a moment to allow my eyes to adjust. There was a set of glass double doors directly across from the door I'd entered. Through the glass, I caught a glimpse of the quiet sanctuary. Wooden beams ran up the white walls at intervals and crisscrossed the high ceiling. A grand pulpit presided over the rows of pews, while a large pipe organ dominated the front of the church.

I had an itchy, guilty feeling tickling the back of my brain. I hadn't been to church in a very long time. I tried to push the nagging feeling aside and rationalize why I had missed so many services the last few years. My work schedule was demanding. Didn't the Bible say that we needed a day of rest? And Sunday was my day of rest. Sunday was also the one day of the week that Eric and I both had off. If I wanted to see my boyfriend at all and actually act like we were together, it had to be on Sunday. On Sundays, he'd whisk me away on his private jet to some random locale where no one knew us. We were always back in plenty of time to return to our everyday lives and pretend we only knew each other through our work.

Standing at the threshold of this church made me realize what a lie I had been living. I had known it from the beginning, but in this place, there was no hiding from it, no rationalizing why it had made sense keep my romance with Eric Sharp a secret for so long. I was a fraud.

If I was willing to admit it, there wasn't a lot of authenticity in my life at the moment. My relationship with Eric wasn't authentic. Sure, it felt that way when we were alone, and all his attention was on me, but that wasn't often. I was certain he never gave me a second thought the other six days of the week. And it wasn't just my relationship with Eric that felt artificial. I worked eighteen-hour days, six days a week, and I loved what I did. I loved Jean Pierre, but what was the point of it, really? Making chocolate creations that most people could never afford? What was I accomplishing? I didn't have a good answer to any of those questions, and that's why I knew I was in real trouble.

Chapter 15

"Bailey?" Juliet said. "The kitchen is down this hallway." She stood at the far left of the entry at another door.

Jethro leaned against her leg like a loyal retriever. I wondered if I would ever get accustomed to seeing a polka-dotted pig at her side.

"I'm sorry." I stumbled after her. "You caught me in a daydream." Or a nightmare, I mentally added.

She beamed and opened the door. "I daydream every time I enter the church too. It's such a special place."

Jethro's hooves made a *tap-tap* sound on the church's wooden steps, and I suppressed a smile. When I'd decided to visit my grandparents, I had expected things to be different from what I was used to, but I'd certainly never expected to be following a pig through a church. I frowned. Nor had I expected murder. Traces of my dark mood returned. There was only one way to fix it, and that was to create my chocolate concoctions.

The musical sound of women talking and laughing floated down the hallway. At the end of the hallway there was a set of double doors. Juliet opened one of the doors and ushered me inside a large room that was half-floored with industrial carpet. The other half was covered with hardwood. A basketball hoop hung from the wall on the side of the room with the hardwood. On the far side of the hardwood, I caught a glimpse of a kitchen.

As much as I wanted to see what the kitchen had to offer, my eye was drawn to the middle of the room, where at least fifteen women—English, Amish, and I guessed a few Mennonite—sat around a massive quilt frame, stitching away at a quilt with some kind of block pattern on it. My grandmother had tried to teach me the art of quilting, but it never quite stuck. I had always been much more interested in what *Daadi* was doing in the candy shop's kitchen. When I was little, he experimented with flavors and created new fudge and candy mixtures. He is the reason I work for JP Chocolates. I learned to love sweets at my grandfather's knee. I bit the inside of my lip. That was why I couldn't let this promotion to head chocolatier slip through my fingers. I wouldn't just be letting myself down; I'd be letting *Daadi* down too. That couldn't be tolerated.

Juliet clapped her hands. Jethro sat beside her like a well-trained dog. "Ladies, ladies, we have a guest."

All the eyes in the room fell on me and studied with me interest. I felt like a bug under a microscope. Some of the women smiled, others waved, and still others watched me with curiosity, as if the jury was still out as to whether I was friend or foe.

"Ladies, this is Bailey King."

"You're Clara and Jebidiah's granddaughter," said an elderly woman working at the corner of the quilt. "My, you look just like your mother."

"June, I was thinking the same thing. It was no wonder Ben King left the Amish when Miranda came to town. She was prettiest girl I ever saw. Ben was smitten from the word go," a younger English woman said.

"It took some time for her to give Ben a chance. I don't think she even tried until he promised to leave the Amish church," another woman said with a chuckle.

The three Amish women around the quilt frame shifted uncomfortably. One of the Amish women I knew. It was the girl from the pretzel shop, Esther Esh. When our eyes met, she quickly looked away. I frowned.

"Bailey," Juliet explained, "is here to create a sweet-treat tasting for Mira Hutton's wedding. She's a famous dessert chef in New York City. Can you imagine that?"

"I'm a chocolatier," I corrected automatically.

The woman who had commented that my mother had given my father a chance only after he left the Amish, squinted at me as if it would make it easier for her to appraise me that way. "What exactly is a chocolatier?"

The English woman to her left elbowed her. "Don't you know anything? It's a fancy name for someone who makes chocolate candies."

The women looked at me.

"That's pretty much it," I said.

"If you are here to make candies for Mira's wedding, you will be working with her mother, Eileen," said the same older woman who'd first spoken. "God speed, my dear, God speed. You're going to need it." She shook her head and resumed her stitching.

"And a suit of armor to deflect the glares she will throw at you," another woman added.

The pair cackled together.

"Really," Juliet said. "You two are horrible." Her chuckle took the bite out of her words. "I'm going to show Bailey the kitchen and where everything is. After that, we could use some help bringing in her supplies."

Juliet moved from the carpet to the hardwood. Jethro dutifully walked beside her. The heels of her ankle boots and the pig's hooves *click-clicked* across the floor. Taking hold of the half-open, pass-through window cover, she grabbed the handle and yanked it up.

Over her shoulder, I peered into the kitchen, and was pleased to see a large mixer, not the industrial one that my grandparents had, of course, but one adequate to create the tasting menu. I also saw stainless steel appliances, including a convection oven that I knew would come in handy since I was working under such a time constraint. The kitchen positively glittered, it was so clean. I made a mental note about that, because I knew that I would have to make it just as clean when I left it later in the day. "This is great! It looks like I have everything I need here."

Juliet beamed. "The church has always had a high-quality kitchen. We have many dinners here, including a free community dinner twice a month—on the first and third Fridays—to help those who are struggling. Simon—I mean, Reverend Brook—is very concerned about taking care of everyone in the community, not just those who fill the pews on Sundays."

I swallowed. Again, I thought of my life in New York. "That's wonderful."

"There is a dinner this evening at six sharp. We will start the cooking around four."

"I'll be out of the kitchen by then," I promised.

"We don't want to rush you off."

"You're not. It was very kind of the pastor to let me use the kitchen, especially on such short notice."

"Simon—Reverend Brook—is a kind man." She leaned closer to me. "But I'm afraid Eileen didn't leave him much choice." She peeked through the pass-through back at the quilting circle ladies, as if to make sure that none of them were listening. "She's a pushy one, that Eileen."

Her comment confirmed the assessment I had already made about the mother of the bride.

She bent and patted Jethro's bristly head. "But you didn't come here to listen to the news about the church, did you? You have work to do. I'll just draft some of the ladies to help bring in those supplies. Is there anything else you need?"

I checked the readout of my cell phone. It had taken so long to make it to the kitchen, between Juliet and the quilting ladies, not to mention Jethro the Pig, that I no longer had enough time to run to the market *and* prepare all of the desserts before Eileen and the bride and groom arrived.

"I hate to be a bother," I began.

"You're not a bother at all. How can we help?"

Within minutes, the ingredients I had brought with me to the church were spread across the counter, and Juliet had dispatched two of the quilting ladies to the local market with my list of additional supplies. It pained me to rely on them, but the women did seem genuinely interested in helping my grandparents, and me, by extension. Two Amish women stood over the stove, stirring chocolate over double boilers. Another one was cleaning the berries and other fruit that my grandmother had purchased at the farmers' market.

Juliet floated from task to task, advising and offering encouragement where she could. Jethro napped in the middle of the basketball court. I was grateful that he wasn't in the kitchen and underfoot.

I blended the berry filling for one of the three varieties of truffles that I planned to make. I hoped that I would have enough time to pop the truffles into the freezer, so that they would harden before the tasting began.

"You're doing a wonderful job, Bailey," Juliet said when she poked her head inside the kitchen. "I'd love to help, but I'm no use in the kitchen. You should ask my son about that. Poor boy grew up on hot dogs and mac and cheese, except when your grandparents fed us. I never have been much of a cook. At church dinners, I always volunteer to serve to avoid being in the kitchen."

I frowned. Except when *my* grandparents were feeding Juliet and her son? What did she mean by that?

Before I could ask, one of the ladies called me over to the double boilers because the chocolate was ready. My questions about Juliet's odd comment would have to wait.

With all the activity in the kitchen, nearly an hour had gone by before I noted that Esther wasn't among the helpers. My brow wrinkled. I thought back to my conversation with the young Amish woman earlier that day, and tried to recall anything that I'd said that might have offended her. I knew she hadn't liked me asking about selling her pretzel shop and about Tyson buying it.

I poured the chocolate into a bunt cake mold that the church had. Once it hardened into the shape of the bunt cake, I planned to fill the shell with a white chocolate mousse.

"What are you going to do with that?" an Amish woman named Lillian asked me.

"I'm going to use it as a serving dish for one of my courses."

She raised her brow. "Why go to all that trouble when you can use a bowl?"

It was a practical Amish question, but not one that I could answer easily, so I posed one of my own. "Did one of your members have to leave early? I thought I saw another Amish woman here. Her name is Esther. Her pretzel shop is next to Swissmen Sweets."

Lillian raised her brow. "Did Esther leave? I didn't see her go." She scanned the kitchen for any sign of the young Amish woman. "It's not like her to leave without saying good-bye. I am her aunt. Did you meet her here?"

"I met her earlier today." I paused. "She was going to sell the pretzel shop to Tyson, I believe, but she mentioned she no longer planned to sell it now."

Lillian frowned, and I immediately saw the family resemblance between her and Esther. "I should go mind the next batch of chocolate boiling on the stove." She turned away from me.

I wasn't getting very far in my questioning of the members of my grandparents' Amish district. Did they refuse to talk to me about Tyson because I was a stranger, or because they had something to hide?

Chapter 16

I heard Eileen Hutton arrive before I saw her. "Juliet!" Her voice echoed across the fellowship hall. "Keep that pig away from me. It will get mud all over my outfit!"

I settled the final truffle on the white plate for the tasting and sighed with relief. I'd made it. I never would have without the help of Juliet and her quilting circle, and I wondered how I would prepare the desserts for the wedding the next day without them. I pushed that concern to the back of my mind to worry about after the tasting.

I peeked through the pass-through between the kitchen and the fellowship hall. Juliet and Jethro stood near the entrance to the hall, across from Eileen and a young couple. The couple held hands, or at least the groom held his bride-to-be's hand. Her fingers weren't wrapped around her fiancé's. Something about the groom's grip made me think he was holding her in place rather than showing her any sort of affection.

Jace Colton had black hair that fell over his dark brows and his dark-rimmed glasses. Every so often, he shook his head in a practiced way to fling his hair out of his eyes.

The girl, Mira Hutton, was as pale as the young man was dark. Her hair was white-blond and her skin was so white, that it seemed to shimmer under the room's harsh fluorescent lighting. Like her mother, Mira wore a dress, but the A-line skirt and bow at the waist made her appear almost childlike, certainly not old enough to be getting married. I knew that the Amish married young, but clearly neither Mira nor Jace was Amish. I wondered what the rush was, especially now that Jace's father was dead.

"Jethro is as clean as can be. Pigs are naturally clean animals," Juliet said in the same cheerful voice she had used to greet me at the church door. "They only wallow in the mud because they don't sweat, and mud keeps farm pigs cool. I can assure you that Jethro has never even seen a mud puddle, although he does enjoy a good soak in the bathtub on hot summer days."

Eileen wrinkled her nose, as if the image of the polka-dotted pig lounging in a bathtub was too much. "So you say. That creature shouldn't be in a house of worship. I'll be sure to speak to Reverend Brook about this."

I glanced at Juliet for a reaction, but she smiled benignly at Eileen's threat. "Let me just see if Bailey is ready for you," Juliet said. "Would you take a seat at the table there?" She gestured at a solitary round table in the middle of the basketball court. The quilting ladies had covered it with a clean, white linen cloth and set it with silverware, glasses, and a pitcher of water. A vase of lovely, deep pink roses sat in the center of the table. Before leaving, the woman who set the table had whispered that the roses were from an elderly parishioner's funeral dinner, which had been held in the fellowship hall the day before. She reassured me that the dearly departed wouldn't mind in the least.

"I hope she is ready." Eileen sat in one of the folding chairs and placed her box-shaped handbag on the floor. "I will not be disappointed by Swissmen Sweets twice in one day."

I ducked back into the kitchen before I could be seen. A moment later, Juliet came through the door followed by Jethro. If the pig had been insulted by Eileen's threat to ban him from the church, he didn't show it, but then again, I didn't know what an insulted potbellied pig should look like.

Juliet cupped her hand around her mouth and said, barely above a whisper, "Eileen, her daughter, and Jace are here."

"I heard," I whispered back.

"Oh, Sweetie." Juliet came to my side. "You look white as a sheet."

"I do?" I asked. I must be more nervous about confronting Jace Colton with his father's death than I realized. I checked my appearance in the reflection of the refrigerator door.

"There's nothing to worry about. Eileen Hutton is all talk. She's harmless really."

I wasn't so sure about that. I pinched my cheeks to combat the pallor of my skin. Then I returned to the desserts and drizzled chocolate around the plates with the three truffles. I added a white and milk chocolate heart on the edge of each plate.

I had hand molded the hearts from chocolate. I wished that I had asked Eileen if the wedding had a theme. If I'd known, I would have been able to make a more specific mold for the theme, but at least this demonstrated that I could do it. There really wasn't anything that I couldn't make out of chocolate. The possibilities were endless if you knew what you were doing, and I knew what I was doing. I knew how to manipulate chocolate. It was the only aspect of my life that was under my complete control.

For the tasting, I had prepared a selection of three truffles, as well as a chocolate-drizzled caramel corn. I could already imagine Eileen turning up her nose at that, but it was all the rage in foodie circles, as she should well know, and if she didn't, I'd be delighted to tell her. There were also individual chocolate-dipped strawberries, ramekins of molten chocolate cakes with caramel and sea salt, and JP Chocolates' famous white chocolate mousse. I hoped that the second option wouldn't be too cakelike for the groom.

I added a final drizzle on the third plate with a flourish.

"You're like an artist stroking her paintbrush across a blank canvas," Juliet said.

I blushed and picked up two of the plates. "That's a fair comparison. I do feel like a bit of an artist when it comes to chocolate. You should see some of the incredible things we have made in my shop back in New York. They really are works of art and far too lovely to eat."

Juliet picked up the third plate. "Let me help you with this."

I nodded my thanks but paused at the doorway. I took a deep breath. I could handle this. Eileen and her family couldn't be any worse that some of Jean Pierre's customers.

"Go on now, Bailey," Julie said encouragingly. "Eileen won't bite." She laughed her wind chime laugh again.

"Here we go," I said under my breath, and before I stepped into the hall, I plastered a bright smile on my face. It was the same smile that I used when dealing with difficult customers at Jean Pierre's shop. "Eileen, it's so nice to see you again."

Eileen narrowed her ice blue eyes at me. "We do not appreciate being kept waiting."

I set the plates on the table. "I'm so sorry to keep you waiting. I had some final touches and wanted everything to be absolutely perfect for you."

"Those look so good," Mira said barely above a whisper. Her eyes slid to her mother as if she were checking for Eileen's reaction to her comment.

Even seated at the round table, Jace retained his hold on Mira's hand. I smiled at the bride and held out my hand. "You must be Mira. Congratulations on your upcoming wedding tomorrow. I'm Bailey King."

Mira pulled her hand from Jace's grasp to shake mine and gave me the tiniest of smiles. "Thank you so much for making the desserts. I know that it must be difficult under the circumstances . . ." Her voice caught, and Jace took her hand again.

Jace shook his hair out of his eyes and watched me with a deep frown on his face. If I hadn't known better, I would have thought that he was Eileen's child instead of Mira, not because of his appearance, but because of his attitude. I extended my hand to him as well. "And you must be the lucky groom, Jace. Congratulations to you too."

He shook my hand. "Nice to meet you." His tone was firm and confident. Nothing like the timid greeting Mira had given me. I tried to assess Jace's level of distress over his father's death. There was no outward sign of grief that I could see.

I glanced at Mira. Her blue eyes were red-rimmed and her black mascara, which had been expertly applied, was ever so slightly smudged. She was certainly more broken up over Tyson's death than his son, or so it appeared.

Eileen sat directly across from her daughter and held herself with ease and authority. Eileen was a woman who knew who she was and how to use her power. Mira, not so much. Mira looked as if her strategy for dealing with any problem was to flee. Maybe that was why Jace was so intent on holding her in place. Perhaps he thought she'd turn into a runaway bride.

"I'm so sorry about your father," I said to Jace, thinking it would be best to address the enormous elephant in the room. There was no point in hiding the fact that we were at the church and not at Swissmen Sweets because his father had died in my grandparents' kitchen. "My grandparents and I are so very grateful that you would still like Swissmen Sweets to cater the desserts for your wedding tomorrow. I know it must be hard for you to be here today, considering the circumstances."

"Right," Jace said.

"Right" wasn't exactly the response I would have expected from a grieving son. What about his father's death was "right"? Maybe Jace was just a very composed guy. Perhaps he was more upset over his father's death than he outwardly appeared.

Juliet clicked a leash on Jethro's collar. "I'll just leave you to it. I'm going to see what Reverend Brook is up to." Juliet led the pig from the fellowship hall. As much as they had startled me when I'd first arrived, I was sorry to see them go. I felt like I had lost the one ally

I had. Well, two, if you counted the pig. Now, I was on my own.

Eileen clicked her tongue. "I don't know why she insists on carrying on the charade. Everyone in the congregation knows that she and Reverend Brook are a couple. It's shameful if you ask me. The pastor's wife has only been dead two years, and he's already moved on to another woman. If I passed away, I would never want my husband to remarry."

"Will your husband join us for the tasting too?" I asked, hoping the answer was no, because I had only made enough desserts for the three people in front of me.

"I'm divorced," she said in a clipped voice.

"I'm sorry to hear that," I said, not at all surprised by this revelation. "I suppose we should get started. I know that you all have a lot to do before tomorrow."

Eileen looked as if she wanted to say something, so I forged ahead. "In front of you we have a trio of truffles. Going left to right, the flavors are pistachio with sea salt, dark chocolate raspberry lemon, and green peppercorn. These are by no means the only truffles that can be made for the wedding, but I wanted to give a sampling, so you'd have an idea of what we can offer."

"These are so beautiful," Mira whispered. "Each piece is like a little sculpture. I've always thought, when I've gone into your grandparents' candy shop, that what they do is like sculpting. I'm a potter myself."

"A potter?" I asked.

She nodded. "I work in ceramics. I have a little studio in town."

Jace cleared his throat.

"It's just a hobby, really," Mira added quickly.

I frowned. It sounded like much more than a hobby to me.

She covered her mouth and gasped. "I'm sorry. It's just been such a horrible day. I wanted to put this off for another time . . ."

"Mira, we already went over this," Jace snapped. "The wedding is tomorrow. There is no other time to put it off to. Unless you no longer want to marry me tomorrow. Is that it?"

Mira stared at her folded hands. "I didn't say that. I just feel it might be too soon after what happened this morning. Shouldn't we postpone out of respect for your father?"

She had a point.

Jace picked up the peppercorn truffle but then set it back on his plate. "He was my father. If anyone should want to postpone the wedding, it's me, and I don't. This is my decision."

I couldn't help but think that the wedding was Mira's decision too. Before I could voice that opinion, Eileen chimed in. "Jace is right, Mira. You can't let what happened derail the plans for the wedding." Eileen picked up her fork and cut the raspberry lemon truffle in half.

I gave a sigh of relief to see that the inside was perfectly shaped.

She picked up one-half of the truffle and ate it. She chewed slowly as if taking in all the flavors. Then she ate the second half of the truffle. While she chewed, Jace picked up the same truffle, popped it into his mouth without preamble, and swallowed it like he was throwing back an oyster.

Mira didn't touch her plate. I suspected that she was waiting to hear from either her mother or her fiancé that the truffle was worth eating.

"It's very good," Eileen finally said.

As if on cue, Mira picked up her fork and cut the first

truffle on her plate in half, but she didn't actually put it in her mouth.

"You said that this next one is pistachio?" Eileen asked.

I nodded, letting out a breath that I didn't even know I had been holding. "With sea salt."

She picked up her fork and cut into her second truffle. She stuck the business end of the fork into the creamy chocolate middle but stopped the fork halfway to her mouth. "Mira, taste one of them, for goodness sake."

The smaller woman jerked away from her mother as if she had been slapped, but then she did what she was told. She picked up one-half of the raspberry lemon truffle and took a tentative bite. I couldn't help wondering if the girl's nervousness had something to do with Tyson's death. Of the three of them, she seemed to be the one most affected.

Eileen finished the third truffle. "These are all very good, Bailey. I must say that I'm impressed, and I'm not easily impressed."

That was a shock.

"Thank you," I said in a tone as sweet as the truffles Eileen had just eaten.

"But—" she began.

I wasn't a huge fan of the word "but" when it came to my creations, but I was certainly accustomed to it, considering Jean Pierre's clientele in Manhattan.

"I'd like to make a few changes," Eileen went on. "Perhaps offer a fourth truffle, something unique and special that no one in Holmes County would have ever had before. If we are going have a New York City chocolatier make our desserts, I want everyone coming to the wedding to be wowed by what you offer them." She made a note on the pad next to her plate.

I nodded. "We can certainly do that. Let me grab the next sampling while you make your notes."

Jace's cell phone rang. He fished it out of his jeans pocket and looked at the screen. "You'll have to continue without me for a moment. I need to take this." He held up the phone as if it stood as some kind of proof.

"Whatever could be more important right now than your wedding? You are getting married in less than twenty-four hours," Eileen said in a huff.

Jace clenched his jaw, but when he tossed his hair out of his eyes, his expression smoothed from irritation to the boredom that seemed to be his resting face. "It's from my office."

"Oh," Mira said. "Yes, it must be important. Yes, you must take the call." She shot a frightened look at her mother.

Eileen folded her hands on the top of the table. "If you must take it, you must take it. Just don't be long."

Jace marched in the direction the kitchen, bumping my shoulder as he went. He didn't make any promises about the duration of his phone call.

Eileen watched him go, a scowl marring her perfectly made-up face. "What on earth could be so important that he had to take the call in the middle of our tasting?"

Mira stared at her hands. I couldn't help but think that she knew exactly why Jace had to take that call, and I sensed it had something to do with his father's murder.

Chapter 17

Before Eileen could protest, I gathered up their empty truffle plates and hurried into the kitchen. I was dying to follow Jace and find out who had called him. I set the plates on the counter, opened the oven door, and removed the molten chocolate cakes from the convection oven where I had left them to keep warm.

I was removing my oven mitts when I caught sight of Jace. He was right outside the kitchen window, pacing back and forth with his cell phone plastered to his ear. His skin was flushed, and even though I couldn't hear the words, I could hear the angry tone of his voice through the window.

I made a split-second decision and shut the oven door, then ran out the back door of the kitchen. The kitchen opened into a small utility room with a stationary tub and a water heater. On the opposite wall from the kitchen, there was a metal door that must lead to the outside.

A petite Amish girl yelped as I barged into the room. She stood at the stationary tub filling a plastic bucket with water. White bubbles sloshed over the sides of the bucket.

"Did a man with floppy hair come through here?"

She stared at me openmouthed.

"Did a man come through here just now?"

She nodded but still didn't speak.

I hurried out the back door, which opened onto a small parking lot. A large green dumpster stood to the right of the door. There was one car in the lot, and the sign in front of it said REV. BROOK.

To the left of the parking lot was a cemetery that looked as if it dated back to the Civil War, at least. Many of the headstones were covered with moss, and all but the faintest impression of the engravings had worn away.

Jace leaned against a large oak tree and gazed into the middle of the graveyard, his cell held up to his ear. His back was to me, and he faced away from the church as he stared out beyond the rolling hills that made up much of Holmes County. In the distance, a buggy crested one of those hills and raced down the other side. As quietly as possible, I closed the utility room door behind me.

For the briefest of moments, I questioned my sanity for leaving the kitchen to follow Jace. For one, Eileen would soon be wondering what had happened to the next tasting plate, if she wasn't already. Secondly, I stood in the middle of the back parking lot. If Jace merely glanced over his shoulder, he would see me. Thirdly, the possibly mute Amish girl knew I was outside spying on Jace. What if she let someone know what I had done?

"I don't care how you take care of it, just do it," Jace

yelled into the phone. "There is no reason to get anyone else involved."

I inched a few steps closer. There was a large headstone at the corner of the cemetery. I hesitated for just a moment before I made a mad dash for it, and then crouched beside it.

"Don't you understand my father has been murdered? The police will be looking at all of his records for a motive. We need to make sure that he doesn't have anything in those records that we need to worry about."

I peeked around the headstone and the ridiculousness of the situation struck me. I had to cover my mouth with my hand to physically hold back a giggle that bubbled in the back of my throat.

The back door of the church opened, and the Amish girl stepped through it. She struggled to carry the heavy bucket of soapy water. In her other hand, she held a scrub brush. She caught sight of me hiding behind the tombstone, and her dark eyes went wide.

Jace turned around and spotted the girl. "I've gotta go," he said into the phone. "You know what you need to do." He shoved the phone back into his pocket and stomped toward the girl.

She set her bucket on the pavement and adjusted her stance as if she were bracing herself for impact.

"What are you doing here?" Jace demanded of the girl.

"I am working."

He pointed at her. "You're here to put more ideas in Mira's head, aren't you?"

The girl stepped back. "I don't know what you mean. I'm very sorry for your loss, Jace. I'm sorry for you and

Mira that this happened, especially at such an important time."

I stared at the pair. It was clear that they knew each other, which wasn't unreasonable in a village as small as Harvest, but Jace didn't strike me as an Englisher who spent much time with the Amish.

From my vantage point crouched by the large tombstone, I couldn't see Jace's face. His back was rigid as he spoke to the girl. "Don't lie. I know exactly how you and the rest of them feel. You're glad he's dead."

The girl stumbled back, knocking her ankle against the bucket of soapy water. Suds and water sloshed over the side. "How can you say that? You know we wouldn't want anything to happen that would ruin Mira's special day."

He took a step toward her. "There you go lying again. Don't pretend you and Emily want me to marry Mira. You have been against it from the start."

I frowned. Emily? Could he mean Emily Esh from the pretzel shop?

The girl licked her lips. "All we want is for Mira to be happy and marry a *gut* man."

"And I'm not a good man?" Jace asked.

The girl didn't reply. Her silence was answer enough.

"Mira and I are getting married tomorrow, and there is nothing that you or any of her Amish friends can do to stop it." With that, he marched around her and stormed back inside the church.

The girl gripped the side of her white apron and stared at the tops of her shoes. When she looked up, her eyes locked with mine.

I stood up, and my knees ached from the sudden release of pressure. I started to walk toward her, but before I could reach her, she picked up her bucket and fled back inside the church.

I was about to follow her when a white and black blur flew across my path and dove into the cemetery.

"Jethro! Jethro! You get back here, you little rascal!"

I turned to see a short round man with wire-rimmed glasses running toward me with a halting gait.

He waved at me. "Stop that pig!"

Without thinking, I bolted into the cemetery after the pig. The graveyard wasn't that large, but there were many places where the small pig could hide.

"Jethro? Come here, buddy," I called, wondering if you could call a pig like you could a dog.

Since the pig didn't come running, I guessed the answer was no. Then I spotted him behind a tombstone with the name TYSON COLTON engraved on the front. I blinked at it as I read the stone more closely. There were two names on the stone. Tyson's and a woman named JEANNETTE COLTON. This must be the stone marking the resting place of Tyson's wife—and Jace's mother. Her death date was thirteen years ago. I glanced back at the church. Jace was awfully young to have lost both of his parents. That made it seem all that more tragic. Maybe this compound loss was why Jace had reacted the way that he did. Maybe there was only so much loss he was equipped to process.

The stone had been pre-engraved with Tyson's name. All that remained was to add the death date, which would be engraved soon, now that he was also gone. I shivered. I knew it was more cost effective to have the stone carved all at once when the first half of a couple died, but I wondered how I would feel if I visited my husband's final resting place and saw my name there every time I went to visit.

Finally, the little man caught up with me. "Did you see him? Do you know which way he went?"

I shook my head to chase away the thoughts of death and dying. "See who?"

He threw up his arms. "The pig!"

"He was right over there a moment ago." I pointed at the stone where I had seen Jethro last.

The man hurried behind the stone. There was a high pitched squeal, and Jethro catapulted himself over one of the low tombstones and ran directly at me. I caught him with an *oomph* as he slammed against my chest. He buried his pink snout in my neck it. It felt cold and wet and tickled my skin.

"There, there," I murmured, patting his back. I didn't know if that was best way to comfort a terrified pot-bellied pig, but it was all I knew to do. "It's okay," I added for good measure. The animal shivered in my arms.

The man wiped his brow and stumbled over a tree root as he approached us. "I turned my back for one minute, and he was off like a shot. He always stays with Juliet. He must have thought that he could find her."

"Juliet left him with you?" I cradled the pig in my arms, and he seemed to be quite comfortable there. I could be wrong, but I thought he smelled faintly of lavender. Not a smell that one would expect when hold-ing a pig.

The man eyed me as if seeing me for the first time. "You know Juliet?"

"I met her and Jethro this morning."

He squinted. "And you are?"

I cradled Jethro in my left arm and held out my right hand. "Bailey King. I'm borrowing the church kitchen for the Hutton wedding."

"Oh, yes, Eileen told me that you were here to make desserts for her daughter's wedding." He looked relieved, as if he'd expected me to say I was someone else.

I found myself squinting at him a little, as he had at me.

"I'm Reverend Brook. We're so very grateful to you for helping with the wedding. As you may have surmised by now, Eileen would like everything to go off without a hitch."

"I have come to recognize that."

"I'm sure." This made him laugh, and the tension in his face evaporated. Instead of a suspicious man, he was transformed into a kindly village pastor. He held out his arms to me, and after the briefest moment of hesitation, I set Jethro into them. The pig gave me a pitiful look as I handed him over.

The back door of the church flew open and Eileen stomped out. "Bailey King, you have kept us waiting long enough. I have half a mind to cancel my contract with Swissmen Sweets. We shouldn't be kept waiting like this." She pulled up short. "Oh, Reverend Brook, I didn't expect to see you out here."

"My apologies, Eileen." Reverend Brook wiped sweat from his brow and tucked Jethro under his right arm like a sack of potatoes. "Juliet volunteered to run some errands for the ceremony tomorrow and left me in charge of Jethro here. He got loose and Bailey"—he glanced at me—"found him for me."

Eileen's nose wrinkled as she took in the small polka-dotted pig in the reverend's arms.

Reverend Brook cleared his throat. "Well, I should get Jethro back inside." He nodded to Eileen. "I'll be in my office if you need me for any last minute wedding questions."

"Everything is well in hand, Reverend Brook."

He adjusted Jethro in his arms. "I wouldn't expect anything less from you."

I felt my brow rise as I watched their conversation with interest. Why did I feel like they were talking about something completely unrelated to Mira and Jace's wedding tomorrow?

Chapter 18

The next thirty minutes going through the final tastings with Eileen, Jace, and Mira were painful to say the least. Eileen nitpicked every dessert I presented. Even when the presentation and taste were flawless, she had some change that she wanted me to make before the wedding. I shouldn't have let her criticism upset me. I was accustomed to Jean Pierre's clients being even more critical than Eileen. What really grated on my nerves was how she treated her daughter. Any time the girl gave her opinion, Eileen shot her down.

I set the last dessert in front of them, the three servings of white chocolate mousse.

"It's almost too pretty to eat," Mira said, barely above a whisper.

I smiled. The mousse was very pretty with a laced heart formed out of dark chocolate sticking out of the top. The chocolate work on the heart was edible and delicate—I'd taken special care to achieve the lacy effect and make each piece identical.

Eileen pointed her spoon at her daughter. "Don't be

ridiculous, Mira. It's meant to be eaten. That's what it's for."

The girl folded her hands in her lap and stared down at them.

Jace, who I thought should come to his fiancée's rescue, plucked the heart from his dessert and set it on his napkin, then broke it in two with such force I wondered whose neck he was envisioning between his hands. Mira winced at the cracking sound the chocolate made and then carefully lifted her chocolate heart from the dessert. She placed it on the white dessert plate at her elbow. Not for the first time, I wondered what the gentle young woman was doing with Jace and how he could be overpowering Eileen's daughter.

"This is lovely," Eileen said, as if it caused her physical pain. "The mousse is well done. I have to say, overall, I am impressed with what you have to offer. We will expect your menu, with the few alterations that I have requested, at the wedding tomorrow."

"How many guests will there be?" I asked.

"One hundred and fifty-four." She announced this number with such precision, I didn't doubt that she consulted the wedding guest list on an hourly basis.

I swallowed. I had one night to make desserts for one hundred and fifty-four guests, with no professional kitchen and no help. I bit down on my tongue to hold back the excuses that bubbled up in the back of my throat as to why that was an impossible task. I'd figure something out.

Eileen stood. "We should be going. There's still much to do on our list before—"

Her litany of last-minute wedding tasks was interrupted by Jace's cell phone beeping. He looked at the screen. "I have to take this."

Eileen nodded. "Our next stop is the caterer."

"And you don't need me, Eileen. I was only interested in the desserts." He jumped out of his chair, pausing only long enough to kiss Mira on the cheek before he ran out of the fellowship hall.

Eileen turned to her daughter. "What on earth was that about, Mira? Why can't Jace just stay off of the phone at least through the end of the tasting?"

"I—I wouldn't know," her daughter whispered, staring at her hands.

"His father was murdered this morning," I said, wondering why I even needed to remind Eileen of that fact. "I think that anyone would be acting different under the circumstances."

"Come along, Mira. We're going now," her mother said. "There's much more we must do before the rehearsal this evening."

Mira nodded solemnly and rose from her chair as if it took an enormous effort to stand up against the weight pressing down on her shoulders. Although still beautiful in her melancholy way, no one would mistake Mira for a blushing and excited bride. She looked more like she would be attending a funeral the next day, not her own wedding. I wondered where and when Tyson's funeral would be, since the family appeared to be so preoccupied with the wedding.

I watched as mother and daughter walked across the fellowship hall. Eileen moved briskly with a perfectly straight back. Mira shuffled with her shoulders slumped.

After they were gone, I went into the kitchen to clean up after the tasting. I groaned when I saw the collection of pots and pans in the sink. Rolling up my sleeves, I turned the faucet all the way to hot.

I was at the church's deep double sink and up to my

elbows in sudsy water when something pinched me on the back of my leg. I jumped three feet into the air, and soap bubbles flew. I knocked a bowl of chocolate syrup off of the counter with my elbow, and it tumbled onto the potbellied pig's head. Jethro shook the metal bowl off, and it clattered to the white tiled floor. I groaned. It would take me all night to scrub the chocolate out of the grout.

"Jethro! You need to behave yourself," Juliet admonished and grabbed a roll of paper towels from the dispenser mounted on the wall. She knelt on the floor and began to sop up the worst of the mess. She looked up at me as she worked. "Bailey, I'm so sorry about that. Jethro is known to nip, but he only nips people he likes. He would never touch Eileen, you see." She lowered her voice as if Eileen were still in the building. "He doesn't care for her much."

The pig looked up at me, and then with his long tongue licked the chocolate off of his white nose. I wiped some chocolate from my cheek. "Jethro's had a busy day. We had a bit of an adventure in the graveyard."

Juliet blushed. "Yes, Reverend Brook told me about that. I had to run an errand and thought Jethro would do all right for a little while alone with the reverend. I do wish the two of them would make up, but they seem bound and determined to dislike each other." She sighed.

I stopped myself from asking Juliet why she was so keen on the pig and pastor liking each other. The answer was as clear as the polka dots on Jethro's back. The woman was completely smitten with the widowed pastor.

She stood and dipped a rag into the soapy water before kneeling on the floor again to scrub the grout. Jethro made short work of the chocolate that was on his face—at least the bits of it that he could reach with his tongue.

"There should be a scrub brush under the sink there," Juliet said. "If you grab it for me, I'll clean up what's left of this mess. Can you clean his face?"

I hesitated. The pig had nipped me but hadn't done any real harm. He'd startled me more than anything.

Juliet smiled. "Oh, go ahead. He nipped you, so he likes you, remember."

I picked up a rag, leaned over and began to clean the pig's bristly head. He stomped his hooves and wiggled his curly tail as I cleaned his face, and I found myself smiling too. The little bacon bundle wasn't that bad after all.

Juliet stood. "See, as good as new."

I stared at the floor. The white tile gleamed. I blinked. "How did you do that? I've tried to get chocolate out of grout before, and it's next to impossible."

"Ahh, well, you've never been a mother to a son, then. If you had, this wouldn't have even been a challenge. Boys are messy, and my son was the messiest when he was little. Thankfully, he has since grown out of that."

"How old is your son?" I asked, expecting her to say eight or ten. Twelve, tops.

"Twenty-eight."

I blinked at her again. There was no way this young woman could have a twenty-eight-year-old son. "You are kidding, right? There's no way you have a son my age."

"I'm very proud of him," She went on. "He's a sh— Jethro! What are you doing?"

Somehow, while we were talking, the pig had managed to climb a foot stool. He had both of his front hooves on the speckled Formica counter, and his snout buried in the plate of leftover truffles. Several truffles rolled across the counter and onto the floor.

Juliet shook her head. "Oh, Jethro."

The pig lifted his face out of the dish, and he had chocolate and raspberry-lemon filling all over it.

"I'm so sorry, Bailey."

I waved away her concern. "It's—"

"Mom?" A deep voice called out. "Are you down here?"

Juliet's face lit up at the sound of the man's voice. "There's my son now." She raised her voice. "We're in the kitchen!"

I turned away from the pig covered in chocolate and found Deputy Aiden Brody standing in the doorway in his navy blue uniform. He removed his ball cap from his head, and tufts of dark hair stood up every which way. He folded his hat in his hands. "I didn't expect to find both of you here," he said. "But I'm glad I did."

Juliet beamed. "You've already met."

Aiden nodded. "At the Kings' shop yesterday before . . ." He trailed off.

I knew he was going to say "before the murder."

"Oh, Bailey, what were you going to say before Aiden showed up?" Juliet asked.

I stared at Aiden, trying to process that the deputy was Juliet's son. "Oh, umm . . . I was just going to say that it's all right that Jethro ate the truffles. Eileen wanted me to make different flavors for tomorrow."

She stared. "And when are you going to do that?"

"Tonight, I guess. I just have to figure out where."

"What do you mean, where?" she asked. "It'll be right here. You'll use the church's kitchen, of course. It's the perfect place. You'll have everything you need, and you'll be close to the reception."

I tried not to look at Aiden. "Is that okay with Reverend Brook? I will be here pretty late tonight. There's a lot to do."

"Leave the good reverend to me," she said confidently.

Aiden made a small sound that came across as a snort.

Juliet shook her finger at her son. "Hush, you!"

He grinned, and then he looked at me, and his smile faded. "I'm glad you are here, Bailey. I need to talk to you about the murder."

My heart sank.

Juliet shook a towel at her son. "What would Bailey know about the murder other than that it happened at her grandparents' shop? I'm sure you have already been over that."

Aiden pursed his lips.

Juliet bent over and patted Jethro's head as if she needed the reassurance that he was still at her side. "Is something wrong?"

He frowned. "I need to talk to Bailey for a moment in private."

"What?" his mother asked. "Why?"

Aiden looked pained. "Bailey?"

I put a hand on Juliet's arm. "It's okay, Juliet. Thanks for all your help this afternoon. I couldn't have done it without you and the quilting ladies. Really."

She frowned. "Well, Jethro and I will clean up the rest of the kitchen for you, so you can head straight home and see your grandparents after you talk to Aiden. I'm sure they are wondering what became of you."

I was sure that they must be wondering that too. I

suspected that Jethro wasn't going to be much help with the cleaning, but I was happy to take her up on her offer. I had a long night of candy making in front of me. I needed to conserve what energy I had, knowing that a good chunk of it would be lost on the conversation that Aiden wanted to have with me. I thanked Juliet, gave her another reassuring smile, and followed her son out of the kitchen.

Without saying a word, Aiden led me across the fellowship hall and out the door.

Outside of the church, I took in a deep breath, basking in crisp country air after working in the church kitchen for so long. I studied the deputy out of the corner of my eye and wondered what he was thinking as we walked down the church steps. Was he focused on the murder? Or was he thinking about his mother and her relationship with the pastor?

I still couldn't quite wrap my head around the idea that I had been with Aiden's mother for a good part of the day, and that his mother was dating the pastor and had a pet pig. Aiden had struck me as coming from much more traditional roots—happily married parents with a dog, probably a Lab. Aiden struck me as a Lab kind of guy.

He walked toward his cruiser and leaned on the fender, facing me. This was going to be much more than a casual conversation about the murder. I had never been so sure about anything in my life.

Chapter 19

Aiden folded his arms, and his jaw was tight. "Bailey, I've been sent to fetch you and bring you to the station for some more questioning."

"About Tyson's death?" I asked, not knowing why I even wasted my breath. Perhaps I wanted to put off the inevitable.

He gave me a tiny smile, and the slightest hint of the dimple on his cheek appeared. "Should I know of another reason?"

My mouth felt dry. "Am I under arrest?"

"No." His answer was firm, but then he added, "No one is under arrest at this time."

At this time. That was telling, too telling in my case.

"We should go," he said.

I stared at the patrol car. "Are you going to make me ride in the back?"

"Nope," he said easily, as if we were just going for a drive to check out the scenery. "You can have shotgun."

If he was trying to put me at ease, it wasn't working. I climbed into the car, and Aiden shut the door after me as if he was a gentleman, and we were on a date.

We drove in silence through the rolling farmland, where there seemed to be a herd of cattle or flock of sheep on every hillside; the trip stirred memories of my childhood summers in Amish Country. I'd grown up in a bustling New England city, and Holmes County had always seemed like some wide-open fairyland to me, where I could run free with little supervision. As a child, I wanted to spend as much time as I could here.

Aiden sat straight in the driver's seat as if propped against a flat board, and his hands were positioned perfectly at ten and two on the steering wheel. He was a man who followed the rules and played by the book. I knew he wouldn't want me to snoop around Tyson's murder. I just wouldn't tell him what I was up to.

Aiden couldn't be more different from Eric, and the thought of it hit me by surprise. Why would I make a comparison between the two men? I had no reason to compare them.

I needed to break the silence before my brain spun completely out of control. "So why do you have to take me to the station? You can tell me now. Your mom isn't here, and I do think it's strange she never mentioned that she was your mother before you arrived."

The right corner of his mouth kicked up in that hint of a smile. "Did she have reason to? Did you talk about me at all?"

My cheeks felt hot, and I was grateful that he kept his eyes on the road and off of me. "No, but I would have thought, when the murder came up, she would have said, 'Oh, my son is a deputy,' or something along those lines."

"There's more than one deputy in the department. How would you make the leap that I was her son?"

"I would have known it wasn't Carpenter. He's way too old and grumpy to be your mother's child."

He did laugh then, and it had a deep, rich sound that made me smile. It was nothing like Eric's laugh, which was an airy *hee hee*. Aiden's laugh was a guffaw that came from deep within him, and I couldn't help but enjoy the sound of it. There I went comparing Aiden to Eric again. I bit the inside of my lip until the pain was great enough that I stopped smiling.

"I'm glad you think my mother's son must be nice."

"You're nicer than Carpenter," I admittedly grudgingly.

He laughed again.

"You never answered my original question about the station."

The laugh died on his lips. "I told you back at the church. We need to ask you a few more questions related to the case."

"It's more than that. After I discovered Tyson's body, you didn't take me to the station. Something must have changed. What is it?"

"Why do you think anything has changed?" he asked.

I gripped the seatbelt, twisting it in my hands. "I'm not stupid, Deputy Brody. You were more than a little uncomfortable when you told your mom where you were taking me."

"I never thought for a moment that you were stupid, Miss King," he said, returning my formal tone. He paused. "New evidence has surfaced, and it would be easier to go over it with you if we were at the station."

"So it's for convenience sake that we are going there?"

He stared straight ahead at the county road. "Yes, among other reasons."

"Do you think I flew all the way from Manhattan, taking the chance of losing the job of my dreams, so that I could kill Tyson Colton, who I'd never even heard of until I arrived here? My grandparents never mentioned him in any of their letters. If you don't believe me, I can give them to you. I have every letter my grandparents ever sent me. They're neatly stored back in my New York apartment. If you are determined to follow every lead, you're welcome to them."

"I don't need to see your letters." His voice was quiet. "I believe you."

I snorted. "You have a funny way of showing it."

"It's true." He took his eyes off the road for a split second to meet my gaze. "You're the granddaughter of Clara and Jebidiah. It's difficult for me to believe that you could kill someone." His voice and expression were so sincere that I almost believed him. Almost.

"You don't know me," I argued. "How can knowing my grandparents proving anything to you about me? Lots of good people have not so good relatives." I knew I shouldn't argue him into suspecting me more. I knew crime was different in Holmes County than in New York, but he couldn't just consider who my grandparents were and assume that I was a good person. *Daadi* and *Maami* didn't know anything about my life back in New York, or that I was an expert liar who had kept my relationship with Eric Sharp hidden for so many months.

"I know that. Believe me when I say that I have seen the least likely people do the most horrible things to one another. It's easy in my line of work to believe that everyone has a bad side." He tightened his grip on the steering wheel so hard, his knuckles turned from pink to white. "In any case, it doesn't matter what I believe to be true. You remain a suspect in this case—the prime suspect—until it's proven otherwise."

I clenched my teeth. "What's your relationship with my grandparents?"

He gripped the steering wheel a little more tightly.

I sat up and pressed my back into the seat. "How do you know them? And I know the connection must be something more than just Harvest is a small town."

He kept his eyes trained on the road in front of him and didn't say a word.

I folded my arms across my chest and cocked my head. I studied the deputy's profile, taking in the shape his face, the curve of his cheekbone, and the slight indentation where his dimple would be had he been smiling. He mostly certainly wasn't smiling at the moment.

He turned to me, and his face broke into a half smile. "Are we in the middle of a staring contest, and I wasn't informed?"

My cheeks flushed, and I dropped my hands to my lap. "I'm only asking because both you and your mother—who looks far too young to be your mother—hinted at having some sort of history with my grandparents. Since you're taking me to the police station to question me about a murder, I think I have a right to know what that history is."

He relaxed his grip on the steering wheel. "I suppose it is a logical question, especially after you spent so much time with my mom." His face softened when he mentioned his mother, and then he smiled. "And Jethro."

I fought a smile. "Yeah, I'd say I've earned a little bit of information since Jethro ate my truffles, and he bit me."

"He bit you?"

"It was just a love nip, or so your mother said."

He laughed. "She would."

"My grandparents could have sold those truffles at their shop or, if the shop's not open, at the market."

His dimple withdrew. "You're right. I'm sorry Jethro did that. My mother insists that he's well behaved, but he's not."

I folded my arms and leaned back into the seat. "Are you avoiding the question for some reason? Is there something about my grandparents that I should know?"

He was quiet for a long moment, and I thought he wasn't going to answer. "Your grandparents are good people, salt of the earth folks, but I imagine you already know that."

I waited.

Finally, he said, "They also helped Mom and me out when we first moved to Holmes County. We owe them everything. I owe them everything."

"Why exactly?"

"They took us in when we had nowhere to go. You know that verse in the Bible where it says, When I was hungry, you fed me. When I was a stranger, you invited me in? They did that for us."

I didn't know that verse. I hadn't grown up going to church and knew very little about what the Bible said other than what I'd gleaned from my grandparents those times we visited them.

I felt my eyebrows shoot up into my hairline. "When was this?"

"A long time ago."

"How long?" I pressed, stamping down my irritation at the vague answer, at all the vague answers I had gotten from him and everyone else in Harvest, even my own grandparents.

He gave me a sideways look. "You ask a lot of questions."

"I'm curious about—" I stopped myself just before I said "about you." I licked my lips. "I'm a curious person. I'm curious about everything, and this has to do with my grandparents, whom I love very much"

"I know you do." He took his eyes off the road for a second and glanced at me. His eyes softened, and then he returned his attention to the road ahead. "You wouldn't have made all those last-minute desserts for Eileen's tasting if you didn't love your grandparents. I don't think anyone puts up with Eileen without some powerful motivation. My mother and I stayed with your grandparents over twenty years ago. I was seven if you want my exact age."

"But why don't I remember you? I spent my summers with them growing up. I would have been here that summer."

"We were gone by the summer and had moved to our own apartment."

"But if you were so close to my grandparents, why didn't I meet you? Where were you all summer? And why did you live with them in the first place?"

His jaw twitched. "I thought you wanted to know about your grandparents, not me."

Clearly, I had hit a nerve with the deputy. We were quiet for a few miles. When I couldn't take the silence anymore, I said, "I'm sorry. I didn't mean to pry."

He sighed. "Let's just get through this investigation,

Bailey. The getting to know each other part can come after that."

I stared at him. What did he mean by that? Before I had a chance to ask, we turned into a large parking lot that literally looked like it had been planted in the middle of a fallow field. On the far end of the lot there was a squat brick building with several wings. HOLMES COUNTY SHERIFF'S DEPARTMENT was emblazoned over the front door. All my thoughts about Aiden's odd comments flew from my head at the sight of the utilitarian building. I gripped the arm rest and closed my eyes, repeating the types of chocolate in my head again. I can't say I found my mantra as soothing as it normally was.

Aiden parked the cruiser in an empty space near the front door. As I got out of the car, Deputy Carpenter came out of the building. "I see you were able to track her down."

I frowned at him. "You knew where I was."

He rubbed his bald head. "That I did, and I told my friend here where to find you. I will say I am a little surprised to see you riding in the front of the cruiser." He eyed Aiden. "It's not protocol."

"Miss King," Aiden said in an even voice, "isn't under arrest."

Carpenter looped his thumbs over his duty belt and rocked back on his heels. "I know you are soft on the Amish, but the sheriff isn't going to be. We both know how this is going to go, don't we?" he asked with a congenial smile on his face.

Aiden's jaw twitched.

Carpenter shrugged. "The sheriff won't go easy on her." He winked at me. "I hope you're tough enough to take it."

Aiden balled his fists at his sides, but slowly, one by

one he unfolded his fingers, stretching them out to their full length. "I'll worry about the sheriff. Now, please move to the side."

Carpenter took the smallest side step to the left.

"Follow me, Bailey," Aiden said as he marched around the Carpenter

I adjusted the strap of my bag over my shoulder and hurried after Aiden. All the while, I felt Carpenter's eyes on my back. "What did he mean when he said that you both knew how this was going to go? And all those comments about the sheriff? What's that about?" I asked in a low voice when I caught up to him.

Tight-lipped, Aiden said, "Just ignore him."

Like that was possible.

Aiden led me into the station. The door opened into a no-frills waiting room. There was a female deputy sitting at the desk, and she smiled at Aiden. "The sheriff has been waiting for you. He said to put Miss King in room three for now."

I bit the inside of my lip and wondered if room three was a jail cell or an interrogation room. Even though Aiden said I wasn't under arrest, I only half believed him. Should I call an attorney now, my parents, or Cass? What if this conversation was the prelude to the sheriff locking me up and conveniently losing the key? I swallowed hard.

Aiden stepped over to what looked like an impenetrable heavy metal door and punched a code into the keypad just above the doorknob. There was a metallic click, and the door opened inward. He inclined his head. "Bailey? This way please."

After a deep breath, I followed his broad back through the door. There was a long hallway to my left, and I could see a large room at the end of it that was divided into cubicles. Instead of moving in the direction of the cubicles, Aiden led me to the right. He stopped at a second door, where he punched in another code. This second door opened into a much shorter hallway. There were four closed doors in all, and a number was stenciled on each door. The door we walked through slammed behind us, and I felt a little like Alice in Wonderland when she had to choose the right door to escape the room she'd fallen into in pursuit of the white rabbit.

In the end, I didn't have to make the difficult choice that Alice had. Aiden made the decision when he opened door number three.

I inched into the room, and he stood in the doorway behind me. "I'll just ask you to wait here," Aiden said. "I'll be back in a minute." He gave me a small smile before he closed the door. As the latch clicked into place, my stomach dropped to the soles of my shoes. As much as I hated being marched around the sheriff's department by Aiden, it was much worse to be left alone in this room for an indefinite amount of time. I tried the door handle and wasn't the least bit surprised to find it locked. If it had been unlocked, I don't know what I would have done. Made a run for it, maybe. I doubted I would get very far, and if the point of me cooperating with the police was to protect my grandparents from having to be put in the same situation, running from the sheriff's department like a guilty party wouldn't help.

I dropped my shoulder bag on the table in the middle of the room and surveyed my surroundings.

It was gray. That was the best way to describe it. Gray walls, gray floor, gray table and chairs. I found the monochromic decor depressing. I wondered if that was intentional, so that the person being questioned would confess just to escape the dull space. On the opposite wall from the door, there was a mirror. I assumed that it was a two-way mirror like they had on the television cop shows, where I could see only my reflection, but the person on the other side could see me. I tapped on the glass and stared into it, squinting to see if I could make out the shape of anyone who might be watching me on the other side. The only thing I saw was my own pale face reflected back at me. I bared my teeth and frowned when nothing happened.

I stepped back from the mirror and circled the room like the tiger I had seen in the Central Park Zoo. Around and around I went. Sitting was impossible. I had to move. Anxiety flowed through my veins. If I stopped moving, I knew the anxious feeling would overpower me. I couldn't let that happen. My skin tingled. Every few seconds I let myself glance at the door, but still no one came. I didn't know how long I paced around that room. Was it ten minutes? An hour? Time seemed irrelevant in the empty gray space, a space outside the confines of time, a space of interminable ending.

Finally, I heard the doorknob turn. I spun around, bracing myself for whoever might enter the room and praying that it was Aiden.

"Well, hello there, Miss King," said the newcomer, who most definitely was not Deputy Aiden Brody. "I've been looking forward to meeting you."

Chapter 20

I had expected Aiden or maybe even Deputy Carpenter to come through the door. Instead there was a heavy-set man with gray hair—as gray as everything else in the small room. Instead of wearing a uniform like the deputies, he had on a rumpled suit and carried a file. He dropped the file on the table. "Why don't you have a seat?" He settled into one of the chairs, which groaned under his weight.

After a beat, I took the seat across from him.

"There you go." He nodded his approval and folded his hands on top of the manila folder. Something about the folder made me wary. He wouldn't have brought it into the room if it wasn't important, and I had feeling that what was inside would not be welcome news to me.

He had a half smile on his face as he studied me. It was as if I somehow didn't live up to his expectations, whatever those expectations might be. "I'm Sheriff Jack Marshall," he said finally.

I nodded and waited.

"Can you tell me again what happened last night?"

His voice was pleasant enough, but the irritating smile remained in place. I knew not to trust the voice.

"I've already told both Deputy Brody and Deputy Carpenter multiple times," I protested.

"Indulge me." He leaned back in his chair as if in a relaxed posture. He moved his hands from the top of the manila folder and folded his arms across his broad chest.

As much as I didn't want to go over it all again, I knew the sooner I answered the sheriff's questions, the sooner I would be able to return to my grandparents. I had been gone so long that I knew they must be worried and wondering what had become of me. They might have gone to the church by now and found that I wasn't there. I wished I'd thought to call their shop phone before Aiden brought me to the station. It was too late for that call. I suspected the sheriff wouldn't look too kindly on me if I whipped out my cell phone just now. So I repeated my story from beginning to end, taking very little breath between sentences because I just wanted to get the story out.

He nodded. "And what were you doing at the church this afternoon?" His question surprised me.

My brow wrinkled. "I don't know what that has to do with what happened at my grandparents' candy shop this morning."

The sheriff straightened up, and the chair beneath him groaned again. "I think it has quite a lot to do with it. Weren't you there with Jace Colton, the deceased's son?"

I folded my hands in my lap. "His wedding is tomorrow. His future mother-in-law scheduled a wedding dessert tasting at Swissmen Sweets for this afternoon. Under the circumstances, the tasting couldn't be in the shop. We didn't have a kitchen to use, so we moved it to the church. Eileen was kind enough to make the arrangements with the pastor so that I could use the church's kitchen."

"Why did you handle the tasting?" He lifted one of his thin eyebrows. The eyebrow looked too delicate to go with his ruddy complexion. "Your grandfather was hired to supply the sweets, not you."

"My grandfather is ill, and remaking everything that would have been needed for the tasting in the time available would have been too difficult for him. My grandparents have been through enough for one day. They didn't need to deal with Eileen too."

"What do you mean by that?" He lowered the thin brows.

I tried not to stare at his peculiar eyebrows as I answered. "I could tell that Eileen was going to be particular about what she wanted for the wedding. I'm used to handling particular people at the chocolate shop where I work in New York, so I stepped in and offered to make the desserts for the tasting. It was Eileen who suggested that we use the church kitchen. I was surprised to see that Jace came, considering."

He arched one of his thin eyebrows. "Considering what?"

The more I stared at the eyebrows, the more I began to realize they were drawn onto his red face. What had happened to the sheriff to cause him to lose his brows? I stopped myself from asking. This probably was not a good time.

Of course, the sheriff knew perfectly well why I was surprised to see Jace at the tasting, but I answered anyway. "Considering his father was just murdered this morning."

He tapped his fingers over the top of the file in a consistent rhythm. I swallowed and tried my best not to stare at it. The folder was making me more nervous by the second.

When neither of us spoke for a long moment, I broke the silence. "Don't you find it odd that Jace wants to go on with the wedding tomorrow? His father hasn't even been dead twenty-four hours. Isn't that a little cold?"

He folded his hands over the top of the manila folder again. "Do you think he should put his life on hold because his father is dead?"

"Not forever, but a day wouldn't hurt, would it?"

The sheriff looked as if he wanted to say something, but I forged ahead. "I don't begrudge him for wanting to go on with the wedding, not really. From what I gathered, he and his father had a difficult relationship. But don't you think they should have waited for a least a day before continuing with the wedding plans?"

"Do you suspect him of something, Miss King?"

I waited for a beat, trying to decide if I wanted to tell the sheriff what I had learned from eavesdropping on Jace in the cemetery. "I overheard him telling someone on the phone to 'take care' of something now that his father was dead, because the police would be searching his files."

The sheriff appeared unimpressed by the information. "Take care of what, exactly?"

"He didn't say."

"Then how do you know it's related to the murder?"

"Because he mentioned his father in the phone conversation," I said, doing my best to keep the frustration out of my voice. I was afraid that my attempt was an epic fail.

Then, his face clouded over. "Let me be very clear,

Miss King. This is a police investigation. I don't want you sneaking around my county, spying on people, and messing with my case."

"I wasn't sneaking or spying," I lied. "I was at the church and overheard the call." I made a point of not mentioning that I had followed Jace outside into the cemetery. "Besides, it shouldn't matter how I heard it. It's an important clue, and one that you should follow up on."

He leaned forward. "Miss King, I will be the one who decides what tips we should follow in this investigation, not you."

"I didn't mean any disrespect, but you have to view Jace Colton as a major suspect in his father's murder. Close friends and family are always the first suspects, aren't they?"

"And were your grandparents close to Tyson Colton's family? Were they among his friends?"

"I severely doubt it." But even as I said this, I thought of the revelation that Aiden had made about my *Maami* and *Daadi* helping him and Juliet when they'd first moved to Holmes County. I couldn't know my grandparents' relationships with anyone in the county, not really. However, my grandfather had nearly come to blows with Tyson in front of Swissmen Sweets. They might have, too, if my grandfather hadn't been Amish and had an aversion to violence. "They're not. They have never mentioned Tyson to me before. I first saw him with my grandfather on the sidewalk the day before he died." As I said this I realized they had never mentioned Aiden and Juliet to me before either, and apparently, my grandparents had been very close to them once upon a time.

His unusual smile broadened. "When he was arguing

with Tyson, you mean? That must have been difficult for you to see."

I didn't say anything.

"Tyson was planning on buying your grandfather's building, am I right?"

"He wanted to buy it, but there was no chance of him doing it."

"Oh?" He arched his drawn-on brows. "Tyson managed to buy the other buildings on the street. What makes you think that he would fail where Swissmen Sweets was concerned?"

"Because I know my grandfather would never sell."

"Why not?"

"Because he has no reason too, and he's stubborn."

"That must run in the family then."

I felt my cheeks grow hot. I finally knew what the Sheriff was driving at. "Tyson's buying up property around Swissmen Sweets has nothing to do with his murder."

"I'm afraid it does," he murmured.

"You have to see how ridiculous it is to consider my ailing grandfather as a murder suspect."

"The only thing I *have* to see is that you are a suspect." He drummed his fingers over the file.

Again, I wondered what was inside. I refused to look at it again. "Deputy Brody already told me that I'm a suspect. I have to be because I'm the one who found the body. I know that."

"And because you have motive." He ran his index finger along the outside edge of the manila envelope.

"What motive?" I asked, even though I knew.

"Motive," he said, "to defend your Amish grandparents." He laughed a mirthless laugh. "The Amish aren't as defenseless as they might seem, and they can take care of themselves. I've been the sheriff of Holmes County for over twenty years. I know."

"Perhaps you don't know them as well as you think," I snapped.

"The Amish pretend to be peace-loving folks." He leaned far across the table, and I could smell coffee on his breath. "But I can tell you stories that would curl your toes. You have no idea what you are talking about."

"My grandparents are Amish." I released my grip on the tabletop. I didn't want the sheriff to see how what he said affected me. I folded my hands in my lap.

"And how does that make you an expert on the Amish people? Do you know any other Amish? They don't come out of a cookie cutter all the same. There are many differences. You would know that if you knew anything at all about them."

"It doesn't seem to me that being the sheriff of an Amish county is a good fit for you if you dislike them so much." My tone was sharp. I was no longer even trying to be polite. I had thought I didn't care for Deputy Carpenter, but this man was worse, just as Carpenter had said he would be. I didn't know how Aiden could work with either of them.

He eyed me. "I grew up in this county, Miss, and I have as much right to it as any of the Amish do, probably more, since I'm a sheriff. You may think you know the Amish because of your family connections, but you're from another world. You have no idea what goes on in my county."

"I don't think—"

He cut me off. "I'm not going to quibble with you over the workings of the Amish communities around Harvest." He folded his hands on top of the manila folder again. "Now, I would like to talk to you about the murder. Where were you between nine PM and midnight last night?"

"I've already told you that I was at the candy shop, trying to sleep."

He arched his thin brow. "You, a city girl, went to bed at nine at night." He leaned back in his chair and folded his arms. "That's a little hard for me to believe."

I frowned. "I was in my room, in my grandparents' apartment over the shop."

"You didn't leave? Not once?" he asked. "In the evening, you went to your room and straight to bed?"

I was quiet for a long moment. "I stepped out for a minute."

A victorious smile crossed his face. "And when was that?"

I remained quiet.

He leaned forward on the table and fixed his dark gaze on mine. "Have you finally decided to tell me the truth, Miss King?"

"All right," I whispered.

Chapter 21

I cleared my throat. "I never lied. No one has asked me where I was at that exact time."

The half smile was back. "Don't you think it would have been helpful to us if you had been more forthcoming with your whereabouts?"

I folded my hands in my lap so that he wouldn't see them trembling. "I didn't know why they would be so important."

The smile disappeared. "Miss King, Colton died sometime between nine in the evening and midnight. Whatever you were doing during that window of time, I want to know about."

I bit the inside of my cheek to hold back another smart retort. I was only prolonging the conversation by talking back. "Around nine, I stepped out of the shop for a minute."

"Did you tell your grandparents you were stepping outside?"

I gripped my hands together a little more tightly. I wasn't going to bring my grandparents into this. "No, they were in bed for the night. My grandfather was ill and my grandmother needed her rest after taking care of him and the shop all day."

"Why did you leave the shop?"

"I needed some air," I said sharply. So much for holding my tongue. I knew it would get me in trouble.

"Why did you need air?"

"Because *Daadi* is ill," I snapped. "And his doctor didn't give me the impression that he would improve. In fact, I think—" My voice caught. I couldn't verbalize what I thought the doctor's expression had told me about *Daadi's* prognosis. Maybe if I didn't say it aloud, it wouldn't be true.

He chuckled mirthlessly. "I didn't realize you spoke Amish."

I wished that I could reach into the air and take the Pennsylvania Dutch word for my grandfather back. It seemed too personal to say in front of this man, whom I disliked more by the second.

I ground my teeth. "Is there anything else you'd like to know?"

"You arrived yesterday just in time to see your grandfather collapse on the sidewalk in front of Tyson Colton. That must have been very hard."

I didn't even bother to respond to that obvious statement.

"How did Tyson react to your grandfather's collapse? Did he offer any assistance?"

"No," I said.

"He was a busy man and had places to be," the sheriff excused. "A busy man, indeed, since he was in the process of buying up as much of Harvest as he could get his hands on, including Swissmen Sweets."

"He wanted to buy it, yes, but my grandfather would never sell. We've already been over this."

"But Tyson was aggressive, wasn't he?"

"According to my grandfather, yes, and he must have been persuasive too. The businesses on either side of my grandfather had already agreed to sell to him. Perhaps you should talk to those shopkeepers."

"Please don't give me any more advice as to how to run my investigation, Miss King."

I snapped my mouth closed.

"So, was that all you did when you left the candy shop? You got some air?" he said, returning to the night of the murder. "You didn't make a phone call?"

"I made one call, yes."

He frowned as if he wasn't pleased that I'd told the truth. Maybe my phone records were in the manila folder, and that was the evidence he wanted to use against me. "Where did you make this call?" he asked.

"Just across the street from the shop. I sat in the gazebo."

"Did anyone see you?"

"I doubt it. Harvest is completely abandoned at that time of night."

"Then what happened?"

"I made my call and went back into the shop and plugged in my phone in the kitchen. The kitchen was fine when I left it. No one was there."

"Did you see anything unusual?"

"The only thing that was unusual was that it was nine o'clock on a pleasant night, and I was the only soul outside. I suppose that's another way Harvest and New York differ."

"And who did you call from the gazebo?"

I pushed my chair back from the table. "Really, why does that matter? It has nothing to do with the murder."

He leaned back in his chair again. "I think it does. How can I be sure that you weren't calling the victim and inviting him to the shop?"

I stared at him. "Inviting him to the shop, so that I could kill him? You can't be serious."

He leaned forward. "I'm deadly serious, Miss King. Earlier in the day, you saw this man upset your *daadi*." He said the Amish word as if were a curse. "So much so that it caused him to collapse and sent him to bed. Maybe you lured that man back to the shop on the pretense that you wanted to discuss selling the shop. The two of you argued, he rushed you, and you picked up the knife and stabbed him. It could be argued that the murder was in self-defense. Tyson was a large man."

I felt sweat gather on my forehead. "You can't be serious. That's not what happened."

"You must be in a hurry to return New York." He lifted the corner of the manila folder just enough to peek inside. "You want to go home and find out if you will be appointed as the head chocolatier at JP Chocolates. Maybe you thought offing the man who you saw harassing your grandfather would allow you to leave the county more quickly."

I laughed even though nothing about this conversation was the least bit funny. "Don't be ridiculous. It was nothing like that. I called a friend back in New York. That's it. He didn't even answer the phone."

"We pulled your phone records. In fact," he said, "I found that you called one Eric Sharp in New York City."

I pressed my hands into my thighs. "Yes. That's my friend."

He waggled those eyebrows again. "Just a friend?"

"I don't understand what this has to do with anything. Yes, I left the shop for a few minutes to make a call to a friend back home. There are some things happening with my work, and I wanted to check in. Eric would know what was going on."

"Miss King, what you're doing with Sharp in New York is none of my concern, but it will become my concern if it cascades into my investigation. Do you understand? It would do you well to be honest with me."

I stared at him for a long moment. I still couldn't bring myself to tell him that Eric was my boyfriend. I wasn't sure what Eric would say if the police asked him to corroborate my story. "Eric's my friend. You should be able to see on the phone records that I never spoke to him or anyone else that night. I didn't talk to him until early the next morning after I'd already found Tyson."

He leaned back. "Now, was that so hard? You'll be happy to know your account matches what we have found as well."

I scowled in return.

"Are you sure your grandfather wasn't giving Tyson's offer some serious thought? If the businesses on either side of him sold and now belong to the developer, Tyson could certainly make life difficult for your grandfather, couldn't he?"

"What do you mean?"

"He'd be a neighbor, and, as such, he could make your grandfather's life difficult. You know all about difficult neighbors, don't you, Bailey?"

"I don't have any idea what you are talking about,"

I said, but it was a lie. I knew precisely what he meant. I prayed I was wrong.

"I just found an interesting police report in my file. That's all. I'm only pointing out the fact that you have a history of violence. Do you deny that?" The smile came again.

I balled my fists at my sides. "I do not have a history of violence."

The sheriff opened his folder all the way this time and lifted out a piece of paper. He didn't show me what was written on the paper. He didn't have to. It could only be one thing.

"If you are referring to the incident that happened at JP Chocolates three years ago, it has nothing to do with Tyson Colton, my grandfather, or this case."

He arched his thin eyebrow. "Doesn't it, though? It proves to me that you have the will to defend yourself and the ones you care about."

I pressed my hands harder into my thighs. "That man was trying to rob Jean Pierre's store. I didn't have a choice."

He shook his finger at me as if I were a naughty child. "You always have a choice, Miss King. Always. You could have given the intruder the money and called the police. That's what you should have done. That's what any reasonable person would do when a thief enters their shop with a gun, demanding money. Any reasonable person would do that, but not you. You put a man in the hospital."

I winced. My mind went back to that horrible day. It was winter and already dark out when I was closing up the shop. A man—a boy really—came into the shop with a gun and demanded that I give him everything we had in the cash register. Cass was with me. He threatened to shoot her too. I couldn't let him kill us, I just reacted. Instead of giving him the money, I hit him with a chair. It was a stupid and dangerous thing to do, and I broke the intruder's arm in the process. I didn't sleep for weeks after the incident. I kept playing what had happened over and over in my head, knowing that my rashness could have gotten both Cass and me killed. The sheriff was right—I should have just handed over the money to the man with the gun, but I wasn't going to admit that now. "All I was guilty of was protecting my employer's property and my coworkers from an intruder, and that was years ago."

"It shows a pattern, a violent pattern, might I add. Tyson tried to break into the candy shop or force his way in . . ." He trailed off.

"That's not what happened." I felt dizzy.

"Then tell me why your fingerprints were the only ones found on the murder weapon?"

It felt like all the blood drained from my face. "I don't know. My fingerprints are on the chocolate knife because I used it earlier in the day to cut fudge. Maybe whoever killed Tyson wore gloves. Don't most murderers know to wear gloves?"

"It seems rather convenient that you were using the knife before the murder."

"It's not convenient, it's true!" I cried, finally losing my temper. "Deputy Brody saw me with the knife when he came into the candy shop to pick up fudge for his mother's quilting circle."

The thin brow went up again. "I know. The deputy

has already shared this with me. All it proves is that you cut chocolate with the knife. It does not mean you are innocent of killing Tyson."

I jumped out of my chair. "I'm telling you I didn't do it! You've wasted so much time on me today when you could be out there finding the real killer. You could be talking to his son, who unlike me, is a viable suspect in his father's murder."

"Have a seat." His voice was cold.

I didn't move.

"Have a seat."

This time he said it with so much force, I fell into my chair with a thud.

"Let me tell you something, Miss King. Everything and everyone around Colton's death has a part to play in the story of this case, and you have a history of reacting violently when threatened. Do you expect me to ignore that?"

"Someone was trying to rob me!"

"Was the money he planned to steal worth being shot over?"

I clenched my hands together in my lap until the knuckles turned white. "That was a long time ago."

"Maybe," he said. "But I would imagine if you reacted that strongly to someone trying to steal from you, you'd react even more violently when someone you care about as much as your grandfather was threatened."

"I didn't kill Tyson Colton." I tried my best to keep my voice even.

He closed the folder and leaned back in his chair. It squeaked under the strain of his shifting weight. "Here's my theory. You went downstairs to check your cell phone messages, as you have already said, and caught

Colton breaking into the kitchen through the back door. You thought he was going to hurt you or your grandparents. You grabbed the closest weapon you could find, which just so happened to be the curved chocolate knife that you used the day before. Colton lunges toward you, and you stab him in the chest. I suppose if you come clean, you can claim self-defense. There are no other witnesses to corroborate that, but I think you have a good shot. Colton must have outweighed you by eighty pounds at least. The jury will be sympathetic, I wager."

"That's not what happened." At this point, I didn't even know why I was wasting my breath arguing with him. In his mind, my guilt was certain, but I couldn't stop myself from saying, "The last time I saw the chocolate knife, it was on the counter in the front room of the shop. I never even used it in the kitchen, so it would not be a convenient weapon to grab in the heat of the moment."

He leaned forward. "If you didn't put the knife in the kitchen, how did it get there?"

"I don't know. I don't know the answer to any of this."

"I don't believe you. You think just because you are from New York City that you can be slick and get away with murder." He smacked the metal table with so much force, I was surprised there wasn't a dent in the surface. "Not in my county. No one gets away with anything in my county."

"If you are so sure, why don't you arrest me then? Don't you have enough evidence to do that?" The moment I asked that question, I regretted it. There was nothing I could do to help my grandparents or find the real killer if I were in jail. I would be completely useless there.

"Let me lay it out straight for you, Miss King. You had means—the knife, motive—your grandparents' business, and opportunity—you were in the building when Tyson was murdered." He glared at me. "Oh, I will arrest you, Miss King. I promise you that, but not until I can make it stick, which I will. Trust me." He stood up and walked out the door. "Don't even think of leaving town. It wouldn't hurt to put a call into a fancy city attorney either."

I stared after him, unable to breathe.

Chapter 22

I pressed a hand to my chest and forced myself to take in a big gulp of air. This wasn't happening. Less than forty-eight hours ago, I was at JP Chocolates putting the final touches on a chocolate showpiece for a Wall Street gala, and today, I was sitting in the Holmes County Sheriff's Department being accused of murder. This couldn't be happening.

There was knock on the door. It was Aiden. I let out another breath. I was so relieved to see him rather than Deputy Carpenter or the sheriff. I didn't think I could face either of them at that moment.

"You're free to go," Aiden said. "I can take you back to the shop."

My knees shook as I struggled to my feet. My body quivered from my toes to the hair on the top of my head as the enormity of my predicament sank in.

Aiden's forehead creased in concern. "What did he say to you?"

"That he's going to arrest me but is waiting until he can make the charges stick," I said, proud of myself that I had been able to control the quaver in my voice.

"But you are free now. He would arrest you if he could. He told me that."

My stomach turned. Was the comment supposed to make me feel better? "What exactly did he say?"

Aiden glanced over his shoulder at the cracked open door. "We shouldn't talk here. Let me take you back to Swissmen Sweets."

Since I wanted to get as far away from the sheriff's department as possible, I didn't argue.

The deputy opened the heavy metal door wide, and I followed him through the winding halls back to the reception area. We didn't run into a single person as we left the building, and that was how I liked it.

Outside the station, I sucked in a deep breath of fresh air, and I was even grateful for the cold bite in the fall wind. There were a few moments inside the station that I was certain I wouldn't be leaving, maybe ever. I wouldn't take being free for granted, and I wouldn't waste my freedom. I had to find out who was really behind Tyson's death.

I would start with the Amish he'd bought property from. There had to be a reason that so many Amish sold out to him all at the same time. Their businesses had been in their families for generations—why sell now? Knowing what I knew about the culture, I couldn't believe that all of them had made the decision for the money. Maybe some of them had, but not all. There had to be another reason, one worth killing for.

I gave the deputy a sideways look as he opened the passenger door of the cruiser for me. He was another puzzle to solve. Why was he helping me? Or was he just trying to make it look like he was, so I would let down my guard?

After I was seated in the cruiser and Aiden climbed into the driver's seat, he started the car and said, "The sheriff is playing a game. As long as he's enjoying the game, you will be free."

I gripped my seatbelt. "What?"

He gave a sigh. "I've seen him do it before on other cases. He enjoys the thrill of the chase before making an arrest. If he arrested you now, the fun would be over. He's not ready to do that yet."

"That's horrible. I'm not a toy to be played with."

"I know that." His voice was sad. "But at least it means you are free now, and we have time to find out who really killed Tyson. So, view the sheriff's behavior as a blessing in disguise."

"*We* are going to find the real killer?"

He glanced in my direction. "We, as in the sheriff's department, not we, as in you and I. You need to go back to the candy shop and worry about the desserts for the Hutton wedding tomorrow. Leave the investigation alone. You'll only make it worse for yourself in the long run."

"I can't do that. I can't just sit by and watch what happens when my entire life is on the line, or when my grandparents are at risk. If I'm arrested, that might be the final act that will stop my grandfather's heart completely. I can't let that happen."

He gripped the steering wheel a little more tightly. "I was afraid you would say that."

Maami and *Daadi* came to mind. I imagined *Maami* pacing in the front room of Swissmen Sweets wondering what had become of me, and *Daadi* clenching the arms of his walker in worry. When I'd left that morning to handle Eileen's tasting, I'm sure neither of them thought I would be gone so long. "My grandparents must be out of their minds with worry."

"They're fine," he said confidently.

"Fine? How would you know that?" I asked.

"I called them and told them you were with me."

"You didn't say I was at the sheriff's department, did you?"

He shook his head. "I didn't think it was necessary to worry them. I only wanted them to know you were safe. That was the important thing. I told you I want to help and find the real person behind Tyson's murder."

I studied his profile. Behind him the sun was setting, and it cast the nearer side of his face into shadow. "Why are so sure of my innocence?"

"I'm not sure of anything."

I shook my head. "Then why do you want to help me? I have a right to know why I have a champion in the sheriff's department when even I can see that all the evidence is stacked against me."

He didn't reply.

"You must have a reason." I wasn't going to let him get away with any more vague answers.

"I owe it to your grandparents."

I stared at him. "Why? Because they took you and your mom in?"

He ran his hands up and down the steering wheel. "Because I have a debt to repay, and this is my chance to do it."

I waited.

He took a breath. "I was born in South Carolina. You may have noticed my mother's accent."

I nodded, still not saying anything. The tension in the car was suddenly ramped up. I found myself gripping my seatbelt as if I needed something to hold me in place.

"When I was seven, my mother and I ended up here in Harvest. We were running away, you see. It's the usual story." He kept his eyes fixed on the road. "My father drank. He hit her. One day, he hit me, and we left while he was passed out on the floor. We never looked back."

"I'm so sorry," I whispered. "Usual or not, it's still horrible."

The car was silent for a long moment, and finally, I had to know the rest. "What does that have to do with my grandparents?"

"When my mother and I stumbled into Harvest, Swissmen Sweets was the first place we went. We had been on the road for a week at that point. We moved from motel to motel, using a new fake name at each one. She was always afraid that my father would come after us."

"Did he?" I asked, barely above a whisper.

"No." His answer was tight, and then he took a deep breath. "When we arrived in Harvest, I begged my mother for a piece of candy from your grandparents' shop. We didn't have the money for even for the smallest piece, but she agreed. We went inside. We were the only customers. I don't know what the Kings saw in us, but before we knew it we had a bed for the night, and I had all the sweets I could eat. They gave my mother a job, and we lived there for a few months until we had saved enough for our own apartment in town."

"I didn't know any of this," I said.

He smiled a half smile. "How would you?"

"I'm sure my father would have said something if he knew that someone was living with my grandparents. I doubt my parents would have purposely kept that from me. I know I would have overheard him and my mother discussing it."

"You were what, six or seven at the time? They might not have wanted to talk about it because of the circumstances with my father."

"But my grandparents never talked about you living here. It was such a wonderful thing they did, why wouldn't they share that story with me?" I asked. "Maybe they didn't tell me because I was so young at the time, but why didn't they tell me later? I was in high school before I stopped spending my summers with them."

"That tells me that, although Amish blood runs through your veins, Bailey King, you don't know much about your heritage." He was smiling now, and some of the tension in the car fell away. "The Amish don't brag about the good they do. That is not the Amish way. They don't do it for praise or recognition. They do it because it's what God wants from them. I think many Englishers like us could learn a lesson or two from them about humility."

That sounded just like my grandparents.

My face grew hot. Would I have done the same thing? Taken in a mother and child like that if I had the chance? I thought about life back in New York, where all I seemed to care about was being made the head chocolatier of JP Chocolates and keeping my relationship with Eric Sharp a secret. I let Eric whisk me around the country on his private jet, but what was it all for? I couldn't remember a time I'd truly helped someone like my grandparents had helped Aiden and Juliet. They'd saved them. The only person I'd ever worried about saving was myself.

Aiden and I were both silent for the remainder of the ride back to Swissmen Sweets.

As he shifted the car into park, I said, "Now that I know why you are helping me, I'm even more grateful for your help, but you don't have to, you know, not really."

"I have to repay the debt."

"Maybe you don't understand the Amish as well as you claim either, deputy. Because I'm sure that my grandparents don't believe there is any debt to be repaid. There never was."

He chuckled, and the cloud that hung over the car seemed to lift as his laughter filled the space. "I suppose that's the core of the reason I could never be Amish, and why I chose to be a cop."

"You thought of being Amish?" I couldn't keep the surprise out of my voice.

"Not seriously, no. I admire their way of life, but it's not for me. To my way of thinking, there are checks and balances, debts to be paid, and scores to be settled." He lowered his voice. "Justice to be had."

"I hope there will be justice in this case," I said, remembering the sheriff's threats.

"Me too," he said.

Chapter 23

Aiden's radio crackled. "Deputy Brody? Please come in."

Aiden lifted the radio from the dashboard. "Brody here."

"The sheriff wants you back at the station. Now."

"I'm on my way." He set the radio back on the dash.

"That was probably about me," I said.

He paused at the intersection of Apple Street and Main Street, where I had parked my rental the day before. It still sat under the apple tree. He sighed. "Colton's isn't the only case we have in the department." After a beat, he said, "But yes, that probably was related to this case."

"You can just drop me off here," I said. "If you have to get back to the station, I don't want to hold you up." I put my hand on the door handle.

Aiden looked at me. "This will get sorted out, Bailey. I won't let the sheriff send an innocent person to jail."

After what seemed like a moment too long to be decent, I tore my gaze away from him. "Thanks, but just know that I won't sit by and wait to be arrested. I need to do something."

"I'm learning that." His voice was softer than it had been before.

I opened the cruiser door, jumped out, and gave the deputy a final wave. Aiden drove away, and I waited until his taillights had disappeared around the corner before I turned up Main Street in the direction of Swissmen Sweets.

My shoulders sagged. I was exhausted from the events of the day. I had been up since one in the morning, when I'd discovered Tyson Colton's body in my grandparents' kitchen. But sleep wasn't an option. I still had to make desserts for one hundred and fifty-four people. It wouldn't be the first time I'd pulled an all-nighter over chocolate, and there was no way I would let my grandparents stay up and help me. They both needed their rest.

I straightened my shoulders and lifted my gaze up from the sidewalk and saw a woman dressed all in black, from her well-cut trench coat to her pointy boots. Purple bangs that were longer than the rest of her black pixie-cut hair fell over her eyes as she struggled to pull an enormous suitcase over the uneven sidewalk.

I blinked. Once. Twice. Three times. I couldn't believe what I was seeing, and the vision wasn't a figment of my imagination. "Cass!"

The woman fighting with the rolling suitcase looked up and squealed. She dropped the suitcase, allowing it to crash to the concrete sidewalk with a *thunk*, and ran at me full tilt.

The impact was reminiscent of a time when I was hit in the chest with a punching bag during a kickboxing class. The kickboxing class had been Cass's idea to help me with my pent-up aggression after the incident with the robber and the chair in JP Chocolates. I hadn't lasted long in the class. Cass was smaller than the punching bag had been, but she put a lot of force behind her leap.

"Bailey! I can't believe I've finally found you!" She stepped back. "You will not believe what I have been through to reach you. If I knew that this assignment would be so arduous, I never would have taken it. You know I love you, but, girl, I have limits, and I passed those hours ago."

I stepped back from her. "Assignment? What assignment?"

"The assignment to drag you home. Jean Pierre sent me to fetch you and bring you back. He and I both agree you would do much better dealing with this murder business from NYC." She brushed dirt off her sleeve. "This is my favorite trench coat. See what I go through just to come to your rescue? The coat will have to be dry-cleaned or sent through a biohazard unit. I'm not sure which yet."

"Wait," I said, blinking. "Where on earth could you have been that you have dirt on your sleeve?" Cass was the most impeccably dressed and clean chocolatier I knew. Sometimes when I was working on a chocolate showpiece, it appeared as if I had rolled in chocolate, but no matter how messy the project, Cass never had a dot of chocolate on her. Now, here she was, standing in front of me with dirt on her sleeve.

"It was terrible, Bai, absolutely terrible. Jean Pierre sent me to Ohio in his private jet, which was glorious. I had cheese and champagne on board. It was nice to see how a world-famous chocolatier lives, and I am certainly going to expect the same from you when you snag JP's position."

I rolled my eyes. "I seriously doubt I will ever have the need for a private jet." Jean Pierre retained ownership in the company. I would have some stock options, but nothing like the buyout he'd acquired when the stocks for his company went public.

"Don't say such a thing. Everyone has a need for a private jet." She took a deep breath. "The flight was lovely, but it all went downhill from there. A taxi came to pick me up from the airport, which was about the size of a mall parking lot, by the way. The van had no markings on it to indicate it was a taxi, but the driver assured me that he was the right one, and when we were underway, he said he had to pick up a few other customers. I objected, but he wouldn't listen to reason."

"I bet you did." I covered my mouth to hide a smile.

Cass caught the smile and narrowed her eyes. "We rambled around the countryside, picking up Amish farmers everywhere we stopped. By the time we got to Harvest, there were seven people crammed elbow to elbow and hip to hip in that van. I don't even think a circus could get another clown in there. All of the farmers were dirty, which is how my coat got ruined. I think I was in that car for four hours, but then again it might have been eight. Time was meaningless after a point."

I bit down hard on the inside of my lower lip. Cass had let me get away with the smile, but a chuckle would not be tolerated. "It sounds to me like you got stuck in an Amish taxi."

"An Amish man wasn't driving," she protested.

My smile widened. "The Amish don't drive cars, so they have Englishers like us drive them from place to place. You hitched a ride on what's known around here as an Amish taxi."

She scowled. "Well, that will be the last time." She shivered. "Surely this county has normal taxis too." She shook her head, and her purple bangs fell over her dark eyes again. "It doesn't matter. I think I remember you saying that you got a rental car for your visit. We'll take that back to the airport and get out of here. Let's go." She turned as if to march back up the sidewalk from where she came.

"Cass, I can't leave."

She spun around and stared at me. "Don't tell me you like it here. Because if you do, I just might have to slap you. You can't possibly like it here. There's dirt. A lot of it."

"There's dirt in Manhattan too," I said.

She folded her arms. "But not on me."

"Didn't Jean Pierre tell you why I was stuck here before he sent you?"

"I know about the murder, of course, but that's no reason for you to stay. That gives you every reason to get out of here. Was there something else?"

Wasn't a murder enough, I wondered, but before I could say it aloud, Cass went on.

"You know Jean Pierre. He was all like 'Oh Cassandra, please jump into my plane and retrieve Bailey. She's been gone too long.'" She said this in a terrible attempt at a French accent. "Is your grandfather worse?" Her face creased with concern.

"He's about the same, but that's not why I can't leave

just yet." I took a deep breath. "I'm a murder suspect. I'm the number one suspect, actually. I was just at the sheriff's department being interrogated by the county sheriff himself. He ordered me to stay in the county."

She blinked at me. "Come again?"

I wrapped my arm around her shoulders. "Let's go to my grandparents' shop, and I'll tell you the whole story there. We need chocolate for this conversation."

Cass slipped out from under my arm. "You can't just say you are a murder suspect and say we need chocolate! I mean I love chocolate as much as the next chocolatier, but Bailey, come on."

I glanced around. There were still a few people walking around the town square—an English couple and some Amish women out for a stroll. All evidence of the farmers' market was gone. "Let's not talk about it out here."

We paused to collect her giant suitcase before setting off toward Swissmen Sweets. Both of us pulled the mammoth piece of luggage down the sidewalk. "If you thought we were heading straight back to New York, why did you pack so much? This thing weighs a ton. I have no idea how you pulled it down the street on your own."

She brushed her bangs out of her eyes. "I know how stubborn you are and thought it might take at least overnight to convince you to come home with me, so I packed enough for a day or two."

"This is enough for a month."

"Not even close."

Shaking my head, I pushed open the glass door to

the candy shop. The front room was empty. "*Maami! Daadi!*"

Cass stared at me. "What did you say?" She looked around the shop and pointed at the crime scene tape across the kitchen. "What the—"

Before she finished that sentence, my grandmother appeared in the door that led to the stairs up to the apartment. "Bailey, dear, is everything all right? Your *daadi* and I have been worried sick about you. Aiden called and insisted that you were safe, but I wasn't as sure." She spotted Cass and smiled. "Hello there, can we help you? I'm afraid the candy shop is closed today."

Cass's mouth fell open.

"*Maami*, this is my friend Cass from New York," I said.

My grandmother folded her hands in front of her starched white apron. "How lovely that you've come for a visit, Cass. Bailey mentions you often in her letters to us."

Cass looked from *Maami* to me and back again. "*Maami*? Letters?"

I gave Cass a small smile, and my stomach twisted. "Cass, this is my grandmother, Clara King."

Cass's mouth opened and closed as she tried to comprehend who *Maami* was. "But she's Amish!"

My grandmother chuckled. "I am that."

Cass turned to me. "Are you Amish? Are you one of those runaway Amish like on television? *Amish Gone Wild*?"

Maami covered her mouth to hide her smile. Her rounded shoulders moved up and down as she failed to hide her amusement.

I bit my lip to hold back my own laughter. I knew

Cass well enough to know that it was never a good idea to laugh at her expense, especially if she wasn't in on the joke. "I'm not runaway Amish. My father grew up Amish, but I was never Amish because Dad left the faith before I was born."

"Your dad was Amish? I think I need to sit down." She glanced at the candy shop. "I assume that you don't have any wine in here, do you? I could use a glass—or five."

My grandmother pursed her lips to hide the smile that I knew was there. "We don't have any spirits, no, but we have fudge."

"Fudge will work." Cass followed my grandmother inside the shop.

Maami patted the front table in the room. "You sit right there, and I'll fetch you a nice big piece."

My grandfather shuffled into the front room of the shop, pushing his walker. I couldn't help but notice that he was breathing harder than he had been that morning. The Amish were proud people, and my grandfather wouldn't want me to draw attention to his poor health in the company of someone he didn't know.

While Cass took in the room, I made introductions.

My grandfather tipped his hat at her. "*Wilkomme*, Cass. It's nice to meet one of our Bailey's friends from the big city."

Seeing *Daadi* had less of an effect on her. Of course, she might have been distracted by the large X of yellow crime scene tape that crisscrossed the door leading to the kitchen.

"I knew there was a murder," Cass said to me, "but

you didn't tell me in your text that it happened in here. That's what the crime scene tape means, doesn't it?"

My grandfather made a pained face.

"It's a long story," I said. "But it has a lot to do with why I can't go back home just now."

Maami set a thick piece of milk chocolate fudge on a plain white plate in front of Cass.

My friend made no move to touch it. "Bailey, what happened?"

Maami took a step back. "I think you girls have much to talk about." *Maami* put her hand on my grandfather's shoulder. "Why don't we go upstairs and let the girls visit for a while? How long will be you be staying, Cass?"

Her dark eyes glanced in my direction. "That depends on Bailey."

I was relieved when she didn't mention that she was there on an errand from Jean Pierre to fetch me. If she had, I had no doubt that my grandfather would have personally put me on Jean Pierre's private jet and sent me back to New York. What *Daadi* didn't know was that the sheriff would most likely view my leaving as fleeing and an admission of guilt.

"You don't have to go upstairs," I said. "I think Cass could use some fresh country air. You can't find air like this anywhere in the city." I stood.

"That's a *gut* idea," my grandfather said. "Fresh air always clears the mind. I'd go out myself if I felt up to it, but I'll stay here and keep your *maami* company."

I felt my brow knit together in concern. Cass frowned. I knew that she caught on that *Daadi* wasn't doing well

"Don't be too long," my grandmother said. "I have dinner ready for you upstairs. I made chicken and dumplings. I know it's your favorite." She nodded to Cass. "There's plenty for you both."

Cass opened her mouth, and I knew what she was going to say. I ushered her toward the door. Before we left, she scooped up the piece of fudge. "Something tells me I'm going to need this."

Chapter 24

As the front door of Swissmen Sweets closed behind us, Cass said, "I think being a vegetarian while I'm here will be a challenge."

"Don't worry about that. *Maami* always has plenty of food in the pantry. I'll be able to make you something to eat."

"Why did you stop me from telling them that I was a vegetarian? Is that a problem for the Amish? Against their religion?"

I laughed. "They won't care, but I thought we'd had enough culture shock for the moment."

She held up her napkin-wrapped piece of fudge. "And there is always chocolate to eat too. I won't starve." She lowered her hand. "Now, are you going to tell me what's going on, or not? Why did you never tell me you were Amish?"

I quickened my pace down the sidewalk, toward the corner where I had left my car the day before. "I'm not Amish. My father was. I told you that."

Six inches shorter than me, Cass jogged to catch up. Her impractical high-heeled boots made a rapid *tap-tap* on the pavement, and for a moment, I was transported to New York by the familiar sound. A wave of home-sickness washed over me. Would I ever be able to return to the city? I wouldn't if the sheriff had his way. I would be spending the rest of my life in a cold, dank prison in Ohio and die of pneumonia.

"I think there is more to the dead guy story than you told me in your text. Was I right that he died in the shop? Is that why the crime scene tape was there? Don't tell me that's how the Amish like to decorate."

"I promise to tell you everything, but first, we have some shopping to do."

"Bailey, what are you talking about? Shopping?" She ran ahead and planted her body directly in front of me, blocking my progress down the sidewalk. "How can you think about shopping? And you don't even like to shop. I have to drag you kicking and screaming into the bou-tiques in the city. You tell me you're a murder suspect, and I learn you're Amish, and you want to go buy a new pair of jeans or something. What the heck?"

I pointed at the rental. "My car is right there. Can you at least wait until we get inside before I tell you?"

"All right." She shook her finger at me. "But I want details, King. Don't leave anything out."

I rolled my eyes and stepped around her. Once we were inside the car, I took a deep breath and told her an abbreviated version of the events of the last two days.

She swore. "This is unbelievable."

I stuck my key into the ignition. "Agreed. I've had some time to get used to the idea."

She grabbed my hand before I could turn the key. "Do you have a lawyer?"

I shook my head. "I'm sure my grandparents don't

know a criminal attorney in Ohio, neither would any of their Amish friends."

She shook her head as if trying to shake something loose. "This is trippy, as my mom would have said. There is no other word that works."

I smiled. Cass had told me some stories of growing up with her hippy mother. In fact, she had told me much more of her life than I had ever told her of mine.

She let go of my hand and reached for her seatbelt buckle. Clicking it into place, she said, "I'll call my brother. I'm sure he knows some people."

Cass's brother had done a couple of stints in prison for white collar crimes such as tax evasion. According to Cass, he'd deserved more time behind bars than he was given. He would know a good lawyer.

"Sometimes it helps to have a crook in the family." She grinned.

I felt tears gather in the corners of my eyes. "Thank you." My voice caught.

She unbuckled her seatbelt and leaned across the car to hug me. "Oh Bai, I know this is messed up, but we'll figure it out. I'm here now. I'll do whatever I can, even if it means punching that mean old sheriff in the mouth." She squeezed me one more time and settled back into her seat, buckling up again.

I wiped a tear from the corner of my eye. "That won't be necessary, but you can start helping me by pulling off an old, culinary school all-nighter."

She eyed me. "What?"

I turned the key in the ignition. "I'll tell you on the way to the supermarket."

She fell back into her seat with a groan. Her purple bangs hid her eyes from sight.

* * *

By the time we reached the supermarket, I had brought Cass up to speed about the Hutton-Colton wedding, and she was already arguing with me about my dessert choices. Some of her suggestions were spot on. I was so grateful she was there. Cass was a world-class chocolatier, but she had just never had the opportunity at JP Chocolates to show off what she could do. I had asked Jean Pierre many times to give her a chance to make one of the big chocolate sculptures for his celebrity clients, but he never had. He always preferred to give those jobs to Caden or me. Thinking of Caden made me realize how close I was to losing the head chocolatier promotion to him. Every day I was away from JP Chocolates, my hold on the promotion lessened.

I turned into the parking lot, and Cass stared out the window. "Look at all those buggies!"

There was a hitching post that ran the length of the parking lot, and six horses and buggies were tethered to it. One of the horses wore a green horse blanket, but the rest were barebacked. It was still early in the autumn. I knew from my childhood visits to Amish Country at Christmas, that in the winter they would all have blankets on their backs.

An Amish man carrying a white plastic bag from the grocery store in one hand held the hand of a young boy in plain dress in the other. The boy carried an open bag of Doritos.

"Am I in some kind of time warp? A time warp where the pilgrims eat Doritos?"

I was about to answer her when I saw Emily Esh climb out of one of the buggies and shuffle toward the store.

I unbuckled my seatbelt. "We have to follow her. Get out of the car. Let's go." I flung open the door and jumped out.

"Wait? What?" cried Cass, who was still in the car.

I was already outside on the lot. I grabbed my purse, slung it over my shoulder, and stuck my head back inside the car. "Do you want to save me from a murder rap or what?"

She unbuckled her seatbelt. "Okay, fine."

Chapter 25

Inside the supermarket, I grabbed a shopping cart. "Try to blend in," I whispered to Cass.

She stared at me. "Bai, I have purple hair. Even I know that's not the norm in these parts."

I spotted Emily in the produce section. "Come on!" I pushed my cart into the aisle.

"If you are going for casual spy, you are failing miserably," Cass grumbled. "You might as well carry a magnifying glass, the way you are suspiciously glancing around. You look like you're either hunting someone—which you are—or afraid you're going to be jumped by a clan of marauders."

I peeked at her. "Marauders? Really?"

She selected five cartons of strawberries. "I think chocolate-dipped strawberries are a must for a wedding. Who are we stalking anyway? I'd like to know the victim."

"She's not a victim." I dropped lemons in my cart and turned away from Emily to face Cass. "Do you see that young Amish girl by the lettuce? She's Emily Esh, the sister of one of the Amish shopkeepers, Esther, who sold out to Tyson Colton before he died. Now that he's dead, Esther's not selling her building anymore."

Cass lowered her voice. "So you think Esther or Emily killed him to keep their shop? But then why sell to him in the first place if she didn't want to move?"

"That's the big question, and Emily might have the answer."

"Wow," Cass said. "Amish Country is a lot more violent than advertised, but this whole time you've been talking, I haven't seen the Amish girl you're talking about."

"What?" I barked, and spun around. Cass was right. Emily was gone. Then I spotted the skirt of a lavender dress, just like I had seen Emily wearing, disappearing around the corner of one of the aisles. I pushed my cart forward. "There she goes," I hissed. "Let's go!"

"You almost ran over my foot," Cass complained, but followed me all the same.

It took a few moments for us to track Emily down.

"She must be a fast shopper," Cass said as we neared the end of the store.

I stopped abruptly when I spotted Emily in the pet aisle. She had a bag of cat foot in her arms and was perusing the other shelves.

Cass ran into my back. "Hey, you can't just stop in the middle of the aisle like that," she cried, loud enough to make Emily turn her head.

I smiled at the Amish girl, and she gave me a tiny smile in return. "Hi, Bailey. I didn't expect to see you here."

I pushed my cart forward and stopped a few feet from where she stood. "We're out shopping for items for the Hutton wedding tomorrow."

"I heard the wedding is still on. It seems odd to

me." She paused. "Considering what happened to the groom." She glanced behind me at Cass.

"This is Cass, my friend from New York," I said.

Cass waved at her, and Emily stared at Cass for a moment longer than was comfortable.

Cass stuck her hand on her hip. "You look as odd to me as I look to you, you know."

Emily's face blazed bright red.

I looked heavenward. Maybe bringing Cass in on this wasn't the best idea I had ever had. I smiled at the girl. "Are you buying cat food for Nutmeg?"

Emily burst into tears and hugged the bag of cat food to her chest.

"Geez, Bai, what did you do to her?" Cass asked.

"I didn't do anything," I whispered.

"Obviously, you did, because the kid is in tears," Cass argued.

Emily wiped a tear from her cheek. "It's just when you mentioned Nutmeg, I became upset. My *bruder* says I can't keep him. They don't believe I can care for anything." She sucked in a breath. "Or anyone." Another big tear rolled down her left cheek. "I'm sorry. You have shopping to do, I'm sure."

I patted the girl's shoulder. "Our shopping can wait. What will happen to Nutmeg if you don't keep him?"

"I don't know." She sniffled. "I'm afraid that my brother might do something drastic to get rid of the cat."

"You think he would kill it?" Cass gasped.

"No! He would never hurt Nutmeg, but I'm afraid he will take him and drop him off at another farm. That's not uncommon out in the country. I couldn't bear it if something happened to Nutmeg. I really think he's too gentle to be an outdoor cat, but Abel absolutely won't have him inside."

"What about your parents? What do they say about the cat?" Cass asked.

Emily stared at her feet. "My parents are dead. I live with my brother and sister now, at least until I marry."

"Are you getting married soon?"

She swallowed. "*Nee*, I am not. But I am twenty. I should be married by *now*."

Cass looked as if she wanted to say something, and I stepped on her foot. She glared at me and took a step away.

Neither Emily's older brother nor her older sister was married, so I didn't see how her being twenty convinced her that she should already be married. But I saw no reason to argue with her or bring to her attention the fact that I was twenty-seven and unmarried. In her eyes, I would be an old maid. She must believe that Esther, who was close to my age, already was.

"I wish I could help," I said.

Her eyes brightened and she held the bag of cat food out to me. "You can! You take him to live in Swissmen Sweets. You keep him until I figure out what I'm going to do."

I tried to give her the cat food bag back. "I don't think that's such a good idea."

"Why not?" the Amish girl asked. "You're right next door to the pretzel shop, and I can visit Nutmeg at your grandparents' shop as much as I want. Your grandparents won't mind."

"I know they won't mind, but my grandfather is ill," I said, still trying to return the bag of cat food. "I'm not sure how he would do with a cat in the house."

"Nutmeg will be very gentle with him," she said.

Hope shone in her large blue eyes. "I don't know what else to do."

"You're her only hope, Obi-Wan," Cass whispered in my ear.

I elbowed Cass in the side.

"Ow," she complained.

"I didn't poke you that hard," I muttered.

"Who's Obi-Wan?" Emily asked in confusion.

"Ignore Cass. She's had long day of travel and isn't thinking straight," I told Emily.

"That's true," Cass agreed good-naturedly.

"Will you take him?" Tears gathered in the girl's eyes again.

"I don't know how my grandparents will feel about me bringing a cat into their home, especially under the circumstances. We can't even go into the kitchen right now. I'm sure the police don't want a cat in there possibly contaminating the scene."

The tears threatened to spill over. "Please. I couldn't bear it if something happened to him. He needs someone to take care of him."

"Oh, geez, Bai, agree to take the cat. We both know that you will," Cass said.

Emily's eyes lit up. "Will you, Bailey?"

I sighed and set the bag of cat food in my shopping cart. "Okay, I'll take him, but the final decision as to whether he can live at Swissmen Sweets is up to my grandparents."

Emily clasped her hands in front of her chest. "I know they will let him stay. Your grandparents are the kindest people in the district."

I couldn't argue with her about that.

"And I don't believe a word of what people are saying," she added.

"What are they saying?" I asked.

"I thought you knew." She furrowed her brow. "They're saying that you killed Tyson Colton."

Chapter 26

"Nutmeg is in my buggy. I can go get him right now for you," Emily said.

I was still reeling from her previous comment. It was bad enough that the sheriff thought I'd killed Tyson Colton, but the members of my grandparents' community too? That stung.

"Do you want me to fetch him now?" Emily asked.

I blinked at her. "What?"

Cass stepped around me. "We have a little more shopping to do. Can we meet you outside in say, a half hour? We'll collect the cat then."

I touched the girl's arm. "Before you go, can I ask you a question?"

Emily nodded.

"Why did your sister agree to sell her shop to Tyson if she really didn't want to?"

She turned pale. "I don't know. Esther doesn't share her plans with me."

"Was she afraid of Tyson? Did he trick her into selling the shop?"

"She wasn't afraid of Tyson, not really." She licked her lips.

"But she was afraid of someone—I can see it on your face."

"*Nee*. We don't have anyone to fear. Abel has always protected us. He is the head of our house." Her voice trembled.

"Is your family in danger?" I asked.

"I—I have to go." She reached for the cat food. "I will buy that. It's the least I can do."

I shook my head. "I got it."

"*Danki*, Bailey." Her blue eyes filled with grateful tears. "I'll wait for you outside." She hurried down the aisle as if she worried I might change my mind if she stayed much longer. She might have been right about that.

When she disappeared around the corner of the aisle, Cass examined me. "All the color has drained from your face. What's wrong? I thought you liked cats."

I shook my head. "It's not the cat. The Amish think I killed Tyson Colton."

"Probably not all the Amish," Cass said.

"Is that supposed to make me feel better?" I groaned.

She reached up and wrapped an arm around my shoulders. "Come on. Let's finish shopping for this wedding you've roped me into. We'll have plenty of time to hash this out while we're buried in chocolate and caramel."

I gave her a hug. "I'm so glad you're here."

"I'm not as glad." She smiled, which took the bite out of her words. "But I'm happy to be here for you. You know I always have your back. You should have told me about your Amish heritage. Sure, I would have teased you mercilessly about it, but it wouldn't change anything. You can always tell me anything. That's what best friends do."

A pang of guilt squeezed in the middle of my chest. "I know." I opened my mouth to start to tell her about Eric, but she turned away before I could get the words out. I sighed and pushed the cart forward.

Twenty minutes later, Cass and I pushed two heavy carts of groceries out through the store's automatic doors. We had enough for the Hutton-Colton wedding and then some, but I would much rather have too much than too little. Harvest, Ohio was not a place that had twenty-four-hour grocery stores, so running out in the middle of the night for one more ingredient wasn't an option.

We loaded the groceries into the rental car's trunk as Emily approached us with the cat carrier. I peeked inside. Nutmeg pressed his striped orange face up against the metal grate and meowed loudly.

"I don't think he likes being in there," Cass observed.

Emily's smooth brow furrowed. "I know. He's been in there most of the day because I've had him with me while I ran errands. I didn't want to leave him on the farm where my *bruder* might get him and take him away, and Esther doesn't want him at the pretzel shop either."

Cass's eyes narrowed. "You know, your brother sounds like a real—"

I stepped on Cass's boot.

Cass grunted and scowled at me.

I ignored her scowl and reached for the cat carrier. "We'll take good care of him."

"I know you will." She stuck her thin fingers through the grate. "I will see you soon, Nutmeg." She gave a strangled sob before running for her buggy. Her lavender skirt flew out behind her in her haste.

After we were in the rental car, Cass narrowed her eyes at me. "You scuffed my boot," she said accusingly. "Do you know how many truffles I had to make to buy these boots?"

"Meow," the cat said from the carrier balanced on Cass's lap.

"See, he agrees with me." Cass patted the top of the carrier.

"Sorry about the boots, but it's not going to do any good for you to tell Emily how awful you might think her brother is. In the Amish world, the man of the house makes the decisions, so if her brother said she can't keep the cat, she can't."

"That's another reason to be thankful I'm not Amish. I wouldn't last a day."

The thought of Cass dressed in Amish clothes made me burst out laughing.

"I'm glad you find this so amusing." Cass peeked inside the carrier. "Well, the first order of business is to give this guy a new name. He doesn't look like a Nutmeg to me."

I started the car. "What does he look like to you?"

"I'm not sure." She peered through the grate at the cat. "Spot? Roy? Mr. Wiggles?"

I shook my head. "So far, Nutmeg is better than those."

"Cuddles? James? Gumdrop? Buddy?"

I sighed, shifted the car into reverse, and backed out of my parking spot.

* * *

Back at Swissmen Sweets, Cass carried in the cat food, litter box, and kitty litter that we'd purchased at the store. I carried Nutmeg, who Cass thought shouldn't be named Nutmeg.

My grandmother met us in the shop's front room. "Bailey, we were wondering what became of you."

I explained to my grandmother about having to run to the store for supplies for the wedding desserts.

She frowned. "I should help you."

I shook my head. "No. Cass is here, and we can do it. She and I have done countless events like this together." I held up the cat carrier. "And we brought you a new guest too."

My grandmother stared at the carrier as if spotting it for the first time. "What is it?"

"It's not what. It's who," Cass said. "Nutmeg the cat, although I personally feel like that's completely the wrong name for him. We're working on coming up with a new one."

My grandmother took the carrier from my hands and set it on the floor. She opened it and the cat gingerly stepped out. He looked around the front room and zeroed in on my grandmother, rubbing his cheek against her skirts.

"Do you think he knows he has to win her over to stay?" Cass whispered to me.

I had been wondering the same.

"Oh, what a sweetie you are," *Maami* cooed. "Isn't he the cat I've seen with Emily?"

I told her about running into Emily at the supermarket and her brother's decision to get rid of the cat.

"Well, yes, we will keep him, for a time at least. Perhaps Emily's brother will change his mind. The poor child. She's been through too much." She clasped her hands. "Your *daadi* is already in bed for the night."

My brow furrowed. "How is he?"

"He's worn out from the day, as I imagine we all are. I'm so very sorry that you have to work tonight on our behalf."

I hugged her. "*Maami*, we're happy to do it. Aren't we, Cass?" I gave her a look over my grandmother's shoulder.

"Oh yeah, can't wait," Cass said in a much less enthusiastic voice.

Maami didn't seem to notice Cass's tone because she said, "Before you go, you need to eat something. I have been keeping the chicken and dumplings warm on the stove upstairs in the kitchenette."

"Yeah, about that," Cass said. "Do you have any salad?"

After Cass and I ate dinner—she had salad and I had the chicken and dumplings—we headed over to the church. Even though it was a short walk across the square, I opted to drive there because it would be easier to unload all of the groceries we'd purchased. And, besides, there was a murderer on the loose. I wasn't taking any chances.

As we arrived, people who had attended the community dinner were filing out of the building. Most were laughing and chatting with each other. There were people in both Amish and English dress.

"They have some kind of service tonight?" Cass asked.

I glanced at the clock on the car's console. It was almost eight in the evening. "A community dinner. That's why we are starting so late. We had to wait until the dinner was over to use the kitchen."

"It's very nice of the church to let us use the kitchen. I mean, they don't know us at all."

"The woman who happens to be dating the pastor is a good friend of my grandparents, so she vouched for me."

"Dating the pastor? That sounds a little risqué for Amish Country."

"This isn't an Amish church," I said. "The Amish don't have Sunday services in a church building. Members of the district take turns having the services in their homes. I used to go to services with my grandparents when I spent my summers here."

"You spent your summers here?" she asked. "Funny you never mentioned that in the last six years we've worked together."

"Let's just unload the car, okay?"

Cass and I walked into the church's fellowship hall a few minutes later, carrying half a dozen grocery bags between us. There was a screech of chairs on the hardwood floor, and everyone in the large room turned to see who the newcomers were. At this late hour, most of the tables were empty, but there were a few stragglers still sipping coffee and chatting, as the members of the church cleaned up around them. Cass, who didn't ever mind being the center of attention, waved at the onlookers as if she was Miss America on a float.

"Cut that out," I hissed.

"I'm just being friendly. You should try it sometime."
She lowered her voice. "There is a lot of flannel in here.
It's like an epidemic, and it's spreading."

Juliet hurried over to me with Jethro, the pinto potbellied pig, waddling after her like a faithful retriever. I
noticed that she had changed into yet another polka-
dotted dress. This one was blue with white dots. "There
you are, Bailey. We are about to clean up, and then we
will be out of your way." She glanced at Cass. "And who
is this?"

Cass stared down at Jethro. Her expression was much
like what mine must have been when I saw the black and
white pig earlier that day. I supposed that I should
have warned her about the swine encounter, but I had
honestly forgotten about Jethro—who was pretty
unforgettable with those black and white dots—in all
the upset of the day. Being accused of murder tends to
make a person forget some details.

Cass looked from me to Juliet and back again. "Isn't
anyone going to address the pig in the room?"

Chapter 27

"Cass, this is Juliet, the woman I told you about who made it possible for us to work in the church tonight." I nodded at the pig. "And this is Jethro."

Cass brushed her purple bangs out of her eyes. "He's a pig. He's a pig, and he's inside a church."

"He is," I said.

Cass stared at the pig. "He has polka dots."

Juliet laughed her tinkling laugh. "Yes, Bailey mentioned the same detail when she met Jethro this morning. You ladies are certainly fashionable. That must be why Jethro's markings are so remarkable to you."

"But he's in a church," Cass said.

I patted her arm. "Just absorb the shock and move on. We have a lot of work to do tonight."

"We'll be out of your hair in no time," Juliet promised.

"There's no rush," I said. "It will take us a little while to unload the car and—" I stopped speaking in mid-sentence when I spotted a man carrying a dishpan full of dirty dishes across the basketball court. As he did, our eyes locked. It was Aiden. He was out of uniform and wearing jeans and a polo shirt. A white chef's apron was tied around his trim waist.

"Hello, Bai. Hello. Are you there?" Cass waved a hand in front of my face. "Juliet asked you a question."

I blinked and broke eye contact with Aiden, who carried his bin into the kitchen. Laughter poured out of the room as the volunteers joked around while washing dishes. "What is it?" I asked.

Juliet smiled. "Do you need any help unloading your car?"

"No, no help is needed." I grabbed Cass by her sleeve and dragged her back into the hallway.

"Hey, careful there, you've already scuffed my boot. You don't want to mess with my coat." Cass wrenched her arm away from me. "What's wrong?"

"Nothing is wrong," I said, knowing my voice was higher than normal.

"Are you afraid of the pig? Is that it?" She peered back into the fellowship hall. "Because he looks pretty harmless to me."

"It's not the pig. I just saw someone in the fellowship hall who I didn't expect to see. It threw me."

She peered back through the door. "Who is it?"

"Stop that!"

She came away from the door. "Who did you see that has you spooked?"

"It was one of the deputies from the sheriff's department. I didn't expect to see him. That's all."

She went back to door and openly stared at the church members cleaning up the dinner. "Is he the one who thinks you killed that Tyson guy? Because I'd like to tell him a thing or two."

I grabbed her sleeve again. "No, it's not that deputy,

but we should be a little more cautious about what we say until we are alone."

She gave me a thumbs-up sign. "Got it."

Cass and I carried the final few grocery bags into the church kitchen and set them on the counter by the others. At least half a dozen ladies bustled around the kitchen, wiping counters and washing dishes. Juliet entered the kitchen carrying a tray of salt and pepper shakers. She was followed by Jethro, of course. I was beginning to see him as her permanent shadow.

Cass openly stared at the pig. She had not reached the acceptance stage in her shock yet.

I walked over to Juliet. "How can we help?"

She shook her head. "You're here to make the wedding desserts. We have everything well in hand."

"We want to help," I protested. "We can't just stand by and watch you work."

Juliet smiled. "That's so kind of you, if you're sure."

"Of course, I'm sure. Cass is too. Aren't you, Cass?" I elbowed my best friend in the side.

"Oww." She rubbed her side. "You really need to stop doing that. I'm starting to bruise."

I raised my eyebrows at her.

"Oh, right, we want to help. I'd love to do it!" She said in mock cheer.

I inwardly groaned. However, Juliet didn't seem to notice Cass's sarcastic tone.

"Well, all right. We could always use the help. And many hands make the work go faster. Perhaps the two of you can wipe down the tables in the fellowship hall. They always seem to be sticky by the end of the meal even if we didn't serve anything sticky. The diners are sort of like toddlers in that way."

Cass wrinkled her nose, but I refrained from elbowing

her yet again. I would really feel bad if she was starting to get a bruise.

"There are extra aprons hanging on those pegs on the wall." She pointed at the aprons. "And I will get the buckets and rags together for you while you put them on."

"An apron?" Cass asked.

Juliet raised her eyebrows. "I just thought that you wouldn't want to get your pretty clothes dirty."

"An apron would be great," I said before Cass could answer. I knew Cass was thinking of the hierarchy at JP Chocolates. Back in New York, in Jean Pierre's place, only the assistants wore aprons. The chocolatiers, like us, wore chef's jackets. At JP Chocolates it was a big deal to trade in your apron for a chef's jacket. After earning hers, Cass had sworn she would never wear an apron again.

I walked over to the wall where the aprons hung and plucked two off the pegs—one for me and one for Cass. I handed her the apron.

She held it away from her. "I said I would never wear one of these again."

"We're in Ohio. No one from JP Chocolates will ever know that you wore an apron. I promise not to tell. Besides, do you really want to take the chance of ruining your clothes?"

She slipped the top strap of her apron over her head. "I'm doing it for the outfit. Let's just be clear about that." She lowered her voice. "I swear if you take a photo of me while I'm wearing an apron, I will haunt you well into the afterlife. I don't want anyone at JP Chocolates hearing about this."

"I'm glad you have your priorities straight." I tied my apron around my waist.

Cass finished tying her apron as Juliet appeared with

two small buckets and clean rags. She held them out to us. "Thank you so much, girls."

I took the buckets from her. "We're happy to do it."

Cass jumped away from me as if she was afraid that my elbow was coming in her direction. "We're very happy to do it," she said.

I handed a bucket to her with a smile. She scowled in return.

Back in the fellowship hall, we split up. Cass started on the left side of the room, and I went to the right. On the first table, I dropped my rag into the soapy water and scanned the room for Aiden. He wasn't there. I was beginning to wonder if I had imagined seeing him when Cass and I first arrived.

Two women cleared the table next to me. Both appeared to be in their late fifties or early sixties. One wore jeans and a sweater, and the other wore a plain gray dress and a white prayer cap on her head.

"No, I'm not going to sell now," the Amish woman said. "I never wanted to in the first place. I wouldn't have if that terrible man had given me half a choice."

"I heard his son might be taking the business over. He might still want to buy."

"I don't care what Tyson's son wants to do. I'm not going to sell. I know that it's a terrible thing to say, but everything will go back to normal now that Tyson's dead. We won't have to worry about what will become of the town now."

The English woman nodded. "That's a blessing. He never cared about Harvest in the least. He just wanted to make money, and this was a way to do it. Colton's company would make a bundle if he got his way and bought all the property on Main Street."

The pair moved three tables over, and I couldn't hear

their conversation any longer. Even though I hadn't finished cleaning the first table, I grabbed my bucket and followed them. I was so focused on hearing the rest of the women's conversation, I wasn't paying any attention to where I was going, and I ran directly into a solid form. Sudsy water sloshed out of my bucket and all over the man's back.

A very wet Deputy Aiden Brody spun around, and I wanted the floor to open up and swallow me whole.

Chapter 28

"I can't believe I did that!" I yelped, brushing water off of him as best I could. "Deputy Brody, I'm so sorry."

He looked behind himself as water ran all the way down his back, over his behind, and down his legs. I tried not to stare.

"I'm so clumsy," I said. "I can't tell you how sorry I am."

He turned around to face me as a puddle gathered on the floor around his feet.

I set my bucket—with the little bit of water that was left in it—on the closest table. "I'll go find something to mop up this mess."

Cass came toward us and openly stared at his back. "Did you throw the bucket of water on him?" she asked.

I covered my face with my hands. "Let me go get some towels." Before either of them could say another word, I ran into the kitchen and ripped the roll of brown paper towels from its holder. The ladies washing and drying dishes stared at me. I didn't pause to explain and hurried back into the fellowship hall.

When I got back to Cass and Aiden, the two of them were laughing.

I ripped off several towels from the roll and handed them to him. "I'm so sorry about this." I squatted on the floor and began to mop up the ever growing puddle. A hand appeared in my line of vision. I glanced up to see Aiden looking down at me with his hand extended. "It's okay, Bailey. No worries." His eyes were kind.

After a moment's hesitation, I took his hand and stood. The moment I was upright, I dropped his hand like I had received an electrical jolt and pressed my own hand into my side to fight the residual feeling of his skin against mine.

Aiden seemed undisturbed by our brief touch. "Your friend here was just telling me about the time when you spilled a vat of chocolate syrup onto a Jordanian princess at some sort of fancy gala. That sounds much worse than what has happened here."

I frowned at Cass. "It was."

She grinned in return.

"Thanks for the paper towels," Aiden said. "I can clean up the floor and go. I was heading home from here, so there's no harm done. Getting splashed with water never killed anyone."

"Clearly you have never seen the *Wizard of Oz*," Cass said.

It was a good thing that Cass was out of elbow range, because I would have poked her for that one.

He grinned. "Don't worry, I won't melt."

"I really am sorry." I apologized for what felt like the hundredth time.

He smiled. "I know you are."

Cass looked from me to Aiden and back again. Her mouth fell into a tiny little O.

Juliet peeked her head out of the pass-through. "Bailey, the ladies are all done in here, so you and Cass can start working on the desserts. I'll be out in a moment. Aiden, don't leave without saying good-bye to your mother." She shook her finger at him.

"Sure, Mom," he said. His dimple was out to its full effect.

"That's your mom?" Cass asked.

He grinned. The dimple practically twinkled. "She is."

I spun around in the direction of the kitchen. "We should get to work."

"I'll see you tomorrow, Bailey King," he called after me.

As we walked to the kitchen, Cass slipped her arm through mine. "You have a thing for Deputy Cutie Pie." She glanced over her shoulder, back in Aiden's direction. "I can see why. He's adorable. That dimple. It could stop a girl's heart."

I groaned. "I do not have a thing for the deputy. Besides, I can't, because I already have—" I stopped myself midthought. I was about to say I couldn't because I already have a boyfriend, but Cass didn't know that.

Cass didn't seem to notice I'd stopped talking and squeezed my arm. "Please tell me you ran at him and dumped soapy water on his back to get his attention, because that's totally what I would have done."

"It was an accident with no ulterior motive, I promise."

She sighed. "Have I taught you nothing? Then why did you run into him?"

I leaned closer to her and whispered. "I was follow-ing two women, who were talking about Tyson's death."

That got her attention. "What did they say?"

"One of them was Amish, and said that now that Tyson was dead, she had no plans to sell her shop to his son or whoever may inherit Tyson's development company."

"Do you think she would have killed him to keep her property? You think an Amish woman knifed someone?"

I grimaced. It did sound pretty far-fetched when she said it like that.

"Who was she? The woman that you overhead saying this?"

"I don't know. I've never seen her before." I peered into the kitchen. Only Juliet, Jethro, and two other English women remained. "She must have left."

Juliet folded a hand towel and set it on the counter. "Bailey, the kitchen is all yours now. I wish I could stay and help, but I should take Jethro home. It's been a long day for him. It's important that he gets his beauty sleep, especially before the wedding."

I glanced down at the pig, who was lying at her feet with his eyes half-closed. I couldn't help but smile. "He does look like he's done in."

"You're taking the pig to the wedding?" Cass asked in a now-I've-heard-everything voice.

Juliet nodded. "I'm invited, and Jethro goes every-where that I do, so yes, he will be at the wedding."

I wondered if Eileen knew about the hoofed wedding guest.

Juliet held out a key to me. "Here's the key to the church. Just lock up when you leave, and I'll collect the key from you in the morning." She slapped her thigh. "Come on, Jethro. Let's go home."

The pig struggled to his feet on the tiled floor and dutifully waddled to her side. Juliet scooped him up and tucked him under her arm. After Juliet, her pig, and the last of the church ladies left, Cass and I got to work. I started two double boilers to begin melting the chocolate. We were going to need a lot of chocolate.

"Let's just work on the desserts, okay? No more talk of guys or murder."

She shrugged. "Fine by me."

After who knew how many hours later, Cass collapsed onto a stool in the corner of the kitchen. "I think I'm dying," she said. "I've pulled all-nighters before, but this is ridiculous."

It was a little after one in the morning. Exactly twenty-four hours earlier, I had discovered Tyson's body in my grandparents' kitchen. I shivered at the thought and set a fourth tray of truffles in one of the church's industrial-sized refrigerators. After putting the tray in place, I closed the door. "I can't believe that we pulled this off."

"We make a good team." She yawned, and her eyes were half-closed.

I wiped my hands on a cloth and walked over to the counter where I had left my purse. I pulled out the rental car's keys and the keys to Swissmen Sweets that my grandmother had given me earlier that evening. We had both known that Cass and I would be returning to the candy shop long after she and *Daadi* were in bed. I moved across the room, picked up Cass's limp hand, and placed the keys in it. "Go back to the candy shop and get some rest. You're going to keel over."

"But we still have to clean up the kitchen." Another yawn.

"I can do that. Take the car and go back."

"How will you get back?"

"I'll walk. It's just on the other side of the square. I don't want to leave the car in the church parking lot. I think Eileen has big plans for the church, its parking lot, and the square for tomorrow's wedding. You'll be doing me a favor by moving the car. I will probably be able to clean up faster without having to worry if you're going to topple over into a bowl of boiling caramel."

She curled her fingers around the keys. "Oh, all right. But how will you get into the shop? You don't want me to leave it unlocked while I go to bed, do you? After a man was killed in your kitchen?"

My brow wrinkled. "No, I don't. Hide the key under the mat in front of the door."

"Won't that be the first place the killer would look?" She yawned. "I mean, even an Amish killer would know to look under the front mat, wouldn't he?"

"We don't know the killer was Amish." I rolled my eyes. "It will be fine. Now go," I insisted. "It will take me just an hour more, at most. And I'm so tired, I've gotten to the point I can do this cleanup on autopilot. It will go faster if I'm alone."

She shook her head. "I don't know how you do it. It's no wonder Jean Pierre hand selected you as his protégé. You're a machine. I'm convinced."

I laughed. "Go."

She struggled to her feet. "Are you sure? I can wait."

"I'm sure."

She nodded and stumbled out of the kitchen. Faintly,

I heard her call as she moved through the fellowship hall. "You owe me, King. Big time!"

Truer words were never spoken.

After Cass left, I made short work of cleaning up the kitchen. I shut the industrial dishwasher and set it to start. I couldn't believe Cass and I had pulled it off. Fatigue washed over me and seeped into my bones. This had been the longest day of my life, by far, and the next day promised to be just as exhausting, between the wedding and the need to clear myself of a murder rap. That reminded me of Cass's brother. I wondered if she'd had any luck getting the name of an attorney from him. I promised myself to ask her in the morning.

I grabbed my shoulder bag from the counter and turned off the kitchen lights. I walked through the fellowship hall and out of the church, flipping off lights as I went. Outside of the church's front door, I closed and locked it with the key that Juliet had given me. I yanked on the door a few times to make certain it was secure. The last thing I wanted was for someone to break into the church because I hadn't locked the door properly. I stuck the key in my jeans pocket. It was interesting that Juliet had a key to the church. Maybe she and the pastor *were* dating. I wondered what Aiden thought about his mother's relationship with the reverend.

I stumbled down the steps into the parking lot and rubbed my eyes. I needed sleep. I couldn't think of Aiden this late at night, especially after the humiliating water bucket incident in the fellowship hall. My muddled thoughts turned to Eric, which was even worse. It was too late at night to face my doomed relationship.

As expected, downtown Harvest was completely abandoned at two in the morning. I walked as quickly as

I dared across the dark square toward the candy shop. The electric porch light next to the candy shop's front door called out to me like a beacon. I knew my grandmother had left it on for Cass and me.

I was just walking by the gazebo when another bright light caught me in the eyes, blinding me. "Where do you think you are going?" a deep voice demanded.

Chapter 29

I held my hand up to cover my face and shield my eyes from the bright light. "Who's there?"

"I asked you a question." The man in front of me held his lantern up high. The light glinted off of Abel Esh's red hair.

I blinked a few times against the glare. "Can you lower the light? It's shining right into my eyes."

"Bailey King." He frowned. "You upset my sister."

I knew that he must be referring to Esther, not Emily. I had a feeling that Emily now considered me a friend, since I had decided to take in Nutmeg. I held a hand in front of my eyes.

Abel lowered the light, so the beam fell on my neck, not directly in my eyes, but it was still plenty bright.

"You scared me half to death!"

"What are you doing out here so late at night?"

I could barely make out his features in the dark. "I was at the church making desserts for tomorrow's wedding."

He frowned. "Wedding?"

I swallowed. "The Hutton-Colton wedding."

He took a step toward me. "Are you a friend of the Coltons?"

I took two large steps back and bumped into a tall evergreen bush. Its sharp branches bit into my back. "No. I'm just making the desserts. I'm not friends with anyone in Harvest except for my grandparents."

He held the lantern up again, and the light hurt my eyes. "You were alone in the church making these desserts?"

His closeness made me increasingly uncomfortable, and I was reminded of the time he had tried to trap me on the square when we were children. This time his tone was much more sinister. "No, my friend Cass was with me. She should be coming along at any moment," I lied, knowing full well that Cass was already inside the candy shop, undoubtedly passed out on my bed in the guest room.

Mercifully, he lowered the lantern. "It is *gut* that you are not friends with the people from the wedding. They are not *gut* people."

Since I couldn't think of anything kind to say about Jace or Eileen, I said, "Mira is a sweet girl."

"She is the worst of them all. She is the one who causes me to worry." He stepped closer to me. As I retreated farther into the bushes, the branches dug even deeper into my back.

Mousy Mira caused this huge Amish man to worry? I couldn't imagine how that was possible. In the short time I had known Mira, I couldn't imagine her worrying anyone, not even a small child or Juliet's pig.

I tried to straighten up and edge my way out of the bushes, but I realized that if I did that, I would touch

Abel. The bushes held much more appeal. "It's late. I have been up all night making desserts. If you don't believe me, you can talk to Juliet Brody or any of the other ladies who were at the church dinner tonight."

The light from his lantern made a geometric pattern on the bushes. "You're friends with Deputy Brody's mother as well. You seemed to have made many friends for being here for so short a time."

"I wasn't friends with Tyson Colton."

He stepped back. "No one was Tyson's friend. It is little wonder he is dead."

I shivered. He said this so coldly, with such little feeling. He didn't sound Amish at all, or at least not what I thought an Amish person should sound like. Perhaps Aiden had been right. My childhood summers in Amish Country weren't enough to fully understand the Amish way of life.

Now that there was some space between us, I straightened up. "Please just let me by. I'm tired, and it's late. I don't think either of us should be having this conversation right now. We might say something we would regret."

He stepped closer to me and forced me into the bushes for a second time. I ignored the pain of the needles piercing my back through my jacket. "I never regret anything that I say or do."

Fear shivered up my spine. There was something about this conversation that felt like we teetered on the brink of something dangerous. Abel was a large man, a strong man. His family's business was right next to the candy shop. The building was about to become the property of a man he clearly despised and that man was now dead, which meant the family could keep the building.

He stepped back, and I went limp with relief. Breath whooshed back into my lungs.

"Outside of making dessert, I wouldn't spend much time with the Coltons or the Huttons if I were you."

I watched as his back receded into the inky darkness. I pressed a hand against my thundering chest as if to hold my heart in place.

Was that a threat? As he walked away, the smell of Kerosene from his lantern wafted in my direction. The scent was strong. It was the same smell I had encountered behind the candy shop when I'd found the broken glass yesterday morning. I had a new suspect to add to my growing list, and he'd just bumped Jace Colton out of first place.

All attempts to keep my cool were gone as I ran full tilt to the candy shop, not once stopping to look over my shoulder.

I sighed with relief when I found the shop key under the mat just where I had told Cass to hide it.

When I was inside Swissmen Sweets, I bolted the door and leaned against it. My chest heaved up and down, and the ambient light from the streetlamps caught the crime scene tape stretched across the kitchen door.

"Meow!" The small cat came out from under one of the candy shelves.

I knelt and held out my hand to him. Nutmeg—or not Nutmeg as Cass would have it—strolled over to me and pressed his velvety cheek into the side of my hand. He began to purr.

"I see now why Emily didn't want to leave you at the mercies of her brother. Who knows what a man like that would do to a gentle creature like you." I shivered at the very thought, and Emily's sweet face came to mind. What must it be like for her to live under her brother's thumb?

Nutmeg mewed and rubbed his cheek against my hand.

I picked up the cat and hugged him against my chest. The cat settled there as if I carried him around all the time, so I took him upstairs with me.

In my bedroom, I found Cass's enormous suitcase just on the other side of the door. Designer clothes, almost exclusively in black, poured out of it. Cass herself was passed out on the bed.

I kicked off my shoes and didn't even bother to change into my pajamas. Fully clothed, I lay on the bed next to Cass. She grumbled and scooted over but didn't wake. Nutmeg curled into a ball on my chest. I stared at the ceiling for heavens knew how long. My mind was so full that it was blank.

At some point, I must have fallen asleep.

I woke the next morning to find Nutmeg curled up in an orange ball at the foot of the bed. Cass was gone, although her clothes were everywhere. At least I knew she was still in Harvest; she'd never leave her clothes behind.

Sunlight streamed into the bedroom through the sheer curtains over the window. Slowly, I sat up, slightly dizzy. I pressed the heel of my hand to my throbbing forehead. Apparently, I was no longer conditioned to stay up all night, as I had been earlier in my career when I had desperately wanted to impress Jean Pierre with my work ethic.

I glanced at the nightstand, where there was an old

battery-powered alarm clock. It was after nine. I had slept longer than I'd thought. I groaned. The honey crisp apple Aiden had given me the day before sat next to the clock. I picked it up and twirled the shiny piece of fruit in my hand. I couldn't bring myself to eat it. It meant something. Exactly what, I had no idea. I set it on the far side of the nightstand, and told myself not to think about it or its benefactor anymore.

Nutmeg sat up, stretched, and began washing his forepaws.

"At least one of us is rested," I said to the cat. I ran a hand through my hair. I needed a bath too. I smelled like chocolate.

Cass walked into the room dressed in black jeans and a black sweater. In New York, I would have thought nothing of her outfit. In Holmes County, she looked like an undertaker, a stylish undertaker, but still. I knew better than to share my thoughts on this point with her.

Her hair was wet as if she were fresh from the shower. She held a hair dryer in one hand and a hand towel in the other. "I can't find an outlet to plug this in."

"The only electrical outlets are in the kitchen. But you can't go into the kitchen. It's a crime scene." I rubbed my eyes.

"Bailey King, are you telling me that I can't dry my hair? I'll be a frizz ball all day. I have standards." She yanked the towel from her head. Her hair stood out in every direction.

I shrugged. "You've gone country."

She groaned, unceremoniously dropped the towel and hair dryer into her open suitcase, and began rifling through her cosmetic bag. "I think I have bobby pins in here somewhere. By the way, I talked to my brother early this morning, and he gave me a few names of criminal defense attorneys that you might want to talk to. I knew he would know all the right people. A couple of them are even in Ohio. My brother has a wide network of lawyers."

I rubbed my eyes. "I'm hoping that it won't come to that."

"Me too." She pulled a compact from her makeup bag. "But it's best to be prepared for these types of things. My brother taught me that. By the way, I'm starving." She dropped her cosmetic bag on the bed and picked up the apple from my nightstand.

She was about to bite it when I yelped, "Don't eat that!"

She stopped the apple halfway to her mouth and cocked her head at me. "Do you want it?" She held out the apple to me.

"I don't want to eat it either."

She stared me. "Bai, I think you have been in the country too long." She set the apple back on the nightstand. "We have to return to civilization—to the real world—where they have hair dryers and outlets and people eat apples."

I forced a laugh. "I'm sorry. I know I'm a little on edge."

"That's one way to describe it," she said.

I hopped off the bed. "I'm going to jump in the shower. I'm sure *Maami* has a huge breakfast waiting for us in the kitchenette. Don't wait for me to eat."

"I won't. I'm starving." She combed her hair and pinned it behind her ears. Her damp purple bangs fell into her eyes.

"You hair looks nice," I said before I left the room.

"Don't mock, Bai," she warned. "Don't mock."

When I returned to the bedroom a few minutes later, feeling at least halfway human again, I found that both Cass and Nutmeg were gone. To my relief, the apple was still there.

I turned away from it and dried my hair the best I could with my towel before throwing it up in a knot on the top of my head.

In the hallway, low murmuring flowed from the direction of my grandparents' sitting room. I walked that way, wanting to see how my grandfather was doing this morning.

Maami's voice floated out of the cracked open door. "Jebidiah, you aren't being reasonable. There's no reason to run yourself ragged for this shop. You've given it your whole life, that's enough. It's time to retire."

I froze midstride in the middle of the hallway and listened.

"*Gott* made us for work," *Daadi* said.

"I know this," she said, and then added something in their language.

"I'm not in denial about my health," *Daadi* protested. "I know my life is at an end, and I am ready for the Lord to call me home. Until that hour, I must work. It is our way."

Maami gasped. "Don't say that you are at the end of your life." Her voice caught. "Bailey and I need you."

A tear rolled down my cheek. I did need him, more than he could ever know.

"We must be prepared for the truth. You must go on without me when the time comes, and if you must sell the candy shop in order to do that, know that you have my blessing. I may have given my life for this place, but I do not want you to."

Sell the candy shop? The thought of it turned my stomach. At the same time, if that's what it took for my grandfather to get well, I'd be happy for him to do it.

They continued their conversation in Pennsylvania Dutch. I stumbled down the hallway into the small kitchenette, where I found Cass digging into a mountain of my grandmother's French toast and scrambled eggs. She waved her fork at me. "If you tell me how many calories I'm consuming, I will stab you with this."

"I won't," I said vaguely, still reeling from the conversation I had overheard in the hallway.

She lowered her fork. "What are you wearing?"

I looked down at my jeans and flannel shirt. "What?"

She wrinkled her small nose. "It's time for us to go home and hit the boutiques on Fifth Avenue, to purge the memory of whatever it is that you have on."

"Cass, please, you've seen me in jeans a thousand times."

"The jeans, yes, the shirt, no." She stabbed a bite of French toast with her fork.

"What's wrong with flannel?"

"Nothing. If you're a lumberjack on a roll of paper towels."

I snorted.

"Bai, this isn't 1994. Grunge is long gone. I don't care what the teens are wearing. Flannel is not back, not for you, not for anyone who works in the city."

I tuned her out as my thoughts wandered back to the conversation I'd overheard between my grandparents just moments ago. Could my grandfather really know that his life is ending?

She dropped her fork on the plate. "Hey, what's wrong? I mean, your shirt is hideous, but if you really like it that much, I won't disown you."

"It's not the shirt." Tears pooled in my eyes. "I think my grandfather is getting worse, not better."

She jumped out of her seat and wrapped her arms around me in a tight hug.

That's all I needed her to do.

Chapter 30

Cass let me go. "What can I do to help?"

"Help me find out who killed Tyson Colton," I said. "The stress surrounding the murder can't be good for his already weak heart."

Nutmeg meowed and rubbed his striped cheek against my leg. I bent over and picked him up. I sat in the chair across from Cass and set the cat on my lap.

Cass pushed the serving plate of eggs across the table to me. "You'd better eat up, then, if we're going to catch a killer."

My stomach turned over again.

"Eat," she ordered. "I know you, Bai. When you're stressed you stop eating. That's not going to work this time."

I spooned a small serving of eggs onto my plate. Nutmeg sniffed it.

Cass picked up her fork again and studied the cat. "What about Pumpkin? Jerry? Buttercup?"

Nutmeg jumped off my lap.

I picked up my fork. "I don't think he cares for any

of those suggestions." I managed to swallow a small forkful of eggs.

Maami stepped into the kitchenette. "There you girls are," she said in a voice so cheerful, I never would have known that just a moment ago she was having such a serious life and death conversation with my grandfather. "How is it tasting?"

Cass touched a cloth napkin to the corner of her mouth. "This is the best thing I've ever eaten. Better than anything you can find in New York, and that includes the bagels."

Maami grinned. "*Danki*. That is quite a compliment. Bailey has sent us fresh bagels from New York before—they are quite *gut*. In fact, I like them more than Amish pie. Don't tell the ladies in my district. I would be excommunicated if they found out."

Cass dropped her fork. "They would do that?"

I laughed. "She's teasing you."

Maami chuckled.

"Nobody told me that the Amish have a sense of humor," Cass muttered.

"Would you like coffee too?" *Maami* directed the question to me as she lifted the coffee pot from the burner and poured the dark liquid into two waiting mugs.

My stomach turned at the thought of coffee, but I knew I would need the caffeine if I had any hope of remaining alert.

"I should not have asked you that, because, of course, I know the answer." She handed one of the mugs to me, and kept one for herself.

Usually, I liked to add cream to my coffee, but there was no waiting for that. If I was going to face the day and clear my name, I would need the caffeine in my system as fast as possible. I took a swig and burned my tongue.

My grandmother shook her head but refrained from comment.

I poured cream into the cup, and she added more coffee. I sipped from my mug a little more cautiously this time. "What are you and *Daadi* up to today?"

She pursed her lips. "That depends on the police. There is no farmers' market today," she said. "I'm hopeful that Aiden will let us back into the kitchen. Everything will need to be scrubbed from top to bottom before we can use it again."

I grimaced. That was certainly true. "Aiden said he knows a company that can do the cleaning for us."

Maami wrinkled her nose. "I can clean the kitchen. I am capable of that."

I shook my head. "*Maami,* this is different. For food safety, you will need the kitchen professionally cleaned. It helps that Aiden knows someone."

"Who's Aiden?" Cass asked after swallowing another mouthful of French toast.

"You met him yesterday at the church," I said. "He was the guy I spilled water on."

Cass gaped at me. "The cute cop?"

Maami wrinkled her brow. "You spilled water on Aiden? Why would you do that?"

"Why didn't you introduce him as Aiden when we met?" Cass watched me over her coffee mug.

Maami watched me too. "He's a very fine young man."

I could tell where this conversation was headed and decided to go on the offensive. "*Maami, w*hy didn't you tell me that you and *Daadi* had taken in Aiden and his mother when Aiden was a child?"

"What?" Cass sat up straight in her seat.

Maami set her coffee mug on the counter. "He told you then. I'm glad of it."

"Why didn't you tell me?" I asked.

"It was Aiden's story to tell. If he didn't want to share it with you, it is not my place to interfere. It's his history. Now that he has, it will be easier for you to trust him." She picked up her mug again and took a sip.

"Why would I have any reason to trust him?" I asked. "He's a member of the sheriff's department. His sheriff has made it no secret that he believes I'm the one who killed Tyson Colton. Aiden suspects me too. He admitted that he did."

My grandmother's face fell and tears gathered in her blue eyes. "How would anyone believe that about you? I just don't understand how Aiden could think that."

She looked so distraught that I backpedaled. "It's his job, and the evidence against me can't be ignored."

Maami closed her eyes for just a moment as if in prayer. "*Gott* will put it all to rights. You will see." She opened her eyes again. "We should not dwell on this. What do you have to do for the wedding today? Do you need my help?"

I shook my head. "Everything is ready for the wedding. Cass and I will set out the desserts while the ceremony is going on, so that they will stay fresh. Since the wedding isn't until the evening"—I shot Cass a sideways glance—"I thought I would show her around town and visit the different places I liked to go as a child."

"*Gut.* It will be *gut* for you to put your mind on other things and not this murder business." My grandmother stirred sugar into her coffee, poured a second cup, fixed it with sugar and cream, and placed everything on a tray. I knew she was taking it to the sitting room to share morning coffee with my grandfather. It was a ritual they'd had for as long as I could remember.

My grandfather always said he was grateful that he wasn't a tradesman or a farmer. Because he lived above the candy shop, he was able to see my grandmother from sunup to sundown every day. I pressed my lips together to hold back the questions on the tip of my tongue about my grandfather's health. I didn't want *Maami* to know that I had been eavesdropping on their conversation.

I wasn't as sure about God putting the murder investigation to rights. It wasn't going that well so far, which was why I had to step in.

I cleared my throat. "We'd better be off then. I don't want to be gone too long in case there is any news from Deputy Brody about whether or not we can open the shop to visitors."

She nodded and lifted the heavy tray from the counter.

I reached for it. "Let me take that for you."

She held the tray away from me. "I've been taking coffee to your grandfather every day for over fifty years. I'm not going to stop until I don't have a choice." Her mouth turned down. With a straight back and her chin held high, she carried the tray out of the room.

Cass clicked her tongue. "Now I know where you get your crazy work ethic from. Does your grandmother ever sit down?"

I shook my head. "Not often enough." I drained the last of my coffee. "Let's go. We have a murder to solve."

"I thought you were going to show me around town?"

"You can see the town while we search for a killer."

Cass stood up and brushed crumbs from her black pants. "I suddenly feel like I am a character in a Scooby Doo cartoon. It goes without saying, but I'm Daphne."

"Who does that make me?" I asked.

"Velma, I suppose."

"Great." I rolled my eyes.

"Would you rather be Shaggy? You don't have the right facial hair for it." She tapped a finger against her cheek. "I never realized it before, but he wears his beard just like the Amish men do. Do you think he's Amish?"

I rolled my eyes again. "Let's go, deep thinker." I walked out of the kitchenette.

She followed me. "I was just asking if it could be possible."

Cass continued her argument that Shaggy was, in fact, Amish as we made our way down the stairs into the shop.

I was about to remind her that Shaggy drove a van, and therefore could not be Amish, when a face pressed up against the shop's front window. I screamed. Cass screamed. The figure jumped back and a muffled squeal came through the glass.

Chapter 31

"Bailey!" *Maami* called from the top of the stairs. "Are you all right?"

I stared out the window and saw Ruth Yoder standing on the other side of the glass with her hand pressed against her chest.

"We're fine," I called back to my grandmother. "Cass startled me."

"Don't pin this on me," Cass complained.

"Shh!" I hissed.

"You all right then?" *Maami* asked with more than a little concern.

"We're fine," I called. "Aren't we, Cass?"

Cass jumped away from me as if anticipating the elbow I was about to throw in her direction. "We're good."

"All right. Be safe today."

We heard the sound of her muffled footsteps making their way back to *Daadi* in the sitting room.

I ushered Cass out the front door of Swissmen Sweets, taking care to lock it as I went. I didn't want the deacon's wife taking the unlocked door as an invitation to enter the candy shop and pester my grandparents.

Across the street on the square, I saw a group of Amish men raising a large white tent. The preparations for Mira and Jace's wedding were well underway. I couldn't see Eileen from where I stood, but I knew she must be over there monitoring every move the men made. It still remained to be seen if she would approve of the desserts Cass and I had made for the reception. Not that she would have much choice but to take them. There wasn't enough time to make any alternatives.

I smiled at the deacon's wife. "Good morning! We're sorry to have startled you," I said, even though her face against the glass had be the reason for our screams.

Ruth lowered her hand from her chest and patted the back of her white prayer cap as if to make sure that it was still on the top of her head. "You should be more careful not to frighten people like that."

"You were the one being a peeper." Cass adjusted one of the bobby pins holding back her hair.

I looked heavenward.

"Who is this?" Ruth snapped at me.

I plastered a smile on my face. "Ruth, this is my friend Cassandra. She's visiting from New York."

The Amish woman looked Cass up and down and didn't appear to like what she found. I had to admit, Cass's hair wasn't as perfectly styled as it normally would be. Her purple and black locks were almost dry, but, as she'd predicted, without the help of a hair dryer they were a tad frizzy. Well, maybe a bit more than a tad. I valued my life too much to make this observation aloud though.

Ruth looked away from her. "I would like to speak to your grandparents."

"I'm sorry," I said, even though I wasn't. "Now isn't a good time. My grandparents are both resting. They had a terrible day yesterday and are still recovering."

She sniffed. "I can imagine. It is not every day that one finds a body in the kitchen."

"I would hope not. That would be really inconvenient," Cass said.

"Maybe you can come back later," I suggested, smiling as brightly as I dared.

"When?" she asked.

I wanted to say never, but instead, I said, "Tomorrow sometime."

"Tomorrow is Sunday, the Lord's Day, and I am the deacon's wife. I have many obligations on that day. I can't come here and call on your grandparents on a Sunday." She adjusted her glasses on the bridge of her nose.

"I guess that leaves you with Monday, then," Cass said.

Ruth frowned. "My husband, the deacon, will be hearing about this." With that, she spun around, sending her dark skirts and black apron flying around her legs, and stomped away from us.

As she marched down the sidewalk in the direction of Main Street's intersection with Apple Street, an Amish woman stepped out of the cheese shop and shook a plain navy tablecloth onto the sidewalk. Crumbs flew in the air. I blinked at her. I recognized her as one of the ladies who'd helped to clean up after the church dinner, the one who'd told her friend that she no longer to planned to sell her shop now that Tyson was dead.

I looped my arm through my best friend's. "Cass, I think we are going to start our day with cheese."

"Come again?" She fussed with one of the bobby pins using her free hand.

"I think we need to visit the cheese shop next door. They have a ton of free samples. You could eat your weight in cheese if you wanted to."

She groaned and patted her flat stomach. "I already ate my weight in French toast. Can't this wait until later? What about the whole, let's catch a killer thing? Have you already given up on that idea? Because if you have, I'm on board with it."

I shook my head. "It can't wait even a second—not if you want me to return to New York free of a murder rap. Visiting the cheese shop is part of the solving murder idea."

She sighed. "I guess I can eat some cheese for a good cause. When I get back to the city, my personal trainer is going to kill me. I can see a million stomach crunches in my future."

The bell over the Cheese Haus's front door jangled when Cass and I stepped inside a moment later. It was after ten in the morning now and there was an Amish girl at the counter. The woman who had shaken the crumbs from the tablecloth was seated at a table behind the sales counter, cutting huge slabs of cheese into three inch bricks.

I also knew the girl in the shop, or at least I had seen her before. She had been the one cleaning the church who had argued with Jace during the tasting. Judging by the way her eyes widened, she recognized me too.

"I've never seen so much cheese in my life," Cass said in an almost reverent tone.

I glanced at her out of the corner of my eye. "There are dozens of cheese shops in New York."

"Sure, but they don't have free samples." She waved her hand down the line of cheese on the counter. "At least not like this, out in the open and ready for the taking."

I suppressed a smile. "I thought you were too full to eat another bite of anything."

"Maybe I'm getting my second wind. Oh look, gouda, my favorite."

I pulled on her sleeve. "Can we focus on why we are here, please? Clear my name, remember?"

She shoved three pieces into her mouth and waved her toothpick at me. "Maybe your being Amish isn't half-bad. You can hook me up with cheese like this, can't you? Do they ship?"

"I'm not Amish," I said for what felt like the hundredth time.

"Can I help you?" The girl's voice trembled ever so slightly.

I smiled at her. "We are just browsing. I saw you at the church yesterday, right? I'm Bailey."

Her eyes were wide. "Maribel," she replied. Then she added, "We have a lot of samples out, but if you'd like to try anything special, please let me know."

Beside me, Cass rubbed her hands together.

"Actually," I said. "What kind of cheese does she have?" I gestured to the woman behind the counter. "If I may, I would love to try that one."

Maribel turned to the woman and said something in Pennsylvania Dutch.

The older woman stood up. She wore a plain blue

dress and black apron. Her white prayer cap was precisely pinned on top of her white head. "You're the girl who was at the church last night." She pointed the knife at me, and then looked at Cass. "You were there too, but your hair looked different." She squinted at Cass.

I grimaced, hoping that Cass wouldn't say anything that would get us kicked out of the shop before I even had a chance to question the shopkeeper.

"This is a new personal low," Cass whispered. "When an Amish person notices how bad my hair is. There's no coming back from that."

The woman behind the counter turned back to me. "You're Jebidiah and Clara's granddaughter, aren't you?" She stared at me. "I should have known. You remind me so much of Clara when she was younger. You're taller, of course, but you have the same bright blue eyes, and you resemble her around the mouth." She set her knife on the table. "I'm Birdie Klemp, and this my granddaughter Maribel."

I smiled at them both. "It's so nice to meet you. My grandparents only have nice things to say about their neighbors."

"We feel the same about the Kings. They have been *gut* neighbors to us. I heard that Clara and Jebidiah's *Englisch* granddaughter was here visiting them. It is nice for you to visit when your grandfather is feeling so poorly."

"Oh, she's not British. She lives in New York," Cass said around a mouthful of cheese. I hadn't even realized that she was again diving into the free samples.

Birdie smiled at her but didn't correct Cass. "I'm so sorry about what has happened. It's just awful. Your grandparents are *gut* people and they have been *gut* neighbors to me these last thirty years. They were especially kind when my husband passed on. Jebidiah always took it upon himself to look in on me to see how I was getting on. I've been meaning to look in on them. Please tell your grandparents that I have been praying for them. I imagine they will have seen the deacon by now."

"I haven't met the deacon yet." I didn't add that I had caught his wife staring into the candy shop earlier that morning.

"Yes." She nodded. "It is his job to make sure everything in the district is running just as it should. I'm sure this has come as a great shock to our deacon and the other leaders of the district." She picked up her knife again. "You'd like a sample of this cheddar I'm cutting? It's our top seller."

"Sure would," Cass said. I was beginning to wonder if she was a hobbit and this stop at the Cheese Haus was her second breakfast.

Birdie cut off a generous piece for each of us, placed them on matching white paper plates, and handed them over the counter.

Cass broke off a piece and popped her into her mouth. "Oh! It melts in your mouth."

I stared at my hunk of cheese. I wasn't able to eat when I was upset, and a huge piece of cheese wouldn't have been my first choice if I could get anything down. "I'll be sure to deliver your message to my grandparents."

"*Danki*. Is there anything that Maribel and I could help you find?"

"I'd like to pick up a few things for my friends back in New York. They won't believe I was in a real Amish cheese shop unless I bring back samples," Cass said.

Birdie blushed. "There's plenty to choose from. It's quite nice to think that fancy people in New York City will be sampling my cheeses. We do have a shipping service, so tell your friends that we can ship any cheeses they like."

"I will," Cass promised, and began wandering around the shop, eating tiny pieces of cheese as she went.

That left me alone with Birdie. I was wondering how I could bring up the delicate topic of her selling her business to Tyson when she said, "I am sorry for what happened to your grandparents."

I raised my eyebrows.

"I'm sorry that horrible man died in their kitchen, but I can't say that I'm sorry he's dead." She covered her mouth with her hand. "I regret I said that. I should have never said such a thing."

Without looking up, Maribel wrapped the cheese that her grandmother had cut in plastic. As she worked, her hands shook. Maribel knew something or was afraid of something when it came to Tyson Colton. Because of Jace's reaction to her, I sensed she had some connection to the family. What had he said? That he thought she and Emily were happy Tyson was dead? It was something close to that.

"From what I heard about him, most people felt the same way," I said. "He didn't seem to be well liked, especially by the Amish."

Birdie pulled back her neck, exaggerating her double chin. "And why would we like him? He was horrible to the entire community. All he wanted to do was buy our property and make us work for him. He didn't care about anyone other than himself."

"I understand he bought this shop," I said.

She pressed her lips together.

"My grandfather told me that before Tyson died," I said, hoping that mentioning my grandfather would remind her that we were on the same side. "Tyson wanted to buy Swissmen Sweets too."

It seemed to work because she relaxed just a little. "I didn't know that for sure, but I'm not surprised. That horrid man wanted to buy up all the businesses on Main Street." She clenched her fists at her sides.

"Why is that? What would he want with all these Amish businesses?"

Again, she pressed her lips together, and I thought maybe I had gone too far this time. "He didn't share his reasons with me, but there are rumors." She sat back down at the table with the cheese and began cutting again.

It seemed that the Amish always had to be doing something productive. Rarely did my grandparents sit still or sit just to chat. They were always doing something else at the same time. In the case of my grandfather, it would be cutting chocolate or stirring caramel. My grandmother would knit or quilt while visiting. Their hands were in constant motion.

I stepped closer to the counter to see Birdie better. "What kind of rumors?"

Behind me Cass exclaimed, "Be still my heart! There are like, fifteen kinds of cheddar over here."

I ignored Cass and focused on the conversation at hand. "What kind of rumors?" I repeated.

Birdie concentrated on her task for a moment, and I thought she wasn't going to answer the question at all. "I heard that he wanted to own all the businesses on Main Street to turn Harvest into some kind of Amish theme park. His vision was an Amish Disneyland."

Chapter 32

"Amish Disneyland?" I squeaked. "Doesn't Harvest already get a fair amount of traffic? I always thought it was one of the most popular spots in Amish Country."

She nodded. "It is, but Tyson wasn't making money off the tourism as it stands now, was he?"

"He wanted to make money off of all the business in Harvest?"

"*Ya*, what else would be want?" She resumed cutting. "I have it on good authority that he would make a handsome profit once he owned everything on Main Street."

"Who told you that?" I asked.

She clamped her mouth shut.

I leaned on the counter and decided to level with her at least a little bit. "I know I'm asking a lot of questions, but you have to understand the situation that my grandparents are in. The sheriff's department is looking at my grandparents closely."

She gasped. "You mean about the murder?"

I nodded.

She frowned, and deep lines creased the sides of her mouth. "How can the sheriff or any of them believe that

Jebidiah or Clara King could do such a thing? It is complete insanity. Anyone who knows them wouldn't believe that." Her frown deepened even more. "Why, Aiden Brody should be ashamed of himself after everything they did for that boy."

"He has to do his job. He's looking into other leads," I said, surprising myself by coming to the deputy's defense.

She shook her head. "He should be doing more to help your grandparents."

"Who told you Tyson wanted to make downtown Harvest into some kind of Amish theme park?"

"I heard it straight from his son's mouth."

My eyebrows shot up. I never would have put Birdie and Jace Colton together as possible confidants. "His son told you his father's plans?"

The deep lines appeared around her mouth again. "He didn't tell me directly. I was sweeping the walk in front of the shop, and he stood at the corner with Mira and told her the whole scheme. He said that it would all be theirs someday when his father died."

I shivered. This sounded to me like a serious motive for murder. Jace had just regained the top spot on my suspect list.

She sighed. "He pointed at all the buildings on this side of Main Street and said that his father was buying up every last one. According to the son, Tyson planned to ask the shopkeepers to stay on and mind the shops. We'd be his employees, you see." She balled her hands into fists at her sides. "Well, I had no intention of doing that. When I turned over my keys to Tyson, I planned never to set foot inside this shop again."

"What else did he have planned?"

"Tours of Amish homes, classes to make Amish food,

and buggy rides around the county. If he couldn't find a real Amish person in Harvest to do it, he planned to hire actors." Her face turned bright red at the thought of someone impersonating an Amish person. "He claimed there was only one thing holding his father back from completing his plan."

"What's that?"

"Your grandfather. Jebidiah King refused to sell Swissmen Sweets to Tyson. Tyson became obsessed with having it, or so I heard. It wouldn't stop him from doing what he wanted to with rest of the town, but he wanted Swissmen Sweets desperately. Jace said that his father had found a way to make Jebidiah sell at last. He said it was foolproof."

"What was it?" I was breathless.

She shrugged. "He didn't say."

"Jace said all of this right in front of you?" I couldn't keep the doubt from my voice.

She shrugged a second time. "Sometimes the *Englischers* don't see us Amish. They think we are part of the scenery and not real people." Her voice turned bitter.

"What about Mira?" I asked. "How did she react to all of this?"

Birdie pulled her chin back again as if in disgust. "And Mira just stood there nodding as if we—"

"*Grossmaami*," Maribel said, and then added something in their language.

Birdie looked sharply at her granddaughter.

"As if you what?" I asked. I knew whatever she was about to say was important, very important.

Maribel stood and set the wrapped blocks of cheese into a green shopping basket. She then took the basket out to the main part of the shop and began restocking the cheddar cooler with the new cheese.

I held on to the edge of the counter. "What were you going to say about Mira?"

Birdie looked over my shoulder at her granddaughter. "It does not matter now."

I thought it mattered. I thought it mattered a lot. But I decided to let it go for the moment. "Did you tell anyone else Tyson's plans for Main Street?"

She frowned. "I told the deacon. That is what you are supposed to do in the church, go to the church elders when you have a concern."

"What did he say?"

"He listened. He doesn't have to share his decisions with me. It's not my place to know."

My eyebrows shot up. "Why not? I would think he'd be worried that someone planned to exploit members of his district."

"The deacon is a *gut* man." She lowered her voice. "The deacon is unwell." She tapped the side of her temple with her pointer finger. "He's very old and is easily confused."

"Why doesn't he retire, so the district can replace him with someone else? How old is the deacon?"

"He's eighty, but Amish deacons and bishops don't retire," she said, as if I had much to learn. Maybe I did when it came to Amish culture. . . .

She went on, "The only way church leaders leave their positions is through death. *Gott* is the one who put them in that place, and He will be the one to remove them."

"So they always stay in their position even when they are ill and cannot do the job?"

She sighed. "Not always. They can choose to step

down if that is what *Gott* wants of them, but that will never happen in the case of Deacon Yoder. His wife would not allow it."

"Ruth Yoder seems to be quite a bit younger than her husband."

"She's twenty years his junior. Deacon Yoder's first wife died young many years ago."

"So when Ruth married him, he was already the deacon," I said. This was an important fact. Had Ruth been power hungry and married the deacon because that was the closest a woman in the Amish community could come to leadership? I frowned. Ambition didn't sound very Amish to me.

"The deacon," Birdie went on without my encouragement, "didn't have any children from his previous marriage, but he and Ruth have six. All are grown now with their own families to care for."

I remembered the remark Ruth had made the day before about all her children staying in the Amish way, while my father—my grandparents' only child—had left the faith.

"Did you tell anyone else in the church about Tyson's plans? The bishop?"

She frowned. "*Nee*. The deacon said it was his place to tell the bishop. It would not be right for me to step over him like that."

"But he might not have remembered to tell the bishop if he is as confused as you say he is," I argued.

"I can't go directly to the bishop. It is not the way in our district. If I were a man, I could, or if I had a husband, I could send him. My husband is dead, so I cannot."

This was an aspect of the Amish culture that I couldn't understand. I understood respecting the hierarchy of the church, but if there was a problem, why not tell as many people as possible? It didn't make any sense to me. And then there was the sexism to contend with. For the first time, I felt eternally grateful to my father for leaving the Amish way. As much as I would have loved to grow up with my grandparents, I couldn't imagine being held back simply because I was a woman.

"When are you moving out of the Cheese Haus?" I asked, knowing full well she had no intention of leaving, but I wanted to gauge her reaction to my question.

She jerked her head back. "Move out of the Cheese Haus? Why would I do that?"

I rocked back on my heels. "You sold your business to Tyson. Don't you still have to move?"

"*Nee.* I'm not going anywhere. The papers were never signed before he died, and I have changed my mind. I will not sell now. I never wanted to when I agreed."

It seemed to me that many of the papers were still unsigned when Tyson Colton was stabbed in the chest. "Why did you agree in the first place?

She pursed her lips, and I had a feeling I'd finally taken the questions too far.

"Bai, do you think Jean Pierre would like baby Swiss or regular Swiss better?" Cass called from across the shop. She stood in front of the display case of Swiss cheese with a tennis ball sized wedge in each hand. At her feet, a red shopping basket was filled to the rim with cheese and jams.

"Regular," I said, shaking my head and turning back to Birdie. "So now that Tyson is dead," I said, "you plan to stay here in your shop."

She narrowed her eyes. "That is what I have told you. I have a right to change my mind. Circumstances are different now. I no longer have a buyer for the cheese shop."

"Did you speak to Jace Colton, Tyson's son? I may not be right, but I am assuming that he will take over his father's affairs, especially since he seemed to think that all of Main Street would be his someday."

"I'm not interested," she said.

"But you were interested when Tyson wanted to buy," I said. "What's the different now? What's changed? Did he threaten you?"

"*He* wasn't the threat," she said, and then winced as if she regretted what she'd just said.

"Was there someone else?" I asked excitedly. This was the second time I had gotten a hint that someone else might have been involved in Tyson's scheme. The first time had been from Emily. "Who was it?"

"No one," she said. "I have already said too much. The past is in the past."

Cass shuffled toward us, carrying her overladen basket of cheese.

I blinked at her. "What on earth are you going to do with all that? How are you going to get it back to the city?"

With a grunt, she hoisted the basket onto the counter. "I flew private, remember? There are no restrictions on how much stuff I can take back to New York." She rubbed her hands together. "I see more shopping in our future."

I groaned.

"I'll just ring that up for you," Birdie said, and then she gave me a pointed look. "So that you can be on your way."

I took the hint. The conversation was over. As I waited for Cass's purchases to be totaled, I realized that

Maribel had disappeared at some point during my discussion with her grandmother. I couldn't help but wonder if that was telling. There was something about Mira that she didn't want me to know.

Cass and I left the Cheese Haus carrying four plastic grocery bags of cheese. The bags were so full that the plastic handles bit into my fingers. I would be happy to set them down, and soon. Across the street, I saw that the wedding reception tent was up, and dozens of people moved around the square carrying chairs, boxes, and flowers. I spotted Eileen in a royal blue suit standing in the middle of the gazebo, directing traffic. I might have been mistaken, but I thought I saw a bullhorn in her hand.

A man approached us at a fast clip from the square. He had a large camera in his hand. My first thought was wedding photographer.

"Bailey King?" he asked.

I adjusted the plastic sacks in my hands. "Yes."

He lifted the camera and took a rapid succession of photographs of me. I was certain my mouth hung open in each and every shot.

Chapter 33

Cass stepped in front of me. "What are you doing?"

He grinned. "I'm from the *New York Star*. I have what I need. Thank you!" With that, he turned and bolted back across the street toward the square.

Cass set one of her shopping bags on the sidewalk. "What was that all about? What is the *New York Star* doing in Harvest, Ohio?"

A bad feeling settled over me, and reciting chocolates wasn't going to take it away.

"Could it be about the murder?" Cass asked. "It can't be anything else, but why would anyone in New York care? I mean, no offense to Tyson or anything, but people are murdered all the time. Is it because you're a suspect and you're from New York?"

That wasn't it. I wasn't a big enough personality to garner the *New York Star*'s attention. The photographer had come to Ohio for a bigger story, bigger than even Tyson Colton's murder. It might be because I was a murder suspect, and I was Jean Pierre's heir apparent at JP Chocolates, or it might be about the other celebrity in my life, the secret one—Eric. I prayed that I was wrong.

I forced a laugh. "Maybe it has to do with the wedding. I wouldn't be the least bit surprised if Eileen called the press about her daughter's wedding."

Cass didn't look a bit convinced. "The *New York Star*, really? They are going to cover her daughter's wedding?"

I knew at that moment I should tell her everything about Eric, but I couldn't form the words. They just wouldn't come.

Cass picked up her bag. "So where do we find Jace to talk to him about his father's plans for Amish Disneyland?"

"You were listening?" I asked.

She snorted. "Hello, I can multitask. Isn't that what chocolatiers do?"

I grinned. "That we do."

"We need to find Mira, too, since she knew about Tyson's plans," she said.

I nodded, realizing that Cass really had been listening to my conversation with Birdie. "But how can we find them? They must be getting ready for the wedding."

"Well, I thought we should go over the dessert menu with them one last time, and if we asked some other questions in the process, we would be multitasking again."

I set the bags of cheese on the sidewalk and hugged her. "Cass, you're a genius!"

"Hey, watch the cheese!" She held the two heavy bags of cheese out at her sides, so that they wouldn't get crushed by my hug.

I let her go. "We need to find out where the wedding party is now."

She adjusted her bags in her hands. "Can we drop off the cheese first?"

Cass and I entered Swissmen Sweets, and *Maami* met us at the door. She engulfed me in a hug, and I held out my bags of cheese to protect them just as Cass had when I had hugged her.

"Wonderful news." *Maami* held me at arm's length. "Aiden has let us back into the kitchen. He made the arrangements with the cleaning company, and they are already here. We might be able to open as soon as tomorrow."

I looked over her head and saw the yellow crime scene tape was no longer marring the kitchen door. "That's wonderful!" I exclaimed. "Where's *Daadi*? I'm surprised he's not here celebrating with you."

Her face fell. "He's not feeling well, and I put him back to bed. I talked to the doctor on the telephone, and he advised more rest. That's what Jebidiah is doing."

My heart lodged in my throat.

Maami squeezed my arms. "Now, don't you make that I'm-about-to-cry face, you hear me? He's resting, that's all. All he needs is a little rest."

If only that were true.

She stepped back. "What's all this?" she asked as if noticing the sacks of cheese for the first time.

"Cheese," Cass spoke up. "I went a little bit overboard, but I know everyone in New York will love it."

"Where are we going to put it?" I asked.

Maami grinned. "The big refrigerator in the kitchen has already been cleaned out. You can put it in there."

"I'll put them away," I told Cass, taking her sacks from her. Even though they were equally as heavy as mine, I knew I could manage them all as far as I needed to go. "Cass, you stay here with *Maami*."

As I made my way to the kitchen, I heard Cass ask my grandmother, "So this means I can plug my hair dryer in there tomorrow?"

I pushed open the kitchen's swinging door and stepped inside. Immediately, my eyes fell to the spot on the floor where Tyson had been. There was a faint stain in the dark tile. A man in a white hazmat suit knelt by the stain and scrubbed at the floor. I looked away to find Aiden watching me from across the room.

"Is it okay to be in here?" I asked, adjusting the heavy bags of cheese in my hands.

The man on the tile peered up at me. "As long as you don't touch the chemical with your bare skin, you should be fine."

I frowned. This was said by a man wearing a face mask. I hurried over to the refrigerator. It was empty. All the food that had been in the kitchen prior to Tyson's murder was thrown away. My grandparents would have to start over again. I shoved the bags of cheese inside the fridge and closed the door.

"Stocking your emergency bunker with cheese?" Aiden asked.

I turned around and came face to face with that blasted dimple. "Umm, no, my friend Cass had the urge to buy cheese for half the population of New York."

"Cass is the friend who was with you at the church last night?"

I nodded. "I'm sorry that I didn't introduce you. I think all politeness went out the door when I dumped that bucket of water on you."

He grinned. "No harm done. As you can see, I'm perfectly fine after the near-death experience."

I rubbed my suddenly sweaty hands on my jeans. I sidestepped him to put some distance between us. Like my close encounter with Abel by the gazebo the night before, this moment with Aiden felt dangerous, but in very different way.

His dimple faded. "So, you just happened to go to the Cheese Haus to buy cheese. You weren't there to talk to Birdie about selling her business to Tyson Colton?"

I folded my arms and felt a combination of relief and disappointment that he had abandoned his flirty tone. "Isn't the amount of cheese Cass purchased proof enough?"

"No," he said. "I asked you to stay out of the investigation."

"Listen, I have to go. I need to head to the church to prepare for the wedding."

He grabbed my arm. "Bailey, I'm telling you to stay out of it. A man is dead. If you keep pushing, you might put yourself and your friend in danger."

I yanked my arm from his grasp. "If you would do your job and find the person who's behind the murder, I wouldn't be in any danger, now would I?"

He dropped my arm as if I had slapped him.

As soon as the words left my lips, I regretted them. "I'm sorry. I shouldn't—"

He shook his head. "Don't be sorry. You're right." He looked away from me. "The crew should be done cleaning up in here soon. You and your grandparents should be allowed back in the kitchen by the end of the day. I see no reason why you can't reopen tomorrow."

"Aiden—" I began.

"Don't you have a wedding to get to, Bailey?" He wouldn't meet my eyes.

I bit the inside of my lip to stop myself from apologizing again. How had things gotten so out of control so fast? Why did I even care what the deputy thought of me? I didn't know him, not really. I turned and left the kitchen without another word.

Back in the front room, I found Cass and my grandmother sitting at one of the small tables at the front of the shop. *Maami* smiled at me. "Was Aiden still back there?"

"He was," I said. As I did, I felt Cass watching me. She knew something was wrong. She knew me even better than my grandparents did. I had spent more time with Cass in the last six years than I had with anyone else.

"*Gut*," *Maami* said. "He's such a kind and generous man. We're so proud of who he has become."

I wondered if my grandmother would have been able to say the same of me if she really knew the person I was, not the person I allowed her to see. The true person hit people with chairs and had secret boyfriends. *Maami* didn't know that Bailey King. Cass didn't even know that Bailey King.

Maami smiled. "I was just telling Cass about the other visitor we had this morning."

"Other visitor?" I asked. I immediately thought of Ruth Yoder. Had the deacon's wife returned to pester my grandparents after Cass and I left?

She nodded. "*Ya*, there was a reporter here looking for you not long ago."

"A reporter?" I did my best to keep the anxiety I felt from my voice.

I felt Cass watching me.

My stomach clenched. It had to be the same guy that Cass and I ran into outside of the cheese shop. "Did he ask you anything?"

She frowned. "He didn't. He only wanted to know if you were here."

"How did you know he was a reporter?" Cass asked.

"I asked him if I could have his name, so I could tell you who stopped by, and he said to tell you he was from the *New York Star*."

It was the same reporter as I feared. I supposed that I should be relieved there wasn't more than one. "I'm sure it's nothing to worry about," I told my grandmother. "It might have something to do with JP Chocolates. I wouldn't worry."

Maami's brow furrowed. "It seems like a long way for him to travel to ask you questions about chocolate. Couldn't he wait until you were back in New York? Or couldn't he have emailed you the questions?"

Cass laughed. "You know about email?"

Maami smiled. "I know it exists. I don't know how it works."

Cass leaned across the table closer to my grandmother. "The truth is no one knows how it works, and don't even get me started on the Cloud."

Maami frowned. "The *cloud*? Like in the sky?" She peered out the window. White, fluffy clouds bobbed like apples through the bright blue sky. Mira and Jace could not have had a more beautiful fall day for their wedding.

"Cass," I said, interrupting their tech talk. "We'd better head over to the church."

"I thought they didn't need you until late afternoon," my grandmother said.

"Oh, I just want to check on a couple of things this morning to be sure we are all set."

Cass rolled her eyes at me when *Maami* wasn't looking.

Once we were outside, I made a beeline for the wedding tent that stood in the middle of the square. Cass jogged after me. "Hey, slow down. The wedding isn't until six. We have a lot of time to find Jace and Mira."

Eileen Hutton remained on her perch in the gazebo. She put the bullhorn to her mouth. "How many times do I have to tell you!" she shouted in the horn. "The white lilies go in the sanctuary for the ceremony, not in the reception tent."

The two young Amish men carrying the vases of canna lilies froze as if they had been caught with their hands in their grandmother's cookie jar.

"The church!" Eileen bellowed into her horn.

The men were off like a shot in the direction of the church. Water splashed out of the vases and leaves flew into the air behind them.

Cass rubbed her ear. "Geez, doesn't she have a volume control on that thing?"

"I'm sure, and undoubtedly, it's on the max," I said. "That's Eileen, the mother of the bride."

Cass winced. "They should require a license to operate a bullhorn, and it should never be given to a mother of the bride."

I agreed with her on that.

Eileen lowered her bullhorn and spotted Cass and me standing at the foot of the gazebo. "Bailey, I wasn't expecting you until later this afternoon. Please don't tell me that there is something amiss with the dessert bar. I have too many problems as it is."

I smiled as warmly as I could. "Everything is fine. We'll set the desserts out during the ceremony so that they will be fresh when the guests enter the reception tent."

"I'm glad someone here has their act together. I wish I could say that for the rest of the vendors." She scowled.

While Eileen spoke to us, the Amish men ran by

with more flowers, throwing furtive glances in Eileen's direction, seemingly relieved that she wasn't looking their way.

"Shouldn't someone else handle all these final preparations?" I asked. "You're the mother of the bride. This is your day too. You should relax and enjoy yourself."

"You would think, but there is no one I can trust when it comes to the wedding. I'm surrounded by a group of buffoons."

"Buffoons?" Cass asked. The corners of her mouth twitched as if she were fighting a smile.

I mentally willed her not to laugh.

Cass stared at her shoes. This was not going to go well.

"Is there anything you need?" Eileen asked. "As you can see, I am very busy."

I opened my mouth to speak, but Cass was faster. "We were wondering if you knew where we could find the wedding party."

Eileen pulled her neck back like a turtle retreating to her shell. "The wedding party? What would you want with them?"

It was a fair question, and I looked to Cass for the answer since she was responsible for eliciting it.

Cass smiled brightly. "Because we would like to make a special dessert for the groom, and we thought his best man or one of the other groomsmen would be able to tell us what he'd like best."

I inwardly groaned at the thought of making yet another dessert for the wedding.

Eileen stared down at her. "I can't tell you where any of the groomsmen are. We were lucky that they showed up for the rehearsal yesterday. I told Mira she should only have had one attendant and left it at that, but Jace was insistent that he had to have four groomsmen. Apparently, that was a sticking point with him about the wedding. It's the only thing that he asked for besides the dessert bar—which I personally still think should have been a cake, no offense to you, Bailey. I compromised to keep the peace."

"That must have been difficult," Cass said.

I had to look away from her to stop myself from laughing. Effortlessly, Cass kept a straight face.

"It was," the mother of the bride said somberly. "It left me scrounging up bridesmaids. I had to pull in a second cousin."

Again, Cass had to look away. I had to stop looking at her at that point, or I was at a real risk of cracking up. "Who is Mira's maid of honor?" I managed to ask.

"The second cousin. Mira wanted to have her Amish friends as her bridesmaids, but of course that would never work."

"Who are they? Her Amish friends, I mean?"

She looked down at her list and made a mark on her clipboard with her pen. "Maribel and Emily. All she ever talks about is that she wished Maribel and Emily could have been part of the wedding."

She must mean Maribel from the Cheese Haus. It was hard for me to believe that there could be another Maribel in Harvest, and I would bet my job at JP Chocolates that Emily was Emily Esh from the pretzel shop, and Nutmeg's former owner. "Maribel from the Cheese Haus and Emily from the pretzel shop?"

She looked up from her clipboard. "Do you know them?"

I nodded. "They have shops on either side of my grandparents' shop."

She returned her attention to the clipboard. "Oh yes, of course."

"Where is the wedding party staying?" Cass asked. "Maybe they are still there?"

"The Amish Door Inn. That's where everyone is preparing for the wedding too. Mira should be in hair and makeup right now. I'll be heading over there shortly, just as soon as I can get the workers under control." She tapped the end of her pen against the clipboard. "There's no point in making anything extra at this point, but if you insist, you may. I won't pay you extra for it though, if that's what you're hoping."

"We wouldn't dream of it," I said.

Cass and I said our good-byes and left Eileen with her bullhorn.

We were still within earshot of Eileen when Cass muttered, "I didn't realize that we needed her permission to speak to her future son-in-law."

"Shhh," I hissed.

Two Amish men carried a long table in the direction of the tent. Eileen held up her bullhorn. "Hey! That doesn't go there."

"At least she didn't call those guys buffoons to their faces," Cass said.

"Yeah," I said, as Eileen ran down the steps of the gazebo after the two Amish men moving the table.

"Doesn't it seem odd to you that the bride doesn't have any friends in the wedding?" Cass asked.

"I suppose if her closest friends are Amish, it's possible. They wouldn't be able to wear whatever bridesmaid dresses Eileen picked out for the wedding, and I can't see her letting them walk down the aisle in plain clothes."

"The bridesmaid dresses that Eileen picked out? Isn't it the job of the bride to pick the dress?"

"I don't think Mira picked much of anything for this wedding. I'm starting to wonder if she even picked the groom," I said.

"We should head to the inn, then?" Cass asked.

I nodded.

Cass waved me forward. "Then lead on, Watson."

I stopped midstride. "Watson? I thought I would be Sherlock."

"Please," she snorted. "I'm always Sherlock. Always."

Chapter 34

The Amish Door Inn was on the outskirts of Harvest at the top of one of the green rolling hills Holmes County was famous for. The rental car whined on its way up the hill.

Cass squinted at the speedometer. "Are you sure this car is safe? It sounds like it's having an acute asthma attack."

"It's fine," I said with far more confidence than I felt. The day I flew into Ohio, the rental car agent had suggested that I wait for a newer car to be cleaned. Instead of waiting, I had opted for whatever they'd had on hand. I had been so anxious to see how my grandfather was doing, I didn't want to wait an extra minute, let alone twenty minutes. It had been a good thing that I had made that decision since my grandfather had collapsed on the sidewalk only moments after I'd arrived. Who knew how long he'd have been lying there if I had shown up twenty minutes later. Tyson certainly wouldn't have helped him.

The inn was a two-story white building with an enormous wraparound front porch. Dozens of people milled around the grounds, peering under bushes and searching the area.

Cass cocked her head. "Do you get a sense that there's trouble afoot?"

I looked at her out of the corner of my eye. "Afoot? Really?"

"Hey, I'm Sherlock, remember. You were the one who dragged me into this whole playing detective thing. You should at least let me enjoy the lingo."

I shook my head, but I had to agree. It did look like something was afoot at the inn.

A sheriff's cruiser pulled into the parking lot as Cass and I climbed out of the car.

"Oh, it's the cute one," Cass said.

I gave her another look. Aiden must have left Swiss-men Sweets while Cass and I had been sidetracked by Eileen and her bullhorn.

"Don't worry. He's all yours," Cass said. "I won't get in the way."

I blinked at her. "What makes you think I want him?"

"Please," she said in return.

Aiden climbed out of his cruiser, and my chest tightened just a little. Guilt washed over me again at how sharply I had spoken to him in the candy shop's kitchen. He frowned when he spotted us. Most likely he assumed that I was meddling in the investigation again. I was, but that didn't mean I appreciated the frown.

I was wondering whether I should stop and talk to Aiden, when a young woman with her hair up in an elaborate twist, marched toward us at a fast clip.

"Bridesmaid," Cass said with one hundred percent confidence.

"How do you know?" I asked.

"You can always tell. You can smell the desperation."

I didn't have time to decipher Cass's cryptic take on bridesmaids because the girl wailed, "She's gone! Have you seen her?"

"Who's gone?" I asked. Out of the corner of my eye, I saw Aiden walk toward us.

"The bride! She fled! We have a runaway bride on our hands. The wedding is off. How will I ever meet one of the groomsmen now? The only reason I agreed to this stupid wedding in the first place was to meet a hot guy. I'haven't seen Mira since we were kids."

I could only assume this was the second cousin.

"A runaway bride?" Cass asked. "Seriously? Are we in a Julia Roberts movie with bonnets?"

I frowned at her. "So not helping."

Cass shrugged, not the least bit apologetic for her humor. I wouldn't have expected anything less.

"You have to find her." The unnamed bridesmaid grabbed Aiden's hand and clung to it. "You have to help us. File a missing person's report or something! Should we call the television news? I would look great on TV."

Aiden extracted his hand from her grasp. "Of course we will look for her, but she's an adult, who has left of her own free will it appears. We won't file a missing person's report until she's missing for at least twenty-four hours, and we mostly certainly won't alert the media until we absolutely have to. I doubt it will come to that."

The bridesmaid pouted. "This wedding is a bust."

"Do you think she's okay?" I asked.

Aiden glanced in my direction. "We will do every-thing we can to make sure Mira is all right, but if we find her and she's left of her own accord, we can't force her to come back."

The bridesmaid paled. I couldn't help but think it was the lost opportunity with the groomsmen and not the fact that her second cousin, the bride, was MIA that turned her smile upside down.

"Where is the groom?" Cass asked.

"I don't know." The bridesmaid was working her pout to full advantage. "Jace and his four groomsmen left a little over an hour ago. We noticed that Mira was gone not long after that."

"If my future husband was goofing off with his friends on my wedding day, I might run away too," Cass said.

"Mira didn't say anything to anyone about leaving?" Aiden asked.

"No!" the bridesmaid wailed. "I'm the maid of honor. If she told anyone, she should have told me. It's my job to keep an eye on her today. Eileen is going to lose it."

She was probably right about Eileen.

"Was Mira upset? Does anyone know where she might have gone?" I asked.

The girl rounded on me. "If we knew that, do you think we would be searching for her in the bushes?"

Cass folded her arms. "Do you really think she would be hiding in the bushes?"

"Is her car here?" Aiden asked.

"Yes, it's right there." She pointed at a silver convertible in the first parking space next to the front door. "That's why we are searching the grounds. She couldn't have gotten far, because there is nowhere for her to go. We're in the middle of nowhere. All there are around here are trees and farmland. I hate nature," she said.

"I have to agree with her on that last point," Cass whispered in my ear. "I'm not a big fan either."

"Shhh," I hissed.

The bridesmaid was right. The inn was in the middle of nowhere. It stood on a hill overlooking the country-side and was surrounded by pastureland dotted by black cows.

Aiden nodded. "We'll do our best to find her. She couldn't have gone far by foot."

Aiden and the bridesmaid headed toward the inn. Cass started to follow them, but I grabbed her arm to stop her. "At the tasting yesterday at the church, it seemed clear to me that Mira wasn't happy, and that her mother and maybe even Jace were railroading her into this marriage. Maybe she finally decided to make up her own mind."

"Kind of late to change your mind though. It is her wedding day."

"At least she changed it before the ceremony," I said. "At least she didn't get into a marriage she would later regret."

"Where do you think she could have gone, then?" Cass asked.

I removed my cell phone from the back pocket of my jeans. "Didn't Eileen say that Maribel and Emily were Mira's closest friends? It stands to reason that she would have run to them. We could call the cheese shop and find out if Maribel is there. If she is, Mira might be there too." As I spoke, I opened the web browser on my phone and found the listing for the Cheese Haus.

Cass frowned. "Do you really think the cheese shop lady will talk to you after the way you grilled her?"

"No, but she might talk to you since you bought so

much." I pressed the number on the screen to make the
call and held the phone out to her.

"Fine." She took the phone from my hand.

"Hello? I was in your shop earlier today. I was the
girl who bought all the cheese . . . yes, yes, everything
with the cheese is fine. I know that my friends in New
York will appreciate it as a gift. It's so very *Amish*. . . .
You're welcome. I called because I was wondering if
your granddaughter, Maribel is there. I . . . ummm . . .
admired her apron and wondered if she'd made it. I
wanted to ask her."

I slapped my forehead. It was very possible that Cass
and I were the worst investigators ever.

"Oh, she's not there. Where has she gone? Oh! Well,
I'd love to speak to her before I head home to New York.
Thank you so much, and again, thanks for all your fabu-
lous cheeses. You're welcome." Cass ended the call.

I arched my eyebrow at her. "You wanted to know
where she got her apron? Really? This after making a
fuss about wearing an apron last night."

"Hey," she objected. "It was the best I could come up
with under pressure, and you'll be happy to know I got
some information for you."

"What?" I said impatiently. I didn't want Cass to drag
this out into one of her long tales. Mira was missing,
and I had a feeling we were racing against the clock to
find her.

"Birdie said that Maribel and Emily Esh went on an
outing in Emily's buggy not long after we left the cheese
shop. Birdie guessed that the girls went to the Esh farm."

"She told you that?" I asked.

"Hey, I just spent a small fortune on cheese in her
shop. I think she would tell me anything in the hope that

I would visit her store again. Do you know where the farm is?"

I nodded. "Let's go." I marched in the direction of the rental car.

When we reached it, Cass opened the passenger side door. "Is it far? Do you think your car will make it?"

"It'll be fine," I said with more confidence than I felt.

Chapter 35

The rental car had a much easier time going down the hill from the Amish Door Inn than it had had going up.

"This contraption has reliable brakes, right?" Cass asked, as she braced her hands against the dashboard.

I tapped the brakes as we cruised down the hill. "Seems to."

"Wow. That makes me feel better. If I die out here, I want my body shipped back to New York. I don't want to be buried in a cow pasture. I want a civilized, urban burial." She fell back into her seat.

"Duly noted."

"So how are we going to find the Esh farm?"

"When I first met Esther, she told me it was out on Barrington Road. My grandparents used to have friends out that way that we visited when I came to town. If it's anything like I remember, there is just one farm on the road. That must be where the Esh siblings live now."

* * *

After several winding twists and turns, during which Cass grabbed the dashboard as if her life depended on it, I finally found the turnoff for Barrington Road.

"I should have taken Dramamine," Cass groaned.

"It wasn't that bad."

"Tell that to my stomach," she grumbled.

A white farmhouse came into view. A few hundred yards behind it was a matching barn that was twice the size of the house. Plain dresses and trousers hung from a clothesline tethered between the house and a nearby tree. A single horse and buggy sat beside the barn, pointing in the direction of the road as if the owner had positioned them that way so that they could leave the farm at a moment's notice.

"What's the plan?" Cass asked. "Are you just going to knock on the door and ask for Mira?"

I pulled the car into the driveway and shrugged. "I could," I said. "Or we could just talk to Mira directly." I pointed to a porch swing on the wide front porch where Mira sat between Maribel and Emily. The three girls sat in a row with their shoulders touching—two Amish and one English.

As we got out of the car, I said, "Let me do the talking."

Cass put a hand to her chest in mock offense. "What? You don't trust me to speak?"

"Not in this situation. Sarcasm isn't going to work with these girls."

"There is always room for sarcasm."

Emily jumped off the swing, which sent the two remaining girls flying backward. The Amish girl ran down the steps of the porch, her black sneakers making a squeaking sound as she moved. "Is everything okay?

Is Nutmeg all right? Is he safe? My brother doesn't know that you have him, does he?"

"Nutmeg is fine. He seems to like it at my grandparents' shop and has made himself right at home."

She gave a huge sigh of relief. "I was just so worried when I saw you. I told Abel that I gave the cat away, but I don't think he would like it if he knew I gave Nutmeg to you."

"Why?" Cass asked.

Emily stared at the tops of her shoes. "Because he doesn't want to hear about anything that makes me happy. It is my punishment."

"Punishment for what?" I asked.

Instead of answering, she asked, "If it's not about Nutmeg, why are you here?"

"They are here about me." A soft voice floated down from the porch.

I hadn't even noticed that Mira had stood up. She did it quietly and gracefully, the opposite from how Emily had moved.

I nodded. "We were looking for Mira."

Maribel came to stand at Mira's side and grasped her hand in a show of support.

"I'm not going back." Mira held her chin up high and spoke with certainty. "The wedding is canceled. I'm not going to change my mind."

"We aren't asking you to change your mind," I said. "I'm actually glad that wedding is off."

Mira's mouth fell open. "You are?"

I nodded. "It was clear to me that you weren't happy."

Tears pooled in her eyes. "I wasn't. I'm still not, but I might be in the future. If you don't want to take me back, why did you come here?" Mira asked, barely above a whisper.

"We heard that you had gone missing, and we were worried about you."

"Why?" Mira asked. "I don't know you."

Emily ran to her friend. "Mira, Bailey is just trying to be nice. Remember, she took Nutmeg when I needed to find him a home. She's trying to help."

"You see the *gut* in everyone, Emily. That's what gets you into trouble most often," Maribel said.

Emily folded her hands in front of her apron and looked down.

"Don't fight," Mira pleaded. "I can't handle any more fighting, not today." She looked at me. "And I didn't go missing. Jace knew where I was. I told him where I was going before I left."

"Jace and his friends went off somewhere. No one is sure where they are either, but we were more worried about you," Cass said.

Mira frowned. "Who are you?"

I stepped forward. "This is my friend Cass."

"I met her and Bailey at the grocery store yesterday," Emily said, seemingly recovered from Maribel's dig at her.

"Cass helped me with wedding desserts last night," I said. "She's a chocolatier like I am."

Mira winced. "I'm sorry you had to make all of those desserts for nothing. I really am."

"It wasn't for nothing," I said. "My grandparents can reopen their shop tomorrow, and we can sell the chocolates there."

She nodded. "I'm glad. I'm glad something good might come out of this mess."

"Why did you agree to marry Jace in the first place?"

Tears gathered in her large brown eyes. "It was what my mother wanted. Tyson, Jace's father, was the wealthiest man in the county. My family is one of the oldest and best connected. She thought it was a good match. It made sense—everyone agreed on that. We had been put on this path since we were children. My mother orchestrated it so that we were always together. I didn't know anything else. I never considered any other possibility."

"Sounds like an arranged marriage," Cass whispered in my ear. "Are you sure she's not Amish too?"

I didn't bother to tell Cass that the Amish don't arrange marriages. I'd share that fact with her later, at a more opportune time. "But if you didn't love him . . ." I trailed off.

"I did love him, at least to start. Jace and I started dating in high school and continued through college. We graduated in May. It seemed that marriage was the logical next step, but by the time we became engaged, I knew his true nature. He was as greedy and self-serving as his father. I knew that and accepted his proposal anyway, because marrying Jace would be a way to get away from my mother. That must sound terrible to you."

"We've met your mother, so not really," Cass said.

I shot her a look, which she of course ignored. If she had been closer I would have stepped on her foot, but she knew to keep a distance now.

"I know this situation is as much my fault as it is Jace's and my mother's. I let this go too far, and now it's out of hand. I would have gone forward with the wedding if Tyson hadn't died. It was his death that convinced me I had to call it off. For all his success and wealth, he was a very unhappy man, and he died an unhappy man. I could see the same for my future. Before I die, I want to at least say I knew some happiness. Even so, I might never have left the wedding party if it hadn't been for Emily and Maribel's support."

Maribel squeezed her friend's hand.

A black Hummer roared up the road, pulled into the Eshes' driveway, and stopped just inches from the bumper of my rental. Jace tumbled out of the passenger side with an open beer bottle held loosely in his hand. He stumbled forward.

"Oh no," Mira whispered.

The two Amish young women flanked her on either side. I didn't know what two Amish girls could do to stand up to a very drunk Jace Colton, but if I had anything to say about it, Jace wasn't getting close enough to them to find out.

Another man close to Jace's age got out of the driver's side, and I was relieved to see that he was sober. At least Jace hadn't been behind the wheel. That was something to be thankful for.

"Mira," Jace slurred as he held up his bottle. "What are you still doing here? Everyone is waiting for us. It's time to get hitched."

Cass wrinkled her nose and whispered to me, "I'd say being a runaway bride was the right choice."

"Definitely," I whispered back.

He took two halting steps forward. "We have to get married, don't we? That was the master plan our parents thought up. God bless them." He spat.

"Really good thing she didn't marry him," Cass hissed.

I nodded. "Jace, I think you should go home and sober up. Your friend can take you back."

His friend kept a distance and made no move to help.

"Brent isn't going to take me home until I say so." He

glanced over his shoulder. "Will you, Brent. Just like my father's pawns, you will do whatever I say, because now that my father is dead, I'm the richest man in the county, and everyone wants a piece."

Brent clenched his jaw. I doubted he would be as obedient as Jace expected him to be.

I tried again. "Jace, Mira has made her decision. You should go home and go to bed. You are going to feel awful in the morning."

He took a swig of his beer. "Go home to an empty house because both of my parents are dead? No, thank you, not interested in going there."

"I know you must be upset by your father's death," I said with as much sympathy as I could muster. "I know you must miss him."

"Miss him?" He barked a laugh. "I hated his guts. He's the reason my mother is dead."

"And a new prime suspect presents himself on a silver platter," Cass whispered in my ear.

"Jace," Mira said in her soft voice. "I'm so sorry if I hurt you."

He glared at her. "You're not sorry. You're as bad as everyone else. You're no better than my father."

Mira jerked back as if he had slapped her across the face with the back of his hand. Her friends closed ranks around her, physically shielding her from his view.

"You should take her in the house," Cass advised the other girls.

They didn't have to be told twice, and they ushered Mira into the farmhouse.

"Hey!" Jace cried as the front door slammed closed after them. "You can't leave me!" He lunged forward.

"Stop!" I stood in front of Jace and held my hand out in the universal sign for stop.

He raised his fist and shook it at me. "Get out of my way, or I will make you move."

"Jace, come on, man. You can't hit a woman," Brent said.

Jace glared at his friend and then bent at the waist and threw up. I jumped back just in time to miss being hit.

"Oh gross," Cass cried.

I couldn't agree more.

Chapter 36

Brent's nose wrinkled in disgust. "Dude, don't puke on your shoes if you think you're getting back in the car."

"It's my car," Jace muttered between heaves. "I can puke in there if I want."

Cass covered her mouth.

I held my finger out to her. "Don't get sick, because if you get sick, I'll get sick."

She turned her back to Jace, pinched her nose, and breathed through her mouth. "I'm trying."

When Jace was done, he stumbled a few feet away and plopped down on the grass as if he didn't have an ounce of energy left. I knew he didn't have an ounce of lunch.

Brent made a gag face. "When Jace asked me to be his best man, I didn't know it would go down like this."

"People seldom do," Cass said.

I was relieved to hear her making jokes again. It reduced the likelihood that she would throw up, which, in turn, reduced my own chances.

Across the yard, Jace groaned and flopped over onto his side like a fish pulled from the sea.

Cass tilted her head in his direction. "He's either asleep or dead."

"Let's go with asleep, okay?" I said.

Cass nodded. "And at least he fell over on his side, so he won't swallow his tongue."

Brent made a face. I was right there with him. "We know about Tyson's plan to make Harvest into some type of Amish theme park, and we know that Jace expected it to all be his someday. Sounds like a great motive for murder to me," Cass said.

Jace struggled to a sitting position. He swayed a little bit but seemed to be holding his own. "I may have wanted to, but I didn't kill my father."

"Who do you suspect killed him? You must have some suspicions." Cass asked.

Brent glared at her. "Why would we tell you anything?"

"Because I'm being framed for Tyson's murder, and I would like to know by whom. One of you might be able to tell me that," I replied.

"I don't know who killed him." Jace pressed a hand against his forehead. "Don't know and don't care."

"Okay," I said. "Then let me ask you this. How did your father buy up all those properties on Main Street? It seems clear to me the Amish didn't want to sell to him."

"My father can talk anyone into anything. Almost anyone," he slurred.

"How did your father convince these people to sell if they didn't want to? What was his trick?" I pressed.

He snorted. "What do you think it was? Blackmail and threats. He was a master at both of those. The Amish have as many skeletons in their closets as the rest of us do. Maybe more, because they are ashamed of more things, stupid things."

"What kinds of skeletons?" I asked.

"Don't know."

"But your father kept those secrets in his office, didn't he? And the day he died you asked someone at his office to destroy the documents." I eyed Brent. "Maybe he even asked you."

Brent's face turned bright red, and I realized that I had guessed right.

"How?" He blinked at me, seeming to come out of his alcohol-induced fog.

"How did I know?" I shrugged.

He nodded.

"I have my sources."

Cass made a sound beside me, but I refused to look at her. Instead, I zeroed in on Brent. "You were the one who destroyed the blackmail documents, weren't you? Don't you know you could go to prison for destroying evidence?"

"I was just doing my job," Brent said, as if that made it all okay.

"Yes," Jace argued. "Brent works for my father's company. He had to do what I said, because the moment my father died, I became the owner and boss of the company."

Brent's brow furrowed together, and I wondered how much longer he would be able to stand working for his "friend."

I frowned. "Did you look at any of the files?"

Brent shook his head. "I didn't want to know what they said. I just shredded them, and took the shredded sheets to the dump before the police showed up."

That was a shame. If Brent had looked at the documents before he had destroyed them, and he had been willing to share the information with me, we might have gotten a new lead. My face fell. I had been so close to getting somewhere with this case, and I felt like I was back on square one.

I turned my attention to Jace. "Why did you ask Brent to do it?"

He still sat in the same position in the middle of the grass. His legs were spread-eagle out in front of him like a Raggedy Andy doll. "Because I still wanted to go through with the plan, and I didn't want the police to find the information and spook the Amish out of selling their property to me."

"All those documents could have given us a long list of suspects. You might have destroyed the police's only chance at solving your father's murder."

He snorted. "They're Amish. Amish don't kill people."

I wasn't so sure about that. "From what I've heard, your precaution backfired. All the Amish who were going to sell to your father aren't interested in doing business with you."

He narrowed his eyes. "Maybe not, but I will find something even greater—a bigger, more impressive project. I'll prove to my father that I can run this business. I don't need his help. I don't need anyone's help."

"And your father didn't trust you with his business. That must have been upsetting," I said.

"He didn't," he snapped. "He thought I didn't care. I do. I do care, but not everything in life is about work. My father would deny it, but he had a lot in common with the Amish when it came to his crazy work ethic. He was just like them in that way. What's so wrong with working hard and playing hard? For my father, it was all about work. All the time. I'd rather have fun." He blinked at me. "You know, I'm glad the wedding is off. I'm too young to get married."

"Did your father threaten the Amish himself?"

Jace doubled up in laughter but righted himself before he fell over "Never. Dad hired muscle to do that. He wouldn't get his hands dirty. That wasn't his way."

My pulse quickened. "Who did he hire?"

He held up his hands. "Don't know. He never told me. He didn't trust me. He was going to write me out of the will and the business. Wouldn't he be mad to know that I have it all now? Whoever killed him did me a favor. If it was you, I'd like to shake your hand." He held out his hand. "Had he lived, I would have nothing. Now, I have it all."

I recoiled from him. "So you don't know any of the secrets your father gathered?"

He shook his finger at me. "Oh, I know some of them." He pointed at the house. "I know Emily Esh was sent away to live with an English family in Indiana because she was pregnant. I know that Maribel's grandmother lied on her income taxes about how much money she made at the cheese shop, so she would have to pay less to the government."

Cass's mouth fell open. I knew I must have the same expression on my own face.

Jace, who was still sitting in the grass, shook his finger at me again like I was a misbehaving child. "See, the Amish aren't perfect, not even close, but do I think they killed my father? The answer is no." He flopped over on his side for a second time and closed his eyes.

"Aww, man," Brent muttered.

"I think it's time for Romeo to head home," Cass said.

I couldn't agree more. I doubted I would get any more information out of him now that he'd passed out for a second time.

"Brent, we'll help you get him back into the car," I said.

Cass wrinkled her nose. "We will?"

I shot her a look. "Yes, we will."

She groaned but joined us at Jace's side. With some effort, we lifted to him to his feet. He was all dead weight.

"Ugh," Cass cried. "His breath is terrible."

I had to agree and covered my mouth with my sleeve.

Brent opened the car door.

"Could they make these seats any higher?" Cass complained. "This is not an ideal car for loading a drunk guy into."

I silently agreed.

Finally, we settled Jace into the passenger seat. His head flopped back onto the headrest.

"Where are you going to take him?" I asked.

Brent sighed. "I guess I'll take him to my apartment until he's slept it off."

"That's a good best man," Cass praised.

Brent scowled, not taking it as a compliment. I don't think Cass had meant it to be one anyway.

Jace's eyes popped open. "I meant it when I said my father was responsible for my mother's death."

"How?" I asked, out of range of his terrible breath.

"He hit her one too many times, and she died in a car accident when she was trying to get away. So, you see, her death was his fault. Because of it, I was stuck with him for the rest of my life, until someone did me a favor and killed him."

I couldn't help but think of how similar Jace's story was to Aiden's, but Aiden's story had a happy ending. Jace's most certainly did not.

"Do you know what she said?" Jace asked us. "Do you know what she said to me right before she left?"

"No," I whispered.

"She said I would better off with my father because he had the money to give me the life and education to succeed. She could have taken me with her, but she didn't, because she thought it was more important that I have money than a loving parent."

"That's rough," Cass said.

That was an understatement.

"I was only nine. Nine." He glared at me as if I was in some way responsible.

"I'm so sorry." It was all I could say. It was all anyone could say.

He dropped his eyes to the grass. "I don't blame her, you know. I only wish she had taken me with her so that I would have died too. That would have been better," he said in a strangled voice, before his head fell back onto the headrest a second time and he closed his eyes. "I have his money now. I earned it. Eileen and I both agreed on that. It was only Mira who wasn't sure. If she really loved me, she would have believed that I deserved everything too."

Eileen?

Brent started to close the passenger side door, and I stopped him. "Eileen knew that your father was about to disown you."

He lifted his eyelids and stared at me with glassy

eyes. "She knew before I did. She was the one who told me and said we had to do something."

"Like kill him?" Cass cried.

His head lolled to the side. "I didn't kill him."

Brent shut the passenger side door and walked around the SUV.

Cass and I stepped back as the Hummer rolled away.

"He claims that he didn't kill his father, but he has a good motive, the best motive—money," Cass said.

I nodded. "And so does Eileen. You heard Mira. Eileen wanted this marriage to happen so that the two families could become one, and so that her daughter, and by extension, Eileen, would have access to Tyson's wealth."

"I'd say," Cass mused, "that she could become angry enough to stab someone given the right motivation."

I swallowed. "Exactly."

Chapter 37

"Now what?" Cass asked when we were safely back in the rental car and headed to Harvest.

"I don't know," I said honestly. "I just don't know. I should probably call Aiden and tell him what we've learned."

Cass's phone rang. "It's Jean Pierre. I had better take this."

I nodded and concentrated on the road.

"*Bon Jour,* Jean Pierre," she said.

Over the line I could hear him yelling at her in French. Cass held the phone away from her ear just as everyone did when Jean Pierre was on a rant. It was the only way to salvage your hearing.

"All right," she interrupted him. "I'll head home today. Not to worry . . ." She glanced at me with raised brows. "Umm . . . Bailey has to stay here another day, but I'm sure she will be back Monday in time for the head chocolatier announcement. . . . I know she will be there. . . . Oh, you want to talk to her? Let me check if she can talk."

I widened my eyes and shook my head.

"Jean Pierre," Cass said into the phone. "I'm sorry. She's busy right now . . . she's in the bathroom. Ate too much Amish food, I'm afraid. It didn't agree with her delicate system."

I groaned.

Cass ended the call. "You owe me big time for that too."

I sighed. "I know, but thank you."

"I guess it's to the airport for me. Jean Pierre has a big client with a last-minute party. He needs at least one of his chocolatiers back fast."

"What about Caden?" I asked.

"Apparently, Caden's buckling under the pressure." She didn't even bother to keep her enjoyment over this announcement out of her voice. "He's out of the running as head chocolatier because of this. It's going to be you, my friend."

I grimaced. Maybe she was right, if I was ever able to leave Harvest. I should be the one at the chocolate shop dealing with this, not Jean Pierre, not Cass. Not for the first time that weekend, I could feel the position of head chocolatier slipping through my fingers, but I refused to lose faith in the fact that I still had a chance

Before I could take Cass to the airport, we had to go back to Swissmen Sweets for Cass to gather her things. I decided that I would call Aiden from the shop, but we had to make the stop quick. There wasn't much time to get her to the private airport in time for her flight. Jean Pierre had already notified the pilot as to when he wanted Cass back in the city.

By the time we got back to Harvest, Main Street was

congested with more vendors and Amish buggies. A caterer's van sat right in front of my grandparents' shop. Again, I parked the rental on the side street. Cass and I got out of the car and walked around the corner.

Cass stared at the Amish men setting up tall round tables around the gazebo for the wedding cocktail hour. "I thought the wedding was off."

"It is," I said.

She cocked her head. "Does it look off to you?"

"Not really," I admitted. Further up the road, two doors down from the pretzel shop, I saw Eileen jaywalk across Main Street in front of an Amish wagon. She didn't even pause to wave her thanks when the buggy stopped to let her pass. "There's Eileen."

"Where's she going?" Cass asked.

I didn't bother to reply. I ran up the sidewalk after the mother of the bride just in time to see her disappear into a shop half the size of the pretzel shop. The purple awning read THE POTTER'S SHED in yellow script. I pulled up short. "This must be Mira's shop."

Cass caught up with me. "What's with all the running? Remember, I can't run in these shoes."

I glanced at her feet and her black boots with the pointy toes and three-inch heels. "You should have worn more practical shoes."

"Fashion first, my dear." She pointed to the door of the potter's shop. "This is Mira's?"

"When I met her at the tasting, she told me she was a potter and her shop was on Main Street. This must be it."

"Did her mother go in there?"

I nodded.

"Then, what are we waiting for?" She put her hand on the doorknob.

"The door might be lo—"

Before I could tell her that the door might be locked, she pulled it open. "Not locked." She grinned and went inside. I followed her.

The shop was tiny and cramped. Shelves filled with pottery for sale crowded the space. There was a table to one side with a laptop computer on it, but the focal point of the room was the back corner, where a potter's wheel stood. The shelves behind the wheel held all the accoutrements that a potter would need. Plastic bowls, sponges, wires, modeling tools, brushes, and other instruments I didn't recognize.

Eileen stood beside the potter's wheel and scowled. "Where is she?"

"Where's who?" I asked.

"My daughter? Who else? The bride who is supposed to be getting married today. The child I did everything for!" She clenched her fists at her sides. "I thought she might be here, but she's not. That ungrateful girl is hiding from me."

"I think Mira's idea to hide is a good one," Cass whispered.

"Shhh," I hissed back.

Eileen glared at us. "Do you know where she is?"

"She was at Emily's farm," Cass said.

I inwardly groaned. Cass shouldn't have shared that information with Eileen.

"She might have been, but she's not now. I was just there." She folded her arms. "What are you doing here?"

"We are looking for Mira too," I said.

She picked up one of the sculpting knives from her daughter's wheel and stabbed it into the wooden shelving. "Your friend just said she was at the Esh farm. Why would you look for her here?"

"Sheesh," Cass gasped, so that I was only one who could hear. "She needs meds."

"Don't lie to me like my daughter has for all these years," Eileen said. "She promised me she would marry Jace, and then we would have everything we needed because of his father's wealth. She has no idea what I had to do to make sure we wouldn't lose that."

"What did you have do, Eileen? Kill Tyson?" I asked.

She picked up one of the unfinished pieces, a large bowl, and threw it against the wall. "Where is she?" she cried.

Cass and I yelped in unison.

"She definitely has enough anger to kill someone," Cass said.

I agreed.

The front door to the Potter's Shed opened, and Aiden stepped inside with his gun drawn. "Eileen Hutton?"

"What?" she snapped.

"You're under arrest for the murder of Tyson Colton. Everything you say . . ." He continued to recite the Miranda warning to her as he walked across the room and cuffed her hands behind her back. She didn't fight him. Cass and I looked on openmouthed.

"I didn't kill anyone!" Eileen yelled.

Aiden held onto her arm. "We found the threatening emails you sent him. You threatened to kill him."

"Maybe I did, but I didn't kill him. I was just protecting my daughter."

Aiden walked her toward the door. "Eileen, you said that you would stab him in the heart if he wrote Jace out of the will. That's difficult to ignore."

Another deputy, one I didn't know, waited at the door and escorted her out of the shop. Aiden turned to me. "What are you doing here?" His eyes narrowed.

"I—we saw Eileen come inside here and—"

"And what? You wanted to see if you could get the two of you killed? The woman stabbed a man in the chest." He threw up his hands. "How could you be so stupid?"

"What proof do you have other than the emails?" Cass asked.

Aiden glanced at her. "Abel Esh came to the station this morning and told us that he saw Eileen enter Swissmen Sweets through the back door with Tyson around ten that night."

"Why didn't he come forward before?" Cass asked.

"He didn't want to become involved. Most Amish don't want anything to do with the police." He returned his gaze to me. "But he came forward because he heard that glass from a broken lamp was found behind the candy shop. He knew it would eventually be traced back to him. He broke it when he was trying to look inside the candy shop's window to see what Tyson and Eileen were doing in there. He knew it wouldn't look good because he had a motive for the murder."

The broken kerosene lamp had been Abel's. "His motive was to protect his youngest sister Emily, who had a baby out of wedlock, and thereby protect his family's reputation in the district," I said.

He nodded and didn't even ask how I knew all of that. Cass looked up from her cell phone screen. "I hate to break this up, but I have to go. If we don't leave now, I'm going to miss my flight. If I do, Jean Pierre will have a hissy fit."

Aiden nodded. "Go. This is finally over."

I met his eyes one last time before I left The Potter's Shed.

Chapter 38

"Daadi! Maami!" I called when Cass and I entered Swissmen Sweets a few minutes later. Nutmeg was the only one who answered.

"What about the name Dr. Pepper?" Cass asked.

I rolled my eyes and spotted a note on the glass counter. I picked it up and recognized my grandmother's handwriting immediately.

*We're at the church helping with the wedding.
We'll see you soon. We hope you and Cass are
having a nice visit.*

"I wish you had the chance to say good-bye to them," I said.

She nodded. "Me too, but there's no time if I want to make the flight. Please tell your grandparents good-bye for me."

I promised that I would.

"I have a feeling I'll be back here anyway," Cass said.

I smiled. "Me too."

* * *

On the drive to the airport, Cass and I were quiet, both lost in our thoughts. Mine were preoccupied with the reality that Eileen was the killer. I knew I hadn't liked her, but I hadn't suspected her until it was almost too late. It was hard to believe it was really all over.

Cass's cell phone dinged, and she removed it from her pocket. At the same time, my cell phone—which lay on the dash—rang. I immediately knew who it was by the ringtone. I made a move to grab it, but Cass was faster.

"You shouldn't answer the phone while driving," Cass said, "especially out here. You might hit a buggy or something."

"Cass, don't—"

But I was too late. The phone was already at her ear. "Hello? Eric? What are you doing calling Bailey? It's Cass Calbera. Who do you think it is? Are you calling about the selection committee?"

I felt Cass watching me. My hand tightened around the steering wheel. I swallowed. "Tell him that I'll call him back later. Now isn't a good time."

Still watching me, Cass repeated my message to Eric.

"Bailey!" I heard Eric yell through the phone. "What the hell is going on over there? I heard from Jean Pierre that you are involved in some kind of murder, and now there is this article in the *New York Star* with your picture. We agreed to keep this quiet!"

I held out my hand to Cass, and she placed the phone into it without a word. I put the phone to my ear. "Eric, this isn't a good time."

Out of the corner of my eye, I saw Cass scroll through

something on her phone. She grew very still as she read whatever was on the screen. A sinking feel fell over me.

"Not a good time?" Eric bellowed in my ear. "Well, excuse me. You know I made space in my busy schedule to call and find out what's going on, and you say this isn't a good time?"

I cringed, knowing that Cass could hear every word of this conversation. She was listening to my side of the call even if she pretended to focus on her phone's screen.

"How did your photograph end up in the *New York Star*? Answer me that," Eric ordered.

My gut instinct had been right about the reporter outside of the cheese shop. He had been there because of my relationship with Eric. How I wished that I had been wrong just this once.

"You need to tell me what's going on! Right now!" Eric shouted.

"I don't have to tell you anything," I snapped.

"Have you even thought for a minute how this could impact me?" His voice was sharp.

"Impact you? What are you talking about? I'm the one who has no hope of being the head chocolatier now."

"Don't be dense, Bailey. Our relationship is all over the Internet. This will ruin the reality show. The angle the producers are going for is the famous bachelor pastry chef in New York. A girlfriend will ruin my image."

My hands were shaking so much, I had to pull the car over to the side of the road and shift it into park. When we came to a complete stop, Cass held her phone out to me without a word. A *New York Star* article about Eric and me was on the screen. The headline read, Sharp Finds A New Love When Secret Lover Charged with Murder.

I grabbed the phone from Cass's hand and read the first line of the gossip article. "While his secret girl-friend, chocolatier Bailey King, was a prime murder suspect in Ohio's Amish Country, pastry chef Eric Sharp stepped out with fashion model Vivian Cone." I scrolled down and saw a picture of Eric kissing Vivian, and it wasn't a peck on the cheek either.

Through gritted teeth, I asked, "Who is Vivian Cone? Does she not hurt your image?"

He stopped yelling.

"What? You don't have an answer for that?" I asked.

"I can explain."

I closed my eyes for a moment. "There's nothing to explain, Eric. It's over. All of it. The lies. The relation-ship. Everything." I ended the call and threw the phone into the backseat of the car. Almost immediately, the phone began to ring again.

"Don't answer it," I told Cass.

"I couldn't answer it if I tried. You threw it way back there. I'm surprised it didn't go through the back window." Her voice was quiet.

I bit my lip and felt tears gather at the corners of my eyes. I had known that I was going to end things with Eric after my first conversation with him while I was in Ohio, but knowing it and actually doing it were two very different things. I hadn't expected it to hurt so much. I started the car again and eased it onto the street. We were less than a mile from the airport now. We'd be able to see it when we came around the next turn.

"Bai, how long have you been dating Eric Sharp?" Cass asked.

I kept blinking. "A few months."

"Just a few months?"

I didn't reply.

When I didn't say anything, she said, "Fine. I'll just ask Eric when I get back to New York. I have a feeling he'll tell me."

I tightened my hold on the steering wheel. "Don't talk to Eric about it."

The private airport came into sight, and I could see Jean Pierre's plane on the tarmac. I pulled the rental car to the guardhouse, and the man inside came out. Cass handed me her ticket to give to him.

He looked over her paperwork and checked her ID. "Have a nice flight," he said, and opened the gate in the eleven-foot-high chain link fence that surrounded the airport.

"If you won't tell me, I don't have much choice, do I?" Cass said quietly as we drove through the gate.

I shifted the car into park twenty or so yards away from the plane. "Fine. Eric and I were dating. Secretly."

"For how long?" Her voice had the quiet tone to it again.

"Almost a year."

"Almost a year! And this is the first I'm hearing about it?"

I felt tears gather in my eyes again, but I didn't know if they were over breaking up with Eric or fighting with Cass. Most likely, it was a combination of both.

"Why didn't you tell me?" she asked.

"I didn't tell anyone. Neither did Eric."

"I'm not *anyone*. I'm your best friend. As your best friend, I have a right to know things you wouldn't tell anyone else."

"Cass, he's on the selection committee for the head chocolatier. You know how it would look." It sounded like a practical reason to keep the secret from her, but I knew it was not.

"And you think I would betray you and tell the world about it. Is that how little you trust me?" She was hurt.

"You would've talked me out of seeing him." My answer was barely above a whisper.

She threw up her hands. "Of course, I would have tried to talk you out of it! Eric Sharp is the most egotistical man in Manhattan, and that's saying something, isn't it?"

I rubbed my forehead. I could feel a headache forming behind my eyes. The plane's engine was so loud I couldn't hear myself think.

Cass jumped out of the car before I could stop her. The pilot waved to her, came over, and removed her suitcase and the bags of cheese from the trunk as I slowly got out of the car. I felt like I was moving under water.

Cass adjusted her purse on her shoulder.

"Cass," I began.

"I think it's good that you're here in Amish Country, Bailey King. You need to figure out what you want, what career you want, what man you want—I saw you watching the deputy—and—" Her voice caught. "What best friend you want, because if you can't tell me that your grandparents are Amish or who you're dating, I'm not sure it's me."

"That's not true. I'm sorry I didn't tell you. I should have trusted you." A tear rolled down my cheek.

"Yeah, you should have." With that she climbed the steps into the plane.

I stepped back and watched Jean Pierre's jet take off with my best friend inside, or maybe my former best friend was a more accurate description. I kept my eye on the plane until it disappeared out of sight. I had a sinking feeling that I'd ruined more than one relationship that day, and the person in that airplane was the greatest loss.

Chapter 39

I drove out of the airport after the plane took off. When I passed the guard house and turned onto the road, I took no care to watch my speed. I wanted to return to Swissmen Sweets and see my grandparents, and have a good cry alone in the guest room. After that, I would get up and try to put my life back in order.

Blue and red flashing lights reflected in my rearview mirror, and I said a word that my grandparents wouldn't be happy with. I pulled the car over to the side of the road. My cry would have to wait.

I watched through the rearview mirror as Deputy Carpenter climbed out of his cruiser. I groaned. It would have to be Carpenter, wouldn't it?

I powered down my window.

"Miss King, what are you doing speeding down the road like your tail is on fire?" He smiled and rubbed his bald head.

"I know I was speeding. I'm sorry. I'll take the ticket and go."

He wasn't going to let me off that easily. "Where were you headed so fast?"

"I wanted to get back to my grandparents."

A slow smile spread across his face. "License and registration."

I reached for my purse and removed the documents from my wallet. As I handed them to him, I noticed the shiny eagle pin that I'd seen the first day I had met him was no longer on his breast pocket. There was an impression on the fabric where it had once been. "What happened to your eagle?"

He scowled. "My what?"

"Your eagle. You were wearing an eagle pin that afternoon when I first saw you at my grandparents' candy shop."

He frowned and peered down at his uniform. His scowl deepened. "I don't think you are in any position to be asking questions, Miss King." He held up my license. "This will be just a minute. I need to give you a thorough checkout."

I didn't argue, although I knew he had already given me a thorough checkout because of Tyson's murder.

"This will just take a minute." He strolled back to his cruiser without another word.

While I waited for Carpenter to return, I unbuckled my seatbelt and reached for my phone in the backseat. Cass had been right. I'd thrown it way back there. Finally, I wrapped my fingers around it and settled back into my seat. I had ten text messages and three voicemails. All were from Eric. None were from Cass. I dropped the phone on the passenger seat.

Carpenter came back to the car and handed me my license and registration through the open window.

"Find anything interesting on your computer about me?" I mentally kicked myself for allowing my smart mouth to get the better of me.

"I found plenty," he said. He handed me a ticket.

I blinked. The cost was two hundred dollars. I hadn't been going that fast, but I knew better than to argue.

He leaned on my car and peered inside. "I heard Eileen Hutton got arrested because of you."

"I didn't have anything to do with it."

"According to another deputy, you were there."

"Aiden?" I asked.

He smiled. "Not Deputy Brody. I didn't know you two were on a first name basis."

He must have heard it from the other deputy who had been there. His radio crackled, and he tipped the edge of his patrol hat at me. "Have a good day, Miss King. I'll be seeing you."

In the rearview mirror, I watched as he strolled back to his patrol car and drove away.

I was pulling out onto the road, too, when my cell phone rang. I grabbed it from the passenger seat. "Eric, this isn't a good time. Can we talk about this later?"

"Bailey, it's Aiden. I'm calling from the hospital." His voice was tight.

"The hospital? What happened? Is my grandfather okay?"

There was a pause. "He collapsed again helping out at the church and was brought here by ambulance."

My hands felt suddenly so cold, I dropped the phone onto the floor of the car. I jerked the steering wheel sharply to the right to get off of the road, and the phone slid under the passenger seat. I swore. "Aiden, hold on, I dropped the phone. Stay on the line."

I heard a muffled reply. I shifted the car into park and turned on my hazard lights before unbuckling and reaching under the seat for the phone. It was just out of my grasp so I lay across the seat, and the gearshift dug into my ribs. Finally, I came up with the phone. Still half lying across the front two seats, I put it to it my ear. "Aiden, are you still there?"

"I'm still here. Are you all right? Did you get into an accident?"

"No, I'm fine."

"You shouldn't be driving while you are on the phone. What happened?" His voice was tense.

"Calm down," I said. "I dropped the phone and it slipped under the seat. Before you ask, I pulled to the side of the road and parked the car before I looked for it. Now, please tell me what is going on with my grand-father."

"He collapsed again. It was at the church. He insisted on helping clean up after the wedding was canceled." He paused. "He fell down the front steps."

"He fell down the steps?" My voice trembled and I could feel the blood drain from my face. "How is he?"

"He's alive. The doctors say that his foot should be all right, but it's his weak heart they worry about. Your grandmother needs you. You have to come."

"Can you give me that address?" I put the phone on speaker and typed the address into the phone's GPS app while he rattled it off. "I'll be there in thirty minutes."

"All right. Be careful, but hurry. You're going to want to hurry." There was such urgency in his voice, I felt sick to my stomach.

Despite the speeding ticket in my purse, I pressed the gas pedal to the floor.

Chapter 40

When I reached the hospital, I was surprised to find Juliet—without Jethro—standing by the emergency room doors. I guessed the hospital was the one place in the county where Jethro wasn't welcome.

Juliet clasped both of my hands in hers. "Thank heavens you made it just in time."

"In time for what?" My voice trembled.

She took me by the hand and led me through the automatic glass doors. She waved at the nurse at the desk. "This is his granddaughter."

The woman nodded as if that meant something to her. Juliet ushered me into an elevator.

"Juliet, what's happening?" I asked.

She only shook her head, and a tear leaked out of the corner of her eye. I knew what was happening, and I felt lightheaded. The floors ticked by with painful slowness.

Finally, the doors opened on the fifth floor. Juliet took my hand and dragged me down the hall. I stared at the beige tiled floor that matched the beige walls. The only color in the place was on the crash carts lining the wall.

I spotted Aiden standing outside the last room on the hallway. His sheriff's department ball cap was folded in his hands.

"Aiden," Juliet called.

He looked up, and I saw such raw pain in his eyes, I lost my breath. "You made it just in time."

Again, I wanted to ask what I'd made it in time for, but I knew.

"Go in," he whispered. "You're the one who should be in there."

I peeked into the hospital room. My grandmother, looking so small, sat beside my grandfather's bed. She held my grandfather's hand in hers, and her head was bent as if in prayer. I tried to stop them, but my eyes traveled to my grandfather's face. His breaths were halting. There were great pauses in between each gasp.

Aiden squeezed my hand and didn't let go.

I don't know how long I stood there in the doorway holding the deputy's hand, but, finally, I pulled my hand away and stepped into the room. "*Maami*?"

My grandmother turned to me, and there were tears in her bright blue eyes.

"I'm so sorry, *Maami*."

She smiled through her tears. "Come here, child. He waited for you." She stood up and offered me the chair. "Take his hand."

Wordlessly, I did as I was told.

Juliet stepped into the room and enveloped my grandmother in a hug. I watched my grandfather's chest go up and down. Each time, I counted the seconds between his labored breaths; they were becoming further and further apart. I leaned close to his ear. "I'll take care of *Maami*. I'll take care of everything. You don't have to worry. I love you."

He took another breath that filled his whole chest, and then nothing. I counted, but the next breath never came.

A nurse entered the room then, and shook her head.

I stared at my grandfather's face. It was without animation. It was peaceful, but empty. He wasn't there any longer.

"I'm sorry, Miss King, he's gone," the nurse said. Her voice had an echolike quality as if she were talking to me through a long cylinder.

I stood up and marched out of the room. I fell to my knees in the middle of the hallway. This couldn't be happening. It was as if someone had reached into my chest and yanked my heart out from the root. Oddly, I wondered if anyone had felt like this when Tyson Colton was killed. In the two days I had spent investigating his death, I was certain the answer was no. As much as this hurt, I found that to be terribly sad.

"Bailey." Aiden stood over me and held out his hand. There were tears in his eyes. I took his hand and gripped it as if it was a lifeline. He pulled me to my feet.

His grip was gentle but firm, and there was a slight tremble in it.

"I should have been here," I said. "I should have been here with her this whole time."

He squeezed my hand, not letting it go. "It happened so fast. You couldn't have gotten here any quicker. He never woke up from his fall."

I pulled away and went back to the room, where I found *Maami,* her head bent in prayer. I went to her chair and knelt beside her, but I didn't pray. I doubted I would ever pray again. She stroked my hair while I cried, just as she used to do when I was a small child, and my heart broke.

"It was *Gotte's* time," she said. "*Gotte's gut* time."

I jerked away from her. "God's good time? How can *Daadi's* death be good?"

"That is the way," she said.

I stood up and marched to the corner of the room. "I can't believe it. I can't believe any good can come from any of this."

"*Gott* uses everything for the *gut* of those who love Him," she said.

"How can you love Him when he's taken your husband from you?" I ran a hand through my hair. "I'm sorry. *Maami,* can I take you home?"

My grandmother's blue eyes pooled with tears. "*Nee.* I want to stay a while longer."

I stared at my grandfather's body. I couldn't stay. He was gone. Holding his cold hand wouldn't bring him back. "I have to go."

"Do what you must, child."

I kissed her cheek and fled the room. In the hallway, I heard heavy steps behind me. "Bailey," Aiden said.

I didn't turn around. Instead I ran away from him.

Chapter 41

I unlocked the front door to Swissmen Sweets and stepped inside. Usually the smell of cocoa soothed me, but I didn't know if I could ever be soothed again. I still couldn't believe that *Daadi* was gone, and on the day the police released the candy shop's kitchen, the same day I lost my boyfriend and my best friend. If God cared for me at all, this would not have happened. At least he wouldn't have taken my grandfather so quickly. He could have given me a few more days at the very least. He could have let me say good-bye.

"Nutmeg!" I called for the cat.

"Meow!" The cry came from the kitchen. I followed his meows and stepped into the kitchen. The blood stain had been expertly removed from the tile. All the appliances and surfaces were sparkling clean. One of the huge mixers was turning a vat of hot caramel over and over. My grandfather must have started the caramel before he and *Maami* left for the church. It was so like him to set right to work so they could open the candy shop the next day. Using a wooden spoon, I scooped some of the hot caramel into a stainless steel bowl.

The least I could do was start the next day's candies. I would start with my grandfather's famous salted caramel fudge. Maybe I was more like my grandparents than I thought. Maybe I needed to always be working too.

"Meow!" Nutmeg called again.

"Where have you gotten to?" I asked the cat, who I could hear, but not see. Not for the first time, I wondered what would happen to the cat when I went back to New York. Would my grandmother keep him? My life in New York had no room for a cat, and that was assuming I still had a life in the city to go back to. By this point, I had surely forfeited the head chocolatier position to whomever else the committee thought was worthy. I'd disqualified myself the moment my relationship with Eric hit the *New York Star*. Jean Pierre must know of it by now.

I set the bowl of caramel on the counter and went in search of the cat. I found him tucked behind the other mixer, the one that was empty. The space wasn't much bigger than the width of a novel. He stuck one white paw out of the tiny cavity.

"How on earth did you get yourself wedged back in there? More importantly, how am I going to get you out?"

He poked his paw out again, and this time it was behind a golden eagle pin. My chest clenched. I had seen that pin before.

I reached for it and folded it in my hand. Nutmeg hissed at me.

I pulled my hand back. "Nutmeg. You've—"

Someone grabbed me by the back of the neck and jerked me to my feet.

Nutmeg wasn't hissing at me after all.

I thrashed about and dug my fingernails into the arm behind me. "Let me go!"

"I wouldn't do that if I were you," Deputy Carpenter whispered into my ear and wrapped his arm around my throat.

As soon as I had the eagle pin in my possession, it all fell into place. Carpenter was the one who'd killed Tyson. He had also been Tyson's muscle, the person who had threatened the Amish. He was the one the Amish were too afraid to speak out against. And why wouldn't they be afraid? He was a sheriff's deputy, and not only that, he was the sheriff's second in command. They had good reason to be afraid. I certainly was.

"Let me go!" I felt my throat closing as I said the words. I tried to jerk my body away from him.

He tightened his grip that much harder. "Don't make this worse than it has to be." He released my neck and grabbed my right arm, twisting it painfully behind my back. Air whooshed into my lungs. As much as my arm hurt, at least I could breathe. Breathing meant I was still alive.

"What's going on? I'll have you charged with police brutality," I croaked, trying to act as if I didn't know full well that he was the killer. "I'll file a report with the sheriff about this."

He snorted a laugh, and I felt his hot breath on my ear. "He won't care. You might not be Amish, but you are close enough for him not to care what becomes of you."

I shivered at having my suspicions confirmed that the sheriff considered the Amish in the county second-class citizens.

"Then I'll report you to Deputy Brody."

"Oh, pretty boy won't come and save you. He's at the hospital pandering to the Amish."

I lashed out at the deputy with my left hand and scratched his cheek with his pin.

He swore but held me fast. I tried to back kick, but he seemed to expect this, and easily avoided my boot.

"Don't move, or I will shoot you right here, so that your grandmother can come home and find your dead body. Wouldn't that be a shame after everything she's been through? Cruel even."

A shiver ran the full length of my body.

He pulled me away from the mixer. Nutmeg made a low-to-the-ground dash to another part of the kitchen. I willed him to hide.

"What are you going to do?" I asked hoarsely.

He threw me against the giant mixer, and the eagle pin flew from my hand and into the vat of caramel. Although small, it was the only weapon that I'd had. I was sorry to have lost it. I looked around the room for some kind of weapon I could use to defend myself.

He held up his gun. "Don't think about grabbing anything else." A thin line of blood trickled from his cheek where I had caught him with the sharp edge of the pin.

"What are you doing here?" My voice was shaky. I couldn't help it.

"That's up to you to decide, Miss King." He grinned. "I think you will make the right decision."

"I'm not one of the Amish shopkeepers you can bully into doing whatever you ask." I refused to allow my voice to shake.

"I know," he said bitterly. "That's what makes you dangerous. I knew when I pulled you over and you mentioned my missing pin, that I had no choice but to come back here and look for it. I knew I must have lost it here.

Your showing up just makes my life easier. Now, I can take care of you at the same time." He took a step toward me. "It's such a shame too. Everyone in town was so enamored with having someone from the big city visiting our little county. You threw it all away because you insisted on poking your nose in where it didn't belong." His smile widened. "Maybe if you had minded your own business, your grandfather would still be alive, because he wouldn't have had to deal with the stress of the murder investigation."

"You framed me for murder. I had to do something to change the sheriff's mind."

He snorted. "There was no hope of you ever changing the sheriff's mind."

"Why? Was he in on the scheme with you and Tyson?"

"No," the deputy snapped. "He wasn't part of it, but any fool can see that he doesn't care for the Amish."

"Why?"

His lip curled. "That's something you will have to discuss with him."

"I don't trust either of you."

He took another step toward me. "Another mistake."

"What's going to happen now?" I held the arm that he had twisted behind my back.

He removed another gun from the small of his back and held it lightly in the palm of his hand. "You're going to shoot me."

"Are you insane?" I took a step back.

"Hardly. I know exactly what is going to happen. You are going to shoot me. Not a death shot, of course, and then I will shoot you in self-defense. I'm a much better shot, so you will have to die, I'm afraid."

"I'm not going to shoot you," I said.

He held up the gun. "Don't you want the gun?"

I stared at it. I did want the gun for the protection it seemed to represent. For protection from this man I knew was determined to kill me. There would be nothing I could say or do to talk him out of it. "How do you know I won't kill you?"

"You won't," he said matter-of-factly.

I didn't move toward the gun.

"If you don't take the gun, I'll just shoot you dead where you stand. Is that what you want? Is that what you want for your grandmother?"

"How will you explain why you shot me, if I have no weapon on me and no way to defend myself," I snapped.

He shrugged. "I'll think of something, and the sheriff will believe me."

"Aiden won't, and neither will the crime scene investigators. It will be obvious that I wasn't trying to hurt you when I was killed."

He smiled. "You would like to think so, but I have been to enough crime scenes to know how to plant a seed of doubt in the techs' minds." He held the gun from the small of his back out to me, hilt first, and then he leveled his own gun at my head. "Take the gun, Bailey, or I will shoot you right now where you stand and worry about the cleanup later."

I grabbed the gun from his hand, and then stepped back.

He laughed and held his gun—the one that had been on his duty belt—in his hand. "I knew you would do that. You're a fighter. I knew that from the moment I met you. It makes you dangerous, but also predictable."

I held up the gun and wasn't the least bit surprised to see it quiver in my outstretched hand.

"Have you ever fired a gun before?" There was almost a teasing sound to his voice.

"It doesn't matter if I hit my mark, does it?" I said it with much more confidence than I felt.

He laughed. "Then go ahead and try."

I leveled the gun at him. I did want to shoot him. He'd killed a man, terrorized a community, and hurt my grandparents. But I couldn't do it. I lowered the gun. "This isn't how it's going to go. You'll have to think of another way. I won't shoot you. I can't." I dropped the gun to my side, and a breath I didn't even know I had been holding whooshed out of my body. I knew I'd made the right choice. It may not have been the wise one, but it was the right one.

He lunged at me, and I jumped to the side. Instead of firing the gun, I dropped it into the vat of caramel. There was no going back for the gun after that. He fell against the industrial mixer with a crash. He cursed. I didn't know if it was in pain or in frustration.

I ran around him while he pushed himself off the mixer.

He reached out to me and grabbed my sleeve, but I slipped out of his grasp.

Behind me, a shot rang out. I didn't stop to see or feel if I had been hit. I would worry about that later. I ran around the kitchen to put the prep island between Carpenter and me. I saw the back door as my escape. Carpenter followed me and now stood on the other side of the island, where I had left the bowl of caramel. Nutmeg jumped onto the counter next to the bowl between the two of us.

I reached out for the cat, because I certainly wasn't leaving him alone in the kitchen with Carpenter.

The cat moved away from me and as he did, he

knocked over the bowl. The caramel spilled on the floor as Carpenter roared and charged me. His feet hit the sticky mess, and he slid back and forth. He lost his footing, falling backward, and then cracked the back of his head on the counter as he went down.

A small pool of blood began to gather around his head.

I took a step toward him. Was he dead?

He groaned.

He was most definitely not dead. I didn't know how long he would be dazed. I kicked his gun out of his hand and sent it spinning across the floor. It had a thin coating of caramel on it before it hit the far wall. I didn't think Carpenter would ever be able to use it again. Not that I thought the law allowed men to have department-issued firearms in prison.

"Bailey!" Aiden called from the front of the shop.

"I'm in the kitchen!"

Aiden bounded through the kitchen door with his gun drawn. Two other deputies came in after him.

One of them swore. "Is that Carpenter? Is he dead?"

Carpenter groaned.

"Not dead," the second deputy said.

"Call EMS," Aiden ordered.

"Already on it," the first deputy said with his radio up to his ear.

Aiden holstered his gun. "Bailey, are you all right?"

"I'm fine." I glanced down at Carpenter. "How did you know that I needed help?"

A small figure stood in the kitchen doorway as if she was afraid to take one step more into the room.

I blinked. "Mira?"

As she entered the kitchen, she held her hands together so tightly they turned white. "When I heard what happened to your grandfather, I knew I had to tell the truth. I called Deputy Brody to tell him about Tyson and Deputy Carpenter's threats. I knew the deputy was in on the scheme because I overheard them once at Tyson's office. I didn't tell you before because Tyson said if I kept quiet, he would protect Emily and Maribel's secrets." Tears gathered in her eyes. "I knew there was no reason to remain silent any longer. Jace called me told me he told you."

"How did you know to come here?"

Aiden looked up from the other deputy. "The desk sergeant said that Carpenter was heading out to make an arrest. He said Carpenter left with a big smile on his face. You were the only one I knew he was dying to see behind bars."

I glared at Carpenter. I would be very happy to see him behind bars. I might even visit him in prison just for the opportunity to see it.

A large form filled the doorway into the kitchen. "What's going on in here?"

"Sheriff!" Carpenter cried.

The sheriff glared at him. "What have you done, Carpenter?"

Carpenter seemed to be more taken aback by that statement than any made so far. "Sir, I swear to you that I didn't have anything to do with Tyson's murder. You have my word."

"Your word isn't good enough, Carpenter. I doubt it ever was. Get him out of my sight."

Aiden cuffed Carpenter's hands behind his back and helped him to his feet. "We'll take him to the hospital first. He's bleeding."

The sheriff glared at Carpenter. "Fine, but I want him under observation the entire time."

The sheriff nodded to me. "I suppose this means I was wrong about you, Miss King." He took a step closer. "Just the same, watch your step while you're in my county. Understood?"

I glared back at him but said nothing.

As the sheriff pushed his way through the kitchen door, I couldn't help but wonder if the sheriff was more upset with Carpenter because he'd murdered someone, or because he hadn't told him about it first.

The kitchen was in shambles again, but Nutmeg seemed to be basking in it. The cat sat calmly on the counter and licked his paw.

Epilogue

The day after my grandfather's funeral, I found my grandmother sitting at one of the wooden tables inside Swissmen Sweets, mixing chocolate batter. It was the first time since she'd comforted me at the foot of my grandfather's hospital bed that I had seen her alone. Since the moment my grandfather passed, she had been under the watchful eyes of the women in her Amish district. I found their quiet vigil to be both a blessing and a curse. I was glad they were around to keep an eye on *Maami*, but at the same time, I longed for a private moment with her. I was relieved to find her alone now, but I wanted to be certain. "Are you alone?"

She laughed. "I came here to get away from them all." She smiled. "The community means well."

"I know they do." I slipped into the chair across from her.

She held a whisk in her hand. "This was your *daadi*'s favorite. I know he was grateful when the bishop let us use electric mixers to stir the chocolate and batter more quickly, but he always said that it never worked as well as the flick of the wrist." She waved the whisk as if it were a wand. "When he could, he would still stir the chocolate by hand."

I smiled. "I do that as well, especially when I'm making something for a special occasion."

She studied me for a long moment. "You're so much like him—determined, hardworking, and stubborn to a fault." Her voice cracked with emotion.

"I take all three of those as compliments."

"You should." She set the whisk in the middle of the table.

"What are you going to do with the shop?" I asked. I had wanted to ask for days.

She frowned. "What I must. I'll sell it. It's time. Even if your grandfather wouldn't accept it when he was alive, it's time."

I grabbed her hand. "Please don't sell the shop. It meant so much to *Daadi*, and it means so much to you still."

"Bailey, I have to sell. There is no other way. I can't live here alone and run the candy shop. It's too much work for me. I can't sell to Tyson Colton, of course, but there will be others. Your grandfather received more offers on this building than I can count. When I make it known that I want to sell, there will be buyers lined up at the door."

"You're not selling," I said, leaving no room for argument.

"Bailey, be sensible. I have already told you that I can't run this place alone."

"You won't have to run it alone. You'll have me." I grinned.

She muttered something in Pennsylvania Dutch. "Don't be ridiculous. You'll be in New York. How can you help me run the shop from there?"

"That's just the thing. I'm not going back to New York. Not now."

Her mouth fell open. "You have to go."

I shook my head. "No, I don't. My time here forced me to take a hard look at my life, and I did't like what I saw. I need a fresh start, and the best way to get that fresh start is to be as far away from New York as possible. I can't think of a place any farther away than Harvest, Ohio."

"But you're not Amish, and this is an Amish business."

I laughed. "And I have no intention of becoming Amish, but that doesn't mean I can't stay and pick up where *Daadi* left off. He taught me about the candy shop business my entire life, and I have learned even more about running a business from Jean Pierre. *Maami*, I can do this."

"*Nee, nee.*" She shook her head like a stubborn toddler. "I won't allow you to give up your dream and your life in New York. Your *daadi* didn't want that for you."

"I'm not giving anything up. Even if I still wanted to be the head chocolatier at JP Chocolates, that chance has come and gone. I gave it up. Cass will be the head chocolatier now."

"How can they do that?" she gasped.

"Because I asked Jean Pierre to do it. Cass has worked just as hard as I have, maybe harder, and has never gotten the recognition she deserves. It's right that she be head chocolatier, and I couldn't be happier for her."

My grandmother smiled. "If you are sure, your grandfather would be so proud."

My relationship with Eric came to mind. My grandfather wouldn't have been proud of how I carried that off, but that was over, and there was no reason to bring it to my grandmother's attention now. "I need to do this for me. I need to start over."

She chewed on her lower lip. "Are you certain?"

"Yes, I'm certain."

Her brow creased. "It won't be the life you're used to."

"I know that, but maybe that's just what I need." I paused. "In fact, I know it is."

Swissmen Sweet
Salted Caramel Fudge

Ingredients
- one pound chopped semi-sweet chocolate or chocolate of your choice
- one half stick of unsalted butter
- three tablespoons pure vanilla extract
- 14 ounce can sweetened condensed milk
- ¼ cup caramel sauce
- coarse sea salt
- non-stick cooking spray

Directions
1. Spray an eight by eight inch pan with non-stick cooking spray. Press a piece of parchment into the pan so that the edges of the paper are just above the edges of the pan. Spray the parchment paper.
2. Mix the chocolate, sweetened condensed milk, unsalted butter, and vanilla in a stainless steel bowl and place it over a saucepan that contains two inches of boiling water. This is a double boiler. Turn the heat to low and stir gently until the chocolate has melted and the mixture is smooth. Pour into the eight by eight inch pan.
3. Heat up the caramel sauce until it is pourable. Drizzle over the top of the fudge. Using a butter knife, swirl the caramel and chocolate mixture. Sprinkle with sea salt. Refrigerate overnight or for at least five hours.
4. Cut into cubes and enjoy.

Read on for a taste of the next
Amish Candy Shop Mystery,

LETHAL LICORICE

Chapter 1

When the pig went missing, I knew there would be trouble.

"Bailey, honey?" Juliet Brody asked me in her sweet Southern drawl. "Have you seen Jethro?"

I looked up from dime-sized bags of homemade black licorice I was stacking in one corner of Swissmen Sweet's competition table. The licorice was my entry in the first round of the Amish Confectionery Competition. The licorice came in a variety of flavors: strawberry, lemon-lime, blue raspberry, orange, peach, and traditional black. The licorice was just one of my candies that would be judged in the competition. The competition had four rounds, and each was more difficult than that last, with only a certain number of competitors advancing to the next round. It was like the NBA playoffs but with way more sugar. No modern cooking implements or methods were allowed in the competition, and that included electricity since some Amish districts didn't allow its use even for business.

Everything had to be done the Amish way, which meant slow and deliberate. I'd thought I was up for the challenge of making candy using the Amish methods, but I was learning that it was much more difficult than I'd realized. It couldn't be more different from how I'd learned to make chocolates and candies as Jean Pierre Ruge's protégé for six years at JP Chocolates, a high-end chocolate shop in Midtown New York City.

"Jethro?" I glanced up and down the row of competition tables. Just like mine, every table was cafeteria length, with a propane stove behind it. A white awning covered each space. At the table next to me, an Amish woman removed the candy thermometer from the boiling pot on her stovetop and poured the sugary liquid into waiting candy molds. If Jethro had been there, I was sure I would have seen him. He tended to stand out. There was no sign of the black and white polka dotted potbellied pig.

"No, I haven't seen him all morning." I tucked a lock of dark brown hair behind my ear. "Is he running loose at the competition? I doubt the competition board would like that. I wouldn't let Margot know he's unattended on the square if I were you."

Margot Rawlings was the village chairwoman and was determined to make sure everything went perfectly for the Amish Confectionery Competition, also known as the ACC. Every year, the competition was held in a different Amish town. The towns had to audition to snag the competition and each one wanted it because it was a big tourist draw. It was quite an accomplishment for a village as tiny as Harvest to win the ACC, especially in Ohio's Amish country, where there were so many better-known Amish communities in places like Charm, Berlin, and Sugar Creek. Margot had campaigned and won the hosting spot for Harvest almost single-handedly from what I heard. She wouldn't let anything mess up Harvest's time in the spotlight as the ACC's host town.

Juliet wrung her small pale hands together. "I just don't know where he could have run off to. It's so unlike him."

"How long has he been gone?" I dropped another bag of licorice on the pile on the table.

She swallowed. "I don't know exactly. I was helping some of the competitors set up their spots, and that took several hours. You would not believe the amount of stuff that some of these people brought for the ACC."

I glanced back at my stack of crates filled to the brim with candy making supplies, pots, pans, and utensils. "I can guess."

Juliet pursed her lips. "There was so much to do that I didn't notice that Jethro was gone until we were done." She clasped her hands together more tightly. "I thought he was there the entire time while I was working. The last time I saw him he was standing in the shade under one of the bushes near the gazebo. When I was ready to leave and went to collect him, he was gone."

I glanced at the large white gazebo that stood in the middle of the village's town square. It was mid-day, and the autumn sun shone down on it like an orange pumpkin ripening in one of the many pumpkin patches scattered around the county.

"I'm sure he's here somewhere. Maybe the crowd spooked him. None of us are used to having this many people in town," I said.

Because of the ACC, the village did have an unusual influx of people. There were thirty Amish candy makers in the competition, and as a rule the Amish didn't travel alone. The competitors came from as far away as Wisconsin and Florida, and some had brought their entire families to Harvest to watch them compete. In the Amish world, that could be as many as twenty additional people. Those numbers didn't even include all the spectators, both Amish and English, who'd come to Harvest to watch the competition. I'd guess there were a couple thousand tourists.

"What if someone took him?" Juilet's voice caught and her accent became more pronounced as it always did when she was upset. "How will I ever know who did it in this crush of people?"

I stepped around the side of my table and gave her hug. "No one took Jethro. I know it. I'm sure he's just hiding somewhere. Why don't we—"

"There she is!" A shrill voice shouted over the din of visitors and candy makers packed into the square. "I demand that you do something about this!"

I let go of Juliet to see a petite Amish woman in a plain navy dress, black apron, and white prayer cap stomping toward me. Her hair was parted in the middle and coiled into a bun at the nape of her neck in the Amish way. The woman was rail thin and couldn't have been more than five feet tall. Despite her small stature, the crowd parted to let her pass like storybook villagers would for a dragon on a raid. I wouldn't be the least bit surprised if she breathed fire just like a dragon. She would be the world's tiniest dragon but that didn't lessen my chances of being burned, and I knew that was just what Josephine Weaver wanted to do. She wanted to burn me out of the competition.

Jeremiah Beiler, the Amish organizer of the candy making competition, lumbered behind Josephine. He was a large, round man who was three times the size of Josephine, but not nearly as fierce even though he sported a luxurious Amish beard. If I had to choose between Josephine and Jeremiah to contend with, the big teddy bear of a man would always win.

Margot Rawlings was a few steps behind Jeremiah. Her short blond hair bounced as she made her way across the village green in Josephine's wake. She looked just as irritated as the Amish woman, but I wasn't sure if it was with me, Josephine, or both of us. Knowing Margot, it was both and probably every other person on planet Earth. She wasn't picky when it came to be being annoyed with people.

When Josephine was within three feet of where I stood next to Juliet, she pulled up short and pointed at me. "She should be disqualified. She's not Amish!"

I looked down at my outfit. Purple suede ankle boots, designer jeans from my life back in NYC, and a pink and purple flannel shirt under a bomber jacket. To complete the outfit, I wore multicolored feather earrings that hung an inch down from the bottom of my earlobes. There was no one in the world who would believe I was Amish.

Jeremiah folded his arms across his ample stomach. "Now, Josephine, we have been over this already. Bailey can compete in the ACC in her late grandfather's place. Jebidiah King's candy shop was accepted into the contest months ago."

Josephine's lips curved into a sneer. "If a contestant dies, I see no reason to allow his relatives to compete, especially if those relatives have turned their backs on the Amish way and become English."

I balled my hands at my sides. My grandfather had died a few short weeks ago and his loss was still too raw for me to take such a comment lightly. "I haven't fallen away from the Amish. I've never been Amish." My words were sharper than I would have liked them to be, but I made no apology.

The tiny woman sniffed. "All the more reason to expel you from the competition. You cannot possibly understand our ways."

"Please, please," Margot said, looking around. "Keep your voices down. There is no reason to cause such an uproar. You will disturb the tourists."

"They should be disturbed. They came a long way to see the ACC, and there is an imposter in the competition."

"Josephine," Jeremiah said as he inched away from her. I wondered if he was moving out of smacking rang. The Amish weren't prone to violence, but I wouldn't put it past Josephine to raise her fists. Jeremiah, now a good two feet away from the angry Amish woman, said, "We have been over this several times already. The board has made its decision and it's too late to change it now."

"How are the Amish to fairly compete if we have to deal with a cheating *Englischer*?" Josephine wanted to know.

"I'm not cheating. I'm making the candies using the same equipment as the rest of you." Now, I was really getting annoyed.

"Clara King should be the one taking her husband's place in this competition, not you." Josephine placed her hands on her narrow hips. "At least she is Amish!"

"Don't bring my grandmother into this," I snapped.

Maami was back at Swissmen Sweets minding the shop. Business would be brisk with all the tourists in Harvest for the ACC, but it certainly would be much quieter than it was on the square at the moment. Quiet was what my grandmother craved. Right after my grandfather had died, she had seemed to be a pillar of strength, going about her life in same orderly way she always had, but as the weeks after his death went by she became quieter, withdrawn, as if she finally realized that her lifelong companion was gone.

Clara and Jebidiah King had truly been together all their lives. She and my *daddi* grew up on the same road. They had known each other since birth. My grandfather said it was love at first sight. As a young child, I would argue that point with him. I told him that babies can't fall in love. He would say, "Sure they can. You fell in love with me when you were a baby." I would protest and tell him that was different because he was my *daddi*. Boy-girl love was another matter. He would shake his head and say, "The soul knows when it's found its match, no matter the age." I didn't buy that at eight. I wasn't sure if I bought it at twenty-seven either, especially considering my own romantic record, or maybe my soul was just as confused as the rest of me.

Juliet, who had been silent up to this point said, "Could it be, Josephine, that you want Swissmen Sweets to be removed from the competition because they just might beat you?" Her voice was as sweet as molasses.

I winced. Even I knew that might not be the best method to deal with Josephine Weaver.

Josephine dropped her hands from her tiny hips. "How can you say such a thing, Juliet Brody? I just want to have fair and safe competition of *Amish* candy makers. My shop, Berlin Candies, has a rightful place in the competition because I am Amish and everyone who works for me is Amish. We do everything the Amish way. Unlike Swissmen Sweets. There have been rumors about the worldly recipes that have been showing up there."

Worldly recipes, really? I wanted to ask her what she met by that exactly, but I thought better of it and held my tongue. It was true that since I'd taken over Swissmen Sweets I had added some new flavors to the many traditional Amish candies and sweets we sold. I'd added lavender blueberry fudge, chocolate cherry ganache truffles, and more. Even if I was going to live in Amish Country, I couldn't leave my life's work as a chocolatier behind. I had worked too hard for too long to master my craft to let it wither and die.

"What we sell at Swissmen Sweets doesn't have anything to do with what I'm entering in the ACC," I said.

"Doesn't it?" Josephine's eyes narrowed. "Shouldn't this competition be for Amish confectioneries? If you are no longer an Amish candy shop, then that's one more reason to disqualify you, and I'm going to make it my mission to do just that."

"Is that a threat?" I asked.

She lifted her chin. "The Amish don't make threats. We make promises."

Sounded like the same thing to me, I thought as Josephine stomped away with Jeremiah and Margot in her wake.

Connect with U s

Visit us online at
KensingtonBooks.com
to read more from your favorite authors, see books
by series, view reading group guides, and more.

Join us on social media

for sneak peeks, chances to win books and prize packs,
and to share your thoughts with other readers.

facebook.com/kensingtonpublishing
twitter.com/kensingtonbooks

Tell us what you think!

To share your thoughts, submit a review,
or sign up for our eNewsletters, please visit:
KensingtonBooks.com/TellUs.

Grab These Cozy Mysteries
from
Kensington Books

Catering and Capers with
Isis Crawford!